Tropical Depression

STORMY WEATHER

BOOK TWO

BA TORTUGA

Contents

Tropical Depression

Cover illustration by AJ Corza

Published with permission

Third edition.

First electronic edition published 2007 by Torquere Press. Second edition 2018 by Dreamspinner Press Inc. Third Printing: November 2019

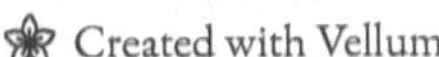 Created with Vellum

Tropical Depression

Stormy Weather: Book Two

The weather in the Florida swamps is looking a little rocky for retired football player, Galen, his laid-back lover, Shane, and their gator, Vic.

When Galen buys into a football team, promoting and wheeling and dealing are the name of the game. He's so busy he hardly gets to see Shane anymore, which means a lot of lonely naps on the couch.

Shane is tied up with managing the bar, covering for unreliable bartenders, and serving drinks to good-time party boys. Used to be Galen couldn't get enough of him. Now he can hardly pry Galen away from the phone, and Shane starts to wonder where he stands in Galen's life. Will things ever be the way they were?

When Galen starts to forget their dates, the pressure builds, jealousy and hurt swirling into a tropical storm. Galen and Shane need to seek shelter in each other before everything they've built is washed away.

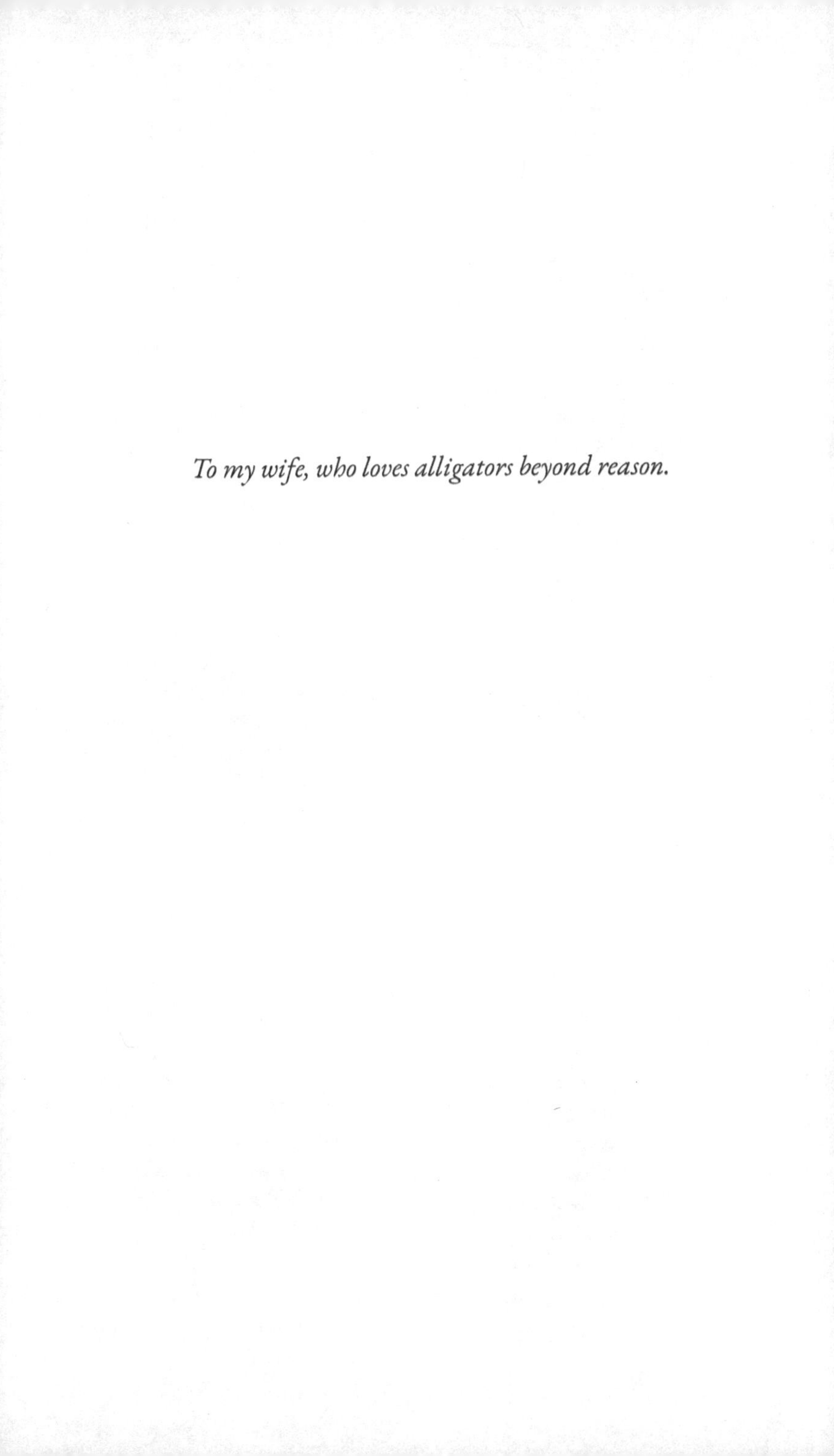

To my wife, who loves alligators beyond reason.

Chapter One

S HANE POURED himself a double, topped off with some lime juice, and knocked it back before toodling out onto the back deck. Man, Sunday afternoons? His absolute favorite. He heard the guitar of the Changos' new song as he hit the door. "Len? Turn the music up? I fucking *love* that song."

The sun was beating down, and his favorite kiddie pool was filled and on the deck, a floaty in the bottom to cushion his ass. The scent of some hunk of meat on the grill was spicy and rich. Mmm... spicy. Galen's come tasted wicked sharp after spicy....

Shane stopped. Blinked.

Okay.

Dude.

He'd only had two.

Three.

Tops.

"Uh. Galen?"

The alligator hadn't been in the pool when he'd filled it this morning....

"Yeah, darlin'?" Len sounded relaxed, happy. Perfectly normal.

"Can you bring me the hose?" He squinted. Man, those claws were *so* bad for his floaty.

"What? You can't be out of water in that thing." But he heard Len coming, dragging the hose. "You make me burn the grilled veggies and... shit."

"Uh-huh." Okay, cool. So. Real alligator. Not a hallucination. Good to know. "Gimme the hose."

Galen handed it over without a word and went to turn it on, then came back to look over his shoulder. "That's pretty good-sized."

"Uh-huh." He took a stance and aimed at the gator's nose, then squeezed the little yellow gun-end-doolie.

The first shot of water hit the gator right on the snout, and all it got him was an open mouth full of teeth and a fucking ominous hiss. That big tail swished, Shane's pool creaking.

"Damn, Shane. Piss him off, why don't you?"

"Well, he's in my pool, Len." He sprayed again, this time in the ass. "What if it shits in it? The floaty's already a loss."

"Well, we can always get another pool, darlin'. We can't get another you." The hose's spray cut off abruptly.

He frowned, blinked at the hose, then back at Galen. "Let up on the hose, Len. I can't move him if you don't."

Galen blinked innocently at him, toes moving off the hose, letting water flow again. The water splashed up in his face, making him shake his head and sputter. "Oh. Oh, you're a bastard. Gonna stick this hose up your ass and fill you up like a balloon."

"Promise?" He got an evil, one-side-kicked-up grin before Galen frowned back at the gator. "'Course it won't be any fun if we gotta watch our asses with this dinosaur. You know, they always say if you distract them with food or something, you can grab them by the tail and move them."

"Yeah?" He nodded. "Okay. You want to distract or grab? I bet we still got some bacon from last night." He thought so anyway. Last night was sort of a blur of fucking and coming and Galen's voice driving him higher and higher and....

Shit.

You can't chase alligators with a hard-on.

"You distract. You're good at it. I'll grab." Galen grinned at him again and popped his butt, then moved around behind the pool.

Shane started wiggling his ass and waving his arms. "Woo! Hey! Alligator! Outta my pool, beast! You got a whole fucking swamp. The green plastic turtle is mine!"

He got another one of those openmouthed hisses, those jaws seeming enormous. But as soon as Galen moved in from the back to grab the tail, that gator whipped around, jaws snapping, making Galen yelp and jump back a good ten feet without ever touching the ground. "Holy Jesus fuck, Shane. Did you see that?"

Shane stood there, hands in the air, blinking. "Uh-huh. I'll buy another pool. They're four bucks at the Walmart."

"And the floaties are what? Two?" Len edged around, grabbed his hand, and hustled him back from anywhere near the edge of the pool. "Which still doesn't tell us how we're gonna get that monster off our deck."

"We could poke him with your pool cue. It's long."

"You even think about it and I'll tan your ass with it. I paid a lot of money for that cue." They stood there and stared as the big old armor-plated monster got comfy again, mouth closing, a satisfied grunt coming from it.

"You'd have to catch me first." He tilted his head, vastly unconcerned about an imminent attack on his ass. "We still got Black Cats and Roman candles?"

"I bet we do. I'll get 'em. See if they're still dry." Galen wandered off, pulling him along until he was another five feet away from the gator.

He leaned against the house, looking, staring. "You look sorta like something on a pirate movie. Or you would, if you weren't in my *pool*, stupid thing."

"Darlin', if he starts talking back? He can have the house, and we'll go to a hotel." Galen came back, hands full of firecrackers.

"Shit, if he starts talking back, we're taking the camera and filming it all." Shane took a couple of Roman candles, trying to remember if you pointed the lit end or the other end.

"Maybe we ought to have supper first. Have a beer. Think on this." Oh. Len was smart. Besides, there was that whole spicy meat thing.

Shane nodded, stepping back toward Galen. "Maybe he'll get bored and go home."

Then they could use the camera for more fun things.

THE GRILLED VEGGIES WERE ONLY A *LITTLE* BURNED. The barbeque-sauced chicken? Perfect. Galen figured he should thank the gator for that, even if he didn't want to get near the damned thing. He peered out the window at the deck. Yup. Still there. It occurred to him that they ought to call animal control. But he had other things to do.

Like Shane. Who was still looking at the Roman candles and mumbling to himself. Lord knew, Shane might burn the house down or something. Sooner or later the gator would move on. Even if Galen had to hook a chicken to a deep-sea line and lure the gator back to the swamp.

Shane? Was more immediate.

Galen wandered over. Hands dropping to Shane's shoulders, he massaged those tight, fine muscles. "You figure those things out yet, darlin'?"

"Mmm...," Shane moaned, head falling forward, shoulders rolling. That gave him all that pretty neck to mark—from the short hair under that gimme cap to the join of Shane's shoulders. "I think so. Mmm. That's good."

"Yeah?" Galen dug in harder, mentally running though his options. Should they fuck nice and hard? Should they play? He listened to Shane's breathing and rubbed, grinning. He figured it depended on how hot Shane got.

The fireworks landed on the table, Shane bending over, ass rubbing against him. "Yeah."

"Well, I figure since you're not using the pool, we can let the gator stay a bit, find something else to do. Just you and me." He pushed hard against Shane's ass, leaving no doubt what he meant. He wanted. Now.

"Oh." Shane rippled, thighs parting, ass rubbing. "I can handle just you and me...."

Sweet. Shane made him crazy, from that tight little ass to the way he moaned, to the heat coming off Shane's skin. Galen bit into Shane's neck, leaving a mark. His.

"Uhn. Toothy bastard." The complaint would have meant more if he hadn't got that full-body shudder, that little cry.

"Better than the gator, huh?" Talk about toothy. Damn. Galen worked at Shane's loose pants and got them shoved down so he could touch skin, slide his hands over ass and thighs and around to cup Shane's cock. "Where else should I use them?"

"Use them?" Shane pushed into his touch. "Fuck, your hands are warm, Len."

"My teeth." Yeah, he was feeling warm all over, wanting Shane like crazy. He didn't think barbeque chicken was an accepted aphrodisiac, so maybe it was the whole "nearly had leg taken off by a dinosaur" thing. Danger made a man want.

He licked Shane's bruise, cupping Shane's balls, stroking the fine hairs.

"Oh." Yeah, that was a happy little groan, that heavy cock jerking against his wrist. "Anywhere. Love wearing your bruises, love the ache of it."

"Mmm. Love seeing you wearing them, darlin'. Just love it." Galen undid his jeans, easing them down too, cock popping out to slide against Shane's ass. Galen shifted, letting his prick slide right into Shane's crease, moaning at the feel.

"Oh. Fuck. Len." Shane leaned forward a bit more, that tight ass pressing against him, squeezing his cock.

"That's the idea, darlin'." Galen laughed, one hand on Shane's body, petting and touching. He brought the other to his mouth, sucking his own fingers, getting them good and wet so he could get Shane ready for him. Then he leaned back some, replacing his cock with his wet fingers, teasing against Shane's hole. "Gonna fuck you right here over the table."

Shane's laughter filled the kitchen, husky and low. "I can handle that. Shit. I can so handle that."

Shane arched against his fingers, taking him deep.

Yeah. Oh, hell, yeah. Galen thrust in, opening Shane quickly, wanting too much to wait.

Shane rode him, fingers scrabbling on the table, trying to get purchase.

He used his free hand to get his cock wet, spitting into his palm and rubbing quickly before pulling his fingers out of Shane, pushing the head of his cock there instead. Then he was able to give Shane a little help, wrapping one arm around his waist and holding him still.

"Oh." That tight hole opened right up for him, Shane's body pulling him in, eager, hot.

"Love." Galen shoved right in, starting a rhythm, hips rocking. "Love the way you feel inside. Love it."

"Uh-huh." Shane nodded, breath panting from him, starting to sweat.

Shane glowed in the light of the overhead lamp, making Galen catch his breath at how much he wanted this man. Still. Always. Galen moved faster, holding Shane up, hand searching out that sweet cock.

"Fuck. Harder, Len. Want to feel it tomorrow." Demanding little shit. Sexy, fine, demanding little shit.

"You," he said between bites to Shane's ear, his neck, his shoulder, "should still be feeling yesterday."

Still, he gave Shane all he had, hips slapping that fine ass.

Shane crowed, riding him just as hard, bucking on his cock. "Short fucking attention span, love."

"Isn't that the truth." His lover was about as focused as a six-week-old kitten. Galen laughed at the idea of Shane chasing string and moved harder, faster, pulling Shane's cock in time.

"Oh. Fuck. Yes. Len. Love!" Shane arched, going up on his toes as spunk poured on Galen's fingers, ass tight as a fist.

"Oh. Darlin'. Yeah." That was all it took for Galen to go right over the edge, his hips snapping as he shot into Shane's tight body.

"Mmm... postbarbeque table fucking...."

He hooted. "Pre-gator-chasing fucking."

Shane cackled. "That fucking beast had teeth the size of your cock."

"That's a frightening image in my head, darlin'." He laughed some more as they pulled apart reluctantly. "We should see if we scared him off with all that noise."

Shane nodded. "If not, there's always the fireworks."

There sure enough always were. As long as he had Shane around.

Chapter Two

S HANE COULD feel the electricity in the air. Storm was coming. Cool.

Victor had finally moved on, left four days ago and hadn't come back, so Shane figured the gator had gone south. Or hibernated. Or did whatever gators did.

They'd gotten plumb used to the bitchy ol' boy too. It was sorta cool—like a garbage disposal and guard dog and freak-show attraction all at once. Vic *really* liked bacon and hush-puppies.

And Miller Light.

Weird-assed critter.

"You think Vic'll come back in the spring, Len?" Shane grabbed the hose and sprayed the accumulated gator funk from the bottom of his pool.

"Don't see why he shouldn't. He knows where the free food is now. Maybe we need to get you a new pool, put this one out for him come then." Galen tilted his head, pausing in the act of folding up a lawn chair, sloe eyes twinkling at him. "Maybe a little farther out in the yard."

He chuckled and nodded. "No shit. Man, the sky's going black out there."

Shane's prick was half-full, interested. He loved the storms.

"Yeah. Wind's picking up too. Gonna be a good year for it." He got a grin, Galen putting the chairs securely away in the little storage thingee next to the house. He watched a minute, admiring Galen's long-assed legs and heavy shoulders and chest.

"You want the grill put up too or just covered?" He dragged the pool over to the shed.

"We should put it up.... I got a feeling about this storm season." They worked together, getting everything stowed away, bumping hips every so often.

"Man, it looks bare out here...." The wind picked up, and Shane gasped, cock jumping.

"Yeah. But there's always the deck railing." Galen came up behind him, hands on his hips.

He leaned into Galen, eyes on the storm. "Did I ever tell you how I'd drive out and watch the storms, jack off as the storm hit?"

"Mmm-hmm. You did. Did I ever tell you I dream about that sometimes?" Galen rubbed against his ass, nuzzled his neck.

"You do? Really?" He reached back, fingers sliding over Galen's ribs.

"Oh yeah. Some of those times when I wake you up in the middle of the night... yeah. Now, of course, some nights I wake you up because I'm dreaming about you in that chair in New Orleans, getting pierced."

"Oh." Fuck, sometimes Len said shit that made him wild, made him stupid with wanting. "Damned near creamed my jeans, knowing you were watching."

"I loved watching." Galen's long fingers started working

his jeans open. "Want to watch you now. Touch yourself for me, darlin'."

Shane groaned a little, felt himself blush, but didn't bother playing the shrinking violet. He was hard and wanting, and Len smelled fucking good, and the wind was bringing that fine storm. He wrapped his hand around his cock, starting slow, dragging his palm over the skin.

Lightning flashed, raising hairs all over his body, making his skin so sensitive. Galen moaned, cheek against his as he leaned over to look. "God, Shane. Damn."

"Fucking cool. The wind, the electricity on the air. Makes me ache for it."

"You look decadent. Fucking amazing." Len bit him. Hard.

"Len!" He jerked, the motion of his hand going a little faster.

Galen urged him on with kisses and nips and hot, hot words, keeping him going as a brilliant fucking light show lit up the sky.

He groaned, hips jerking, eyes wide as hell. His nipples were hard, cock stiff as stone, balls aching. "Soon. Shit. Want to wait for the rain...."

"It's coming, darlin'. I can feel it. Just hold on." Galen reached down, hand cupping his balls, pulling them down and away from his body, stalling him.

His head fell back, breath panting out of him, thighs hard.

"So pretty." The rain finally broke, pouring down on them, warm and good, the storm right on top of them.

"Yes...." He started pumping in earnest, rubbing against Galen, so fucking hot for it.

Galen rubbed right back, hand joining Shane's finally, squeezing, pulling hard.

"Oh. Oh." Shane arched, one hand on the deck railing, hips rocking insistently. Another bright flash of lightning showed, and he jerked, coming hard enough to make his teeth click together.

"Shane. Oh fuck." Galen pushed him up against the rail so hard the breath whooshed out of him, rubbing against his ass hard and fast, groaning and jerking.

His face was turned up to the rain, eyes blinking, flying with it.

Galen finally stilled, panting hard. "Oh, love. Yeah."

"Uh-huh. Damn. Damn, Len." He laughed, rubbed their cheeks together.

The wind picked up, practically tossing them off the deck. "Shit." Galen laughed. "We should go in."

"Yeah. Yeah." They headed for the house, the thunder booming behind them.

Galen slipped his hand into Shane's, pulling him along, turning to kiss him as they got in the door, lips wet with rain. The kiss was fiery, rain-soaked bodies pressing together like a hand in a glove.

They stripped off sopping wet clothes, letting them fall on the tile floor of the kitchen. Galen squeezed his ass when it was bare, lifting him against that big body, skin warming so fast.

"Fucking love you, Galen Frost." He dove into another kiss, shaking as the lightning hit close by.

Jerking against him, Galen grunted, took the kiss hard and deep, tongue pushing in. They moved until his back hit the door, Galen pressing right in, humping against him. One of his legs wrapped around Galen's hip, tugging them closer together, nails dragging right on up Galen's spine.

"Uhn. Darlin', you're just...." He loved it when Galen lost the words, gave up, and started biting and sucking, bruising his skin.

Shane started moaning, babbling, promises, and threats just pouring out of him. The glass rattled behind his head as the wind swept past the house, adding to the excitement of

Galen's cock against his belly, Galen's hands on his skin. Galen grabbed his other leg, pulled it up until he was wrapped around Galen's waist.

Sweet fuck, the man was strong. "Need. Galen, fuck."

"Uh-huh. Need you. I... oh shit, lover." He could tell Galen was close again already, could feel it in the jerky rhythm, the wet cock.

He leaned forward, bit Galen's earlobe hard. "Got me. For fucking ever."

"Yeah. Oh, darlin', yeah." They rocked, Galen pushing him hard, cock finally jerking against his lower belly, hot spunk covering his skin as Galen shot.

"Mmm...." He rubbed, nuzzling Len's jaw, Len's neck.

"Damn, Shane. What you do to me." He got a grin, Galen's eyes so dark, so hot.

"Wasn't me. Was the storm." He winked, bit Len's bottom lip.

"It was both. You get me going when the air is still. You get to me by breathing. We could go to bed. You could do me."

"Ooh." His breath caught in his chest, and he nodded. "I could. I'm a big fan of our bed."

"Hang on, then." Oh, caveman. Galen literally hoisted him up a little more and carried him to the bedroom. Shit.

"Fuck, you're something. Think I'll keep you." He held on, squeezing tight as the lights flickered. "We're going to spend the evening in the dark, I'm thinking."

"There's worse things." Galen dumped him on the bed so he bounced. "We could light some hurricane lamps."

"We could. We could just fuck like bunnies in the dark." He reached for the lube.

"That's a good plan." Crawling on the bed, Galen reached for him, kissed him hard. "How do you want me, darlin'?"

"Get comfortable." He smiled, nuzzled in some. "I want to make you need."

Galen settled, stretching out long and strong on the sheets. The rough hair on Galen's belly and chest and thighs had his hands itching to touch. "Can't wait."

The lightning flashed again, and Shane spread Galen's thighs, bending to lap at his flat belly. "Not going to make you wait."

"Mmm."

Oh, he could taste Galen's come on that skin, taste heat and want and need. He slicked his fingers and rolled the heavy, warm balls, not teasing so much as enjoying, touching.

"Mmm. Good." Hips rolling, muscles bunching, Galen purred for him, stretched and showed off a little.

He hummed, wanting, watching, tongue sliding along Len's cock as his fingers stroked that tight little ring of muscles.

Legs spreading, Galen opened for him, exposing everything. Those balls still hung heavy, Galen's cock showing interest, but showing signs of their earlier play too, growing slowly. He could take his time, see and smell and taste everything.

He did too, licking at Galen's cock and balls, but lingering over that belly and those sharp hipbones and those softer-than-fuck inner thighs. When the lights went out, it made things even slower, nothing but the occasional flash of lightning showing him the way.

That and Galen's moans, his ragged breathing whenever Shane hit a particularly sensitive spot.

He sucked up a dark mark on Len's leg, then spent a long, sweet time shifting to lap at that tiny ring of muscles, loving the dark, deep sounds Len gave him.

"Shane." His name was a threat, a promise. A plea. Galen moved up, digging his heels into the bed and lifting for him. He cupped that fine, muscled ass, thumbs spreading his lover wide. He pushed in close, licking and loving, the heady scent of Galen making him as dizzy as a horsefly on a string.

"Need you, lover." Galen groaned, rocking against his mouth, cock hard now, hot, balls drawing up.

He nodded. Fuck, yes. He was aching for it, way down deep in his soul. Shane slicked himself a bit, not wanting to push himself any closer, then set the tip of his cock against that wet hole.

"In. In me, darlin'." Galen opened up, took him in just like that.

"Oh." He leaned down, lips brushing Len's nipple, collarbone. The heat was just.... Damn. "Love."

"Good." Arching up, Galen took him in deep. So deep. One of Galen's hands cupped the back of his head, pulling him down for a kiss that scorched, would have made steam if they were still out in the rain. He wrapped one of his hands around Galen's hip, pulling them together, driving them deeper and faster. Galen urged him on with harsh sounds, with hands and mouth. That tight body gripped him, squeezed him. He finally slid his hand around, grabbing Len's cock and pumping. He needed. Now.

"Fuck! Shane. Yeah." Moving even faster, Galen humped up, hands scrabbling against his skin, short nails digging in.

"Uh-huh. Come, love. Come on. Fuck." He arched, rocking in deep, eyes rolling.

Galen grunted, cock jerking in his hand, a deep flush covering that wide chest. His head snapped back, hips slamming into Len as the lightning flashed, blinding him as he shot.

"Oh. Oh, darlin'. Yeah." Galen petted him, brought him down easy. "Good."

"Uh-huh." He nodded, eyes rolling. "Good. Love."

The rain pounded against the windows, the lightning flickering, their bed warm and dry and good. Galen was solid under him, chest rising and falling against him, hands pulling him close.

"Helluva way to start the storm season, darlin'."

"Mmm... the best." He just snuggled, boneless as a sleepy kitten. "Absolute fucking best."

Shane blinked, eyes closing as he almost drifted off. "You think Victor's okay?"

"I think he's holed up somewhere with a pretty girl gator, fixing to make with the vacation in the south." They curled up together, the house strong against the storm.

"Cool." He nodded, the image of Vic in sunglasses with some lady gator fluttering her lashes making him grin. Yeah, too fucking cool.

Chapter Three

"**L**EN, YOU wanna run out to the store?"

"Len, you wanna go out to the bar?"

"Len, you wanna go have a beer with Wade?"

For fuck's sake, he'd been listening to this shit from Shane for days.

Galen's phone rang, and he grabbed for it, itchy as hell and hungry for something to do that wasn't fucking or sitting on his ass watching TV or moving money from one investment to another. "Frost."

"Galen? Hey, man, it's Frank. Frank Waters? You remember me?"

Frank Waters. Frank Waters. Come on, Galen. Think. Think. "Sure I do, man. How's it going?"

"You totally don't remember me, man. I'm wounded. Seriously."

Well, fuck. Then, boom. All of the sudden he remembered Waters—a publicist and all-around money guy out of Arkansas, he thought, one of those go-getters with a trophy wife and the perfect social media. "Shut your mouth, Frank. Of course I remember you. You and me went to that little hole-in-the-wall restaurant in New Orleans. Barbeque shrimp, you remember?"

"I do. Cool. Cool. You interested in a business proposition?"

He shook his head, a grin splitting his lips. Lord have mercy. "That was delicate."

"Who has time for delicate these days? I have this great opportunity to buy a semipro team, man. One we can run like they ought to be run. You're on my short list of guys."

Guys with money, he bet. "Am I now?"

"You know it. You have always had a head for business, you're a former player, and you look good on camera. That's what I need for this project. I'll send it to you."

He rolled his eyes and sighed, listening to the sales pitch with half an ear, waiting for the opportunity to break in and just say "Hey, I'll get back to you," and when it happened, he took that chance and hung up.

The pitch came in, and he started reading, surprised to find himself a little intrigued by the prospect, by the forecasted numbers. This could make some cash, could genuinely be successful.

Damn.

"Len, you wanna go—"

"Shane, can't you run down and clean the fucking bait shop or something? I'm fucking busy, and it's pouring out there."

"What?"

"I'm working, huh? Numbers."

"Right, because I'm not any good at those."

"That's not what I—"

"Right. I'll be in the bait shop, cleaning. It's a talent."

Shane turned heel and stormed out, and Galen sighed. Fuck a duck sideways. He hadn't meant to.... Goddamn it.

He turned back to his computer and shook his head. He'd

let Shane cool down, read this e-mail, and then go apologize. Too much steady rain made him a bitch.

THE WEATHER WAS FOUL. NOW, GALEN FROST LIKED his storms as much as the next man. Hell, with Shane around, he really got off on them. But this was a tropical storm that was too damned dangerous to get out in, and they'd been cooped up inside for nearly three days this time.

A man could only play so much coffee table volleyball.

He was getting snarly, and Shane was still pouting because he'd yelled—which he hadn't; he'd just... grumbled—and now Galen fucking *itched*. He needed to do something. Anything.

The offer to let him buy in on a team if he would do half of the marketing and cold calling and wheeling and dealing wouldn't let up, wouldn't give him a break. Galen had told Frank he'd think about it, and he was, but that really wasn't what he wanted to do right then. Not really.

So he settled on doing Shane.

Galen was in the mood to play. To draw it out. He hit the bedroom while Shane was scrubbing the kitchen sink, little ass wiggling as Shane danced along to the music he had on. He set things up, rearranged a bit, and lit a couple of hurricane lamps, then stood back to survey his arrangements. Yeah. That would work.

Nodding once, he went to collect a bottle of whiskey, a couple of soft washcloths, and Shane. "Hey, darlin. You done sulking?"

"I don't sulk. I was... pondering." Right. Pondering. Shane. Uh-huh.

"Pondering, huh? Well, I've been pondering something too, darlin'." He moved up behind Shane, let Shane feel just what gutter his mind was in.

"Oh." Shane wriggled, rubbing right into him, eager bastard. "I like your ponderings."

"Yeah? Then you'll like my plotting even more. Wash up and come to the bedroom." Galen sucked up a mark on the side of Shane's neck and wandered off, knowing Shane would follow. Soon. Sure enough, Shane came sauntering, damp shirt off, jeans unbuttoned.

Perfect. Galen distracted him a little by grabbing him and kissing the fire out of him, tongue pushing in deep. Shane fed him a low little cry, one hand curving around the back of his neck, holding them together.

Hell, it was distracting him too. God, he loved kissing this man. Wasn't nothing like it in the world. Except maybe fucking that ass. He waltzed Shane over to the bed, pushed him down, and came down on one knee beside him, pulling at those jeans. It didn't take more than a wiggle and a tug and all that skin was bared to him, tanned and lean. That sweet little ass bounced on the bed, cock filling and dark on Shane's flat belly.

"Mmm. Oh, darlin', you are a treat, for sure." He leaned down, bit at Shane's thigh, licked Shane's cock. "Here, sit up a bit."

Shane's fingers slid over his face, petting, loving on him as that belly rippled, Shane sitting up. Fuck, he had to taste that too. He nipped Shane's belly, licked Shane's navel, coming up to pull the tiny nipple rings with his teeth.

"Oh. Oh, that. Damn." Shane went all shivery and tight for him, nipples hard as little rocks.

Hell, yeah. He loved all over Shane, licking, biting, mouth moving. Little moans came from Shane, and Galen soaked them in, fingers running all over, finally moving down Shane's arms. He took Shane's left wrist in his hand, lifted it to his mouth to bite hard at the tender skin before moving fast, reaching for the locking cuff he'd gotten and tethering Shane right to the bed.

Shane's sweet blue eyes were still rolling from the bite, cock jerking hard by the time Shane realized he was bound. "Damn, you're fast."

"It wasn't easy, darlin'. I was a little wrapped up in you." He grinned, kissing Shane's nose. "But I got plans."

Shane's right hand came up, cupped his jaw, tugged him in for a deep, hard kiss, Shane wanting him something fierce.

He gave, kissing, tasting, hands sliding on Shane's skin, ending on that sweet cock, giving it a nice tug. Taking Shane's free hand, he brought it down before replacing his own hand with Shane's, wrapping Shane's fingers around the hard length.

Galen moved back, off the bed, more damned reluctant than he thought he'd be. He sat in the big easy chair he'd pulled up and poured himself a whiskey. "Looks like I'm ready for the show, lover."

Shane's eyes met his, hungry and hot, dragging over his body. "Show?"

"Mmm-hmm. You're gonna touch yourself for me. I'm gonna watch." He sipped his whiskey, licking the edge of the glass, knowing Shane liked the taste in his mouth.

Shane watched his tongue, hand moving nice and slow, thumb working the tip on every upstroke.

Yeah. That was it. He was gonna tease the hell out of Shane, let Shane tease him. Then he was gonna fuck Shane so hard they'd both run out of pent-up energy. He growled deep in his chest. "So fucking hot."

"Just want you." He could see Shane's balls start to tighten as Shane spread for him, letting him see everything.

"You make me crazy." Shifting, Galen slid down in the chair, popping the button on his jeans. He sipped again, watching Shane, letting the need build in his gut.

Shane's hand slipped down to stroke and tug on those soft balls. That made Shane moan, shift, ass sliding on the sheets.

Damn. When he found he was massaging his own cock through his jeans, Galen sat up, put his hand on the arm of the chair. "Harder. Touch yourself a little harder, darlin'."

"Harder." Fuck, he loved to see that throat work, see those lean hips start to roll and thrust.

"Uh-huh. I want to see you feel it. Want to know you're working it. For me." His nipples were as tight as Shane's, his cock shoving and prodding.

"Want you to fuck me." Shane bent his knees, toes curling into the sheets. The bed was rocking, Shane's eyes on him, begging, burning.

"I will, Shane. I will. Promise. I need you ready." He grinned, his own hips rising and falling, heavy denim rasping against him. "There's lube there. On the nightstand."

"Perv." Shane groaned, reached for the tube. One-handed and horny, Shane took a bit, but he finally got those fingers slick. The sight of Shane's fingers driving deep—two, then three—was inspiring.

So fucking inspiring that he tossed back the last of his whiskey, let it burn all the way down, then stood and shucked his shirt and jeans. "Come on, lover. Get good and open."

"Uh-huh." Shane licked his lips, hips bucking, cock slapping that flat belly. "Need."

"Yeah. Want you bad, Shane." It was good, telling Shane what he wanted, what he needed. Looked like Shane liked it too. Galen went over, stood out of range of Shane's hand, grabbed the lube, and slicked up his cock. Shane's body fucking shifted, reached for him, begged for him. Those bright eyes were on his cock, tongue slipping out, balls drawing up tight-tight. His own balls were pulling up, his belly rigid, muscles jumping. "Gonna fuck you so good, Shane. Gonna make it hot."

"Always. Always do." Shane went rigid, eyes rolling. "Sweet fuck."

That was all he could take. Galen's control snapped and he lunged, coming down on top of Shane, making sure that trapped arm wasn't pulled too tight. He took a kiss, feeding Shane the taste of good whiskey, tasting hunger and want. Shane drove right back, rubbing against his belly, hotter than the hinges of hell.

"Fuck, darlin'. Burn me alive." He got the head of his cock lined up, Shane's fingers sliding away from that hot hole. Took him no time at all to slip right in, push in deep in one hard surge.

"Yes." Shane hissed the word, free hand dragging down his spine.

Hot. Tight. Shane's ass was a dream, making his eyes roll in his head. Galen growled, the sound deep, fucking feral. He bit Shane's lower lip, lifted Shane's hips in his hands, and started thrusting good and hard, his body demanding he move. The little low sounds poured out, Shane bracing himself against the headboard, riding hard.

Close. Man, he was fucking close, right on the razor edge, just like that. "Shane. Yeah. Come on, darlin'."

"Uh-huh. Love. Fuck." He felt it fucking everywhere, Shane going tight as a virgin, milking him as heat sprayed over that flat belly.

"Fuck!" Galen slammed into him again and again, finally shooting hard and deep into Shane's body, a deep moan torn from him.

Shane moaned, lips sliding and dragging over his skin.

Galen panted, chest heaving. "Damn, lover. What you do to me." He kissed Shane slow and deep, the kind of drugging, long-assed kiss you could only achieve after you came.

Shane wrapped around him, tongue sliding and slipping alongside his. "Was good, Len."

"Mmm." Good was an understatement. Galen almost collapsed, but he figured he ought to unlock Shane's cuff first. He let Shane go, snuggled right in. "And I'm not feeling the least bit snarly."

"Mmm... no. Not snarly. Not pissy. Just right."

"Yeah." Galen put a hand under Shane's butt, pulled him so close. Let it storm. He had Shane, and that was all right with him any day.

Chapter Four

MAN, MANAGING a bar was hard work. Not impossible or anything, but slinging suds was more fun than doing deposits and hiring and firing and dealing with suppliers and shit. Shane sighed and started counting cash again, trying to make the numbers add up.

Twenties. Tens. Fives. Ones. Quarters.

The radio changed songs, and he jerked, coins going flying, realizing he'd been sleeping on his desk, dreaming about counting dimes. God damn it.

5:00 a.m.

Already.

Maybe he'd sleep here tonight. Call up to the house and tell Len he wasn't driving.

Yeah.

Except. Damn. Sleeping with Galen. Snuggling.

Pancakes.

Oh, man. Pancakes. Galen made good goddamned pancakes.

He grabbed the deposit bag and started stuffing it full. Safe. Then pancakes. Then snuggling.

Go him.

GALEN WOKE UP ABOUT 4:00 A.M., AND WHEN HE reached over to Shane's side of the bed, all he felt was empty sheets. No Shane. Just him and the silence and the big bed....

Shane was staying at the bar again, he reckoned. Goddamn.

He rolled up, reaching for the phone to call and make sure Shane was okay. He didn't pick up the handset. If Shane was asleep, Galen didn't want to wake him. Bartender's hours often left folks with insomnia, and Shane could go for days without actually going to bed.

He stared at the empty side of the bed. His shoulders rose up around his ears. Fuck.

Galen slid out of bed and padded to the bathroom. Once he'd washed up, he made his way to the kitchen. He leaned on the door of the fridge for a while, staring into the light without really seeing dick. Then he wandered out to the deck. The smell of water in the air should have soothed him, but it just made him miss Shane.

Maybe he ought to hop in the truck and go to the bar. He had visions of sweeping Shane off his feet and loving him into wanting to come home again.

More and more when it got late and Shane was still doing the deposit, he would stay at the bar.

Not cool.

Finally Galen headed to the workout room. He would lift weights and do sit-ups until he was tired enough to go back to sleep. That way he didn't bother Shane, and he could wear himself out a little without having to resort to warm milk or a shower or something.

Galen sat on the weight bench before lying back under the bar. He knew he should have a spotter in the house at least, but these days he rarely had that either.

He hefted the bar and started doing reps.

Enough physical exercise could make a man forget almost anything. Even how crappy it was to wake up alone.

IF HE HEARD "WELCOME TO THE JUNGLE" ONE MORE goddamned time tonight, he was going to rip someone's head off and shit down their neck.

Oh, man. That was a gross fucking thought.

And all Galen's fault too, he was sure of it. Shane poured another round of shots and barked at Will to get his ass to the back for another keg before nodding over at big, dark, and hung at the corner of the bar.

Galen looked like maybe he was tired of the fucking song too.

Lord, they were busier than a one-legged man at a butt-kicking competition, and the crowd was starting to rumble a bit at the edges. Including Galen. Every time the guy in the "Gators Do it in the Water" T-shirt bumped Galen's arm, the man got a glare, one Shane knew well enough to avoid at all costs. Too bad Gator Boy didn't.

He headed over, fixed Gator Boy with a look. "You need something else to drink, man?"

"Huh? Yeah! Hell, yeah! Give us all another round. Including the big guy here." The guy jerked a thumb at Galen, and Shane was just close enough to hear the growl.

He arched an eyebrow over at Len, almost—almost, now,

he was getting a little fucking tired—tickled. "You want another one, big guy?"

"From you? Yeah. But on my dime, not his." He knew Galen would never start anything in his place. Not after that one time where he'd lost his job and all. But it was still fun to see those sloe eyes pin the guy in place and that upper lip curl with contempt.

He nodded. Galen's money wasn't good here, hadn't been in forever, not since he'd moved up the ladder from bartending to managing. He poured the kids a round, then got Galen a shot of the good stuff and wiped the bar in front of Galen clean.

"Man, what is your fucking problem? Giving this guy the best seat and better fucking booze than anyone else?"

Shane arched an eyebrow. "Kid, I don't have time to play with you. Take your drinks and go on."

The guy made to reach across the bar and grab him, but that hand never even made it past the pretzels. One of Galen's big football-player's hands clamped on the guy's wrist.

"You're about to have a problem, son, you don't back off."

There was this pause, right before shit hit the fan, where everything kinda went still. Shane was extremely familiar with it, and in his experience, it meant grab the José Canseco, bay-bee.

He wrapped his fingers around the neck of the bat right about the time Gator Boy took a swing at Galen and one of his drunk friends raised a beer bottle up to whack Len in the head.

Oh, he didn't think so.

Galen always did have eyes in the back of his head. Even as he backed out of range of Gator Boy, he ducked the bottle, and the sound of Galen's fist hitting flesh sounded *loud*. Galen had a way longer reach than Gator Boy.

Shane was up and over the bar before Jake and Will could blink, wading right in with a snarl, bat swinging.

"This."

Thwack.

"Is."

Pow.

"My."

Thud.

"Bar!"

Smash.

Lord, that one guy turned into five like nothing going, like cockroaches coming out of a broken wall. Galen snarled at one who got too close to Shane, and damned if the asshole didn't go down like a felled tree under Galen's punch. Will was on one side of him, and that big feller they hired to play bouncer waded in, and suddenly it was a fucking free-for-all—bodies and fists and bottles flying—and fuck, he hated getting hit in the face, man. It made Len crazy too. He could tell by the way Galen started really meaning it, not playing anymore. He'd only seen Len that mad once before. Ever. And that had been the start of a shitty couple three weeks.

By the time everything was said and done, they'd cleaned the place out but for the core group of regulars, who all stood around with their teeth in their mouths.

Shit.

Damn.

"Everybody okay?"

"Yeah."

"S'all good, buddy."

Everyone sounded pretty chipper. The only one who didn't answer was Len.

He turned to give Len a good once-over, wrist twinging as the bat swung some. Man, people were easier to hit, but the recoil? Shit. "Galen?"

Galen stared at him, nodding slowly, those black-on-black eyes... well. They were on fire. He could see muscles jumping under Len's skin.

Oh.

Damn.

Upstairs.

"Office?"

"Uh-huh." God, no wonder Len had stayed quiet. That one word held a wealth of need, and Len turned abruptly and walked off to lead the way.

"Will. Bar. Holler if you need me." He didn't wait for the answer, just followed his own personal redneck right up the stairs.

He made it right in time to see that high, tight ass disappear as Galen opened up the office and went on in. Shit, he could smell the man. He'd bet Len had opened his jeans right up. The thought made his cock throb, made it press against his zipper and demand attention. He locked the door behind him, the bat clattering to the floor.

Len was on him before he could even blink, pressing him back against the door to kiss him, hands hard on his shoulders. Fuck, yes. Shane groaned, fingers twisting in Galen's shirt and tugging hard. Their lips split, they kissed so hard, the tinge of blood joining the burn of whiskey.

They started getting naked, their clothes falling to the ground, and he figured they were going to burn up when Len stopped, growling a little and pulling back. Before he could ask what the hell was wrong now, Len touched his cheek, fingers moving slow and careful.

"They bruised you, darlin'."

"They were drunk bastards looking for a thrill." He leaned into the touch, not easy, but hard enough that it stung some. He knew Galen, knew that bruise would make that man snarl for days.

"Well, it's my job to leave marks, damn it." Oh fuck. Galen did, leaning down to bite at his shoulder, stinging like crazy. Yeah. Hell, yeah.

His cock jumped like it could push its way right out without any help. "Then get to it and quit rumbling."

"Uh-huh. Get up here." Len lifted him, stripped off the rest of his clothes so fast he almost had rug burn. That man amazed him with the simple strength in those arms.

"You... you're something." He leaned in, got himself a good, hard kiss, grateful as hell his prick and his zipper were no longer in speaking distance.

"I just want you, darlin'. So bad." He could feel it too, against his leg. Galen's cock rubbed and rubbed, leaving wet trails. And the kisses. Fuck, they were making his head spin.

"Uh-huh." Okay, that was brilliant, but damn. He just. Fuck. Shane crawled up Galen's body, pushing close and doing his best "hump like a bad puppy" impression.

The world spun and his ass peeled away from the door as Galen moved them, finally plunking him down on his desk. Bracing one hand on the desk, Galen covered him, coming right down between his spread legs, their cocks rubbing like crazy.

"Uh-huh." He groaned, reaching up to pull them closer. "Come on."

"Yeah, darlin'. Yeah. I want...." Galen moaned, nipping at his chin and neck, that heavy beard stubble scraping his last fucking nerve.

"Right here." He bucked, ass slapping the desk hard enough to sting.

"I know. Oh Jesus, I know." Galen bent and wiggled, and that hot prick rubbed at him, all down the underside of his cock and along his balls, then lower.

"Galen...." He wasn't one to beg, but goddamn, he was on fucking fire, balls to bones. "Please. I fucking need."

"Need... what, darlin'? Say it." Len wasn't laughing at him, wasn't asking him to beg either. Len just liked to hear it. Bastard.

He pushed himself up so their chests slapped together, his lips right next to Len's. "Fuck me. Hard. I have to feel you right fucking now."

He got a kiss as a reward, Len lining right up. There wasn't going to be any sweet fingering or lube or anything, and that was fine with him. Len always slid right in like he belonged there. Like now.

Oh, hell, yes. They groaned together, breathing into each other's mouths for a second before they started moving, Galen slamming into him and giving him what he needed.

Their bodies slapped together hard enough to leave more bruises, Galen's hips smacking his ass. The hand Galen wasn't braced on pulled at him, lifting him even more. He couldn't last long, so he didn't try. He just held on and did his best to add his strength to Len's, meet each thrust and make it good for both of them. Cords stood out in Len's neck, and those dark eyes stared right down at him as Len went a little crazy, fucking him like there was no tomorrow. Then Galen groaned, going still for a few seconds before shooting right inside him, hard and deep, those strong hips snapping.

"Galen." He didn't have enough breath to scream or holler, but whispering that one word had to be enough, because he lost it, heat spreading over his belly.

Galen moaned for him, forehead dropping to touch his own, their sweat dripping into his eyes. "Damn, darlin'."

"Uh-huh." He nodded and swallowed, staring up into Galen's eyes. Yeah. Damn.

"You okay? They didn't hurt you, did they?" Oh, Len would worry about that *now*.

"Nah. Just knocked me around some. You?" Of course, if

Galen could fuck like that *hurt*, they were going to have a talk about holding out on his ass.

"M'good. I was more pissed than anything." They moved a little, Galen pushing him to one side to sort of flop half on him, half on his desk. "Your blotter is hard."

"You noticed that." There was also a pack of postie-notes digging a valley into his left buttcheek, but he could live with that.

"I did. You have a couch somewhere, yeah?" They weren't moving. He noticed that too.

"Uh-huh. Eight feet to the left, give or take six inches."

"Okay. We can make it there, no problem." It was a bumpy ride, but damned if Len didn't haul his ass right over there.

He settled right in, clinging a little. "You're gonna be sore in the morning. You're not used to beating the fuck out of strangers."

Len nuzzled his cheek, right where that damned bruise sat. "Not anymore. But for you, darlin'? I'd take on the world."

That? He so believed. Balls to bones.

Chapter Five

G ALEN FIGURED he was busier than a one-armed paperhanger. He'd finally taken Frank up on the football offer, and he was spending way more time on the phone in his home office than he was in the bait shop or at the bar, for that matter. He just wasn't getting out as much.

It was Shane's bartender Jake who called him one evening, asking him to come down.

"Something wrong?" he asked, punching formulas for a concession stand dealie into his computer.

"Well, it's slam busy, and there's a bunch of college kids in here, and I worry. We have a few call in sicks, you know?"

Jake was a pretty cool head, so if he called, that meant he was pretty worried something was gonna get rowdy. Galen checked the weather. Yeah, it might have a bit of a blow, and that always made the crowd crazy. He sighed.

"Sure, I'll be over in a half hour or so, yeah?"

Jake grunted. "Thanks, man. See you then."

Hanging up, Galen signed off with Frank on the IM and got up to put on his good jeans and some boots. Shane liked that look. And if Shane knew he was coming just because Jake thought the man deserved a little help on a busy night? Galen would need all the ammunition he could get.

MAN, THE BAR WAS *ROCKING*.

Shane had been running his ass off since three. One bartender had called in sick, and both barbacks, and it was fucking Saturday. Tomorrow? Heads were gonna roll.

Of course, working the bar meant regulars bought him drinks and tipped him, laughing at his old jokes, the old teases. By nine thirty or so, he was fucking buzzing, things just zooming. Damn. Damn, but he didn't remember shit being so... crazed. Sparkly.

Still, the money was flowing, the faces coming back for more, laughing with him.

The one face he *hadn't* seen all night popped up right about then, Galen in his usual low-slung jeans and black hat, leaning against the bar down at the end, waiting patiently for him.

He poured his lover a Jack and waltzed his way down the bar. "Hey, stranger."

"Hey, darlin'. Man, it's buck wild in here tonight."

"No shit. That new little prick Jim didn't show. Bastards. Still, making some money, so woo, yeah?" He winked, turning as Jake tapped his arm.

"The table in the back bought you another shot, boss. You want me to comp them a round?"

He chuckled. "Sure. One round. House booze."

He knocked the shot back, saluted the table.

Galen looked at him closely, then looked at his big old gold watch. "You might oughta stop with that one, darlin'. It's only ten, and you're looking happy."

"Only ten? Shit. It feels like it's been forever tonight." Forever and ever, the music going faster and faster. Len was right, though. Damned lights were trailing like nothing going, and damn if he wasn't spinning a little.

The frown deepened on Galen's face. "Shane? Darlin'? You okay?"

"Yeah. Yeah, just blinky some. You know? Not used to working...." He got sidetracked again, some customer coming up and hollering in some weird fucking foreign language.

"I guess that.... Are you sure?" Galen was looking at him, eyes serious, hand coming out to hold him there when he would have flitted off. He blinked down at Galen's hand, tilted his head. The man had beautiful hands. Just amazing and square and dark, and man, Galen needed a ring.

A ring?

Would look cool.

"Shane?" Now Galen sounded kinda pissy. What had he done? "Can you get a break?"

"It's real busy, man." He caught sight of himself in the mirror behind the bar, blinking as he saw about ten of him. Cool. Be really cool if they could all tend bar too.

"I know it." Holding him in place, Galen waved at Will and Jake. "Shane needs ten. Can y'all handle it?"

Will nodded. "Yeah, man. We're cool."

Shane looked over at Galen, and that pissed look was still there.

Shit.

He hated that look.

"Cool. Thanks, guys." Galen walked him all the way down to the end of the bar, holding his hand over it before hauling him off to the bathroom. Galen closed the door and turned on the lights before turning to tilt his head up.

"Dude. Len. Bright. Sparkly. Damn." Whoa. Trailers....

"Fuck." The curse was low, vicious. "Your eyes. Shane... what have you been doing?"

"Working?"

"Darlin'. I know it's busy... but you didn't pop anything to keep you awake, did you?" It wasn't really a question. Galen sounded like he knew the answer.

"Awake?" He blinked again, pretty sure he was missing something. "I slept with you last night, Galen."

"I know, darlin'. I mean tonight. To keep you going." Galen's hands were leaving tingles all over his cheeks and neck.

Fucking cool.

"I didn't take. Well, I mean I had a couple three, but it's a bar. You know? Booze."

"I know, darlin'." That pissed-off look was completely at odds with the way Galen touched him. "Someone is going to die."

"Uh.... Now?" He pushed closer, eyes closing against the light.

"Yeah. Now. Not you. Goddamn people." Galen pulled him close, lips moving on his skin.

"Oh...." He shivered, gasped. It was like little fires burning all over him, which would be creepy if it didn't feel so fucking hot. "Wow."

"Yeah. Wow. Who can I call to come fill in?"

"Huh? I gotta work, Len. My barbacks didn't show. The tall one and the ugly one. I'm just on break."

Galen shook him a little, making his skull rock like he had baby head. "Pay attention, Shane. Someone slipped you something. You're only gonna get freakier. Who can I call that's not on tonight?"

"Aaron. I can work, Len. Honest. I didn't take anything." He caught sight of the ten other Shanes in the mirror again. That was beginning to creep him out.

"I know you didn't mean to, darlin'. You stay here. I'll call

Aaron. Then we're going home." The door opened and closed, the sound really loud for a second, then muffled again as Galen left him alone.

Well, as alone as any guy could be with ten clones standing around....

Shit.

He stood for a bit, sort of watching the way the floor moved with the music before he reckoned he needed to do something constructive. Not construction, because it was the wrong season, and Galen wouldn't let him play with the nail gun after the last deck incident.

Just when he was about to start cleaning the toilet with his fingernails, Galen knocked and came back in. "What are you doing?"

"Uh.... Constructing? No. That's not it. Constructiving. Being construction. Shit." He closed his eyes, counted to some number between ten and fifteen. "Cleaning."

"Yeah. Wash your hands, darlin'. We'll go." Galen led him to the sink and washed his hands for him when he closed his eyes. "Aaron is coming in, and those guys buying you shots were long gone. No one to kill."

"No? Well, that's probably okay. We're not zoned for killing." The soap smelled like cucumbers. How fucked-up was that?

"Not unless you're related to the kill-ee. This is Florida, after all. Come on, darlin'. Let's get you out of here." So gentle. Galen's hands were so gentle.

"You want to dance first?" Hell, if he was off work? It was the first Saturday he'd had free in forever....

"Oh, darlin'." Galen led him out, all the way out, ignoring everyone. "We can dance at home, yeah?"

The wind was blowing, and he swore it was talking. "Yeah. That's cool. Then we can dance naked." He grabbed his car keys, looking for the Jeep.

"We can. I can strip you down and rub all over you." The keys went flying off in the wind, and Galen took him to the big old truck Galen had, hoisted him up in the cab, and strapped him in.

Man, that was some wicked, stunning wind. He swore to God, he saw his Jeep driving itself home, and they were moving out of hurricane country. Honestly, what did the wind need with his Jeep? Victor? Now he could kinda go there. Sort of. Except Victor had short little gator legs, and the Jeep was a standard, and, man... it would *suck* to have to manage the clutch that way....

There. Galen had the kind of legs you needed for driving. They hit both pedals, and Galen had long arms too, so he could shift and steer, though maybe Victor could do that with his teeth. Galen had nice teeth.

One of those long arms moved, Galen's hand landing on his thigh. "You okay?"

"Yeah. You know, you're a much better driver than Victor." He stroked Galen's fingers, heart beating a million miles a minute.

"You think?" A sideways kind of smile came his way, and suddenly they were home. Just like they'd flown. Maybe the wind was good for something.

"Yeah. Man, we're home." He looked around, frowned. His Jeep hadn't made it home yet, though.

"We are. We can dance. Come on, lover. Let's get you inside."

He nodded, let Galen ease him through the wind, into their house. "You pissed at me, Galen?"

"No, darlin'. Not at you. Not ever." They got inside, and Len locked the door and seemed to relax some. Which was good, 'cause, man, was Len wound too tight.

He reached up—and up and up and up and, shit, Galen

was getting taller in his old age—and started rubbing Galen's shoulders.

"Mmm. Feels good, darlin'. I promised you naked. Let's get you some water first." Len was being so nice. When he sounded so mad.

"Water." He leaned up for a kiss, the room spinning a little.

"Uh-huh. A big old glass of water." He got his kiss, light and sweet and too short, damn it.

"Okay." Shane really wasn't thirsty, but he had learned it was easier to go along with Len on stuff like this. The man was... single-minded. Determined. That was good when it came to sex, so he put up with a lot of other times. The water was all sparkly in the glass. Maybe it was bubbly water.

He could see himself in the bubbles, floating up and up like those guys in that show with the candy factory and the little orange singing midget-weirdos. Fucking creepy.

"Shane?"

Galen's eyes were way prettier than the water, so dark Shane could hardly distinguish the pupil from the iris.

"Darlin'? Are you feeling sick?"

"No. Weird. My heart's fluttery. Not sick. I don't think. I love you, yeah? Love how you call me darlin'."

"I love you too, darlin'. You know that, yeah?"

If he closed his eyes, he could drink the water. And Galen rewarded him with a kiss, so that was okay.

He leaned in, breathing Galen in, holding on, swaying to the beat of Galen's heart. His own heartbeat was like a weird counter-rhythm. They could dance to that. Galen swayed right along with him, arms warm and steady around him.

Fuck, he loved this man. Really, really. And not like a goofy, stupid love with hearts and cupids and shit, but like....

Uh.

Something way cooler.

Galen hummed, low and sweet, that whiskey voice melting right into his skin and running through his veins. It made the weird feeling better, made his heart a little less freaked out. He could feel every individual whisker on Galen's face rubbing against his cheek.

Oh yeah. He held on, happier than he'd been in forever—which was fucked-up, because he'd been happy a lot with Galen.

"You like the dancing, darlin'? This what you wanted?"

"Mmm... so good to me, Galen. Always give me what I need."

"I try. Even when you don't want it." Galen laughed, nuzzling him again, kissing his throat. Then those lips fastened right over the pulse point on his neck, and Galen sucked up a mark.

"Oh...." His belly went tight, the sensation huge, crashing over him and making him gasp. "Galen!"

"Crazy, isn't it, darlin'? Makes everything huge." Galen bit down on the bruise, making it throb.

"Uh-huh. Fuck." He held on, panting, a little worried. "I'm gonna be okay, yeah? It's all okay?"

"It is, darlin'. I promise. By tomorrow you're just gonna have a bad hangover. I've got you. You know I'd never let anything hurt you." Galen pulled him to the couch, curled around him. "I love you."

He nodded, settling right in, fingers sliding over Galen's arms, fascinated by the soft dark hairs. Galen was talking, he could hear it, but it was sort of buzzing in his ears in a low rumble, and finally Galen kissed him again, tongue easing into his mouth. Oh, that was much better than trying to work out when Galen started speaking Swahili. Pushing him down on his back, Galen came down on top of him, heavy and hot. They still had their clothes on. That seemed wrong.

"Mmm... naked." It was like magic, how those eyes went black.

"Yes. Don't let go. Don't let go, Len. Need you."

"Not going to, darlin'. What do you need?" Galen had him, held him, touched him all over, just petting.

He frowned, kept his eyes closed. "Shit's spinny."

"I got you. It will wear off, if I'm remembering right. You feeling sick at all?"

"Not really, just... wigged."

Worried, maybe.

Itchy, some.

"Good. I mean, not good that you're wigged, darlin'. But good you're not gonna puke." Galen shifted, rolled a little, got him up in Galen's lap. "Someone slipped you something."

"Why? What?" He was doing the baby-head thing again. Bizarre.

"I don't know, Shane. Someone at the bar. Those guys buying you shots? I could tell by your eyes." One big hand cupped his head, holding it still, cradling his skull.

Oh, dude. Yeah. They'd given him that first shot over at the table, all of them laughing and.... No....

"My eyes." He tried to look, crossing his eyes and making himself dizzy as all fuck.

"Don't. It won't do anything but make you dizzy." Galen kissed his forehead. "If you were gonna get sick off it, you would have by now. We just have to ride it."

Safe. Galen kept him safe. "We. Cool." If Galen was there, he'd be cool. Home. "I don't have my Jeep here."

"I know. We'll get it when you can drive again."

"Tomorrow." He nodded, cheek ending on Galen's shoulder. "Thank you."

He wasn't sure what *for*, but he was thankful.

"You're welcome, darlin'. And I swear to God, I ever get

my hands on them? I'm gonna kill them." The muscles under his cheek went hard, tension going through Galen's body.

"Bet it was an accident." Nobody wanted to hurt him. He was pointless. No. Harmless. Well. No threat.

"And I bet they wanted you, darlin'. You're special." Galen stroked his back, his hip. "No one gets you but me."

"No. No one but you. Never wanted anyone else after that first night. Blew my mind. Even in the Jeep when it was bad between us, I couldn't with anyone but you."

"I know. I know, darlin'. You blow my mind."

Oh, there. There was the good growly. He petted that pretty belly, humming. "Yeah. Blow you...."

"Yeah. I'll count on that sometime soon."

He actually got a laugh. Go him. Galen settled them nice and comfy, pulling the throw down off the back of the couch to cover them.

"Mmm... feels good." His head was heavy, whole body feeling weighted down.

"Yeah. You always do." Galen had to be doing something, something tricky to make him sleepy.

"You learned voodoo in New Orleans without me...." Shane would have to kick Galen's butt.

"Yep. While you were out getting pierced. Just wait until I summon up your Jeep."

The laughter rippled right through him from Galen's chest. Like butterflies.

"Oh, that would be so cool...."

But Len was gonna have to wait. He was tired.

Maybe even already sleeping.

GALEN WAITED UNTIL SHANE WAS GOOD AND ASLEEP, maybe sometime around six in the morning, and called his momma. He needed to talk, knew Shane would never really get why he was so mad, and maybe he didn't want Shane to. He loved Shane just as happy as he was.

Oh, that sounded bad. But his momma understood. She had seen him at his lowest.

"Hey, Momma," he said. "I didn't wake you, did I?"

She chuckled, her morning voice almost as rough as his. "No, honey. I been sitting and drinking coffee nigh on a half hour."

"Oh, good."

There was a long pause where he didn't say nothin', and she listened to him breathe. Then she asked. "What's wrong, baby?"

"At the bar tonight. Last night. Someone slipped Shane a Mickey, Momma."

"Oh." He could hear her draw a breath. "Oh, honey. Is he all right?"

"Yes, ma'am. He's sleeping it off. I just... damn."

"They didn't get you, did they?" She sounded downright worried now. And, hell, she had good reason. He'd been a damned junkie once, and when he'd come crawling to her to apologize, he'd been as wrung out as she'd ever seen him.

"No." Rage filled him when he thought of Shane's pupils, drawn up like tiny pinpricks. "Shane takes way better care of me than he does himself."

"Bullshit, honey. He's a big boy. You have to trust him, all right?"

"I do! It's all the other assholes I don't trust."

"Well, he's gonna meet a lot of assholes at a bar." She sighed, the sound as concerned as it was fond and exasperated and... Momma. "Are you coming for Thanksgiving?"

"I am. We are."

"Good. I want Shane here this year."

"Yes, Momma."

She wasn't trying to change the subject, he knew, and she listened to him rant and rave when he started up again and never said a word when he threatened murder and mayhem. In fact, the only thing she got het up about was when he told her how Shane was looking forward to Victor the gator coming back.

Then all she said was "That boy needs a dog."

He talked until he was hoarse, and he could tell she was worried about him. Hell, who could blame her? He hardly ever spilled his guts. Finally he sighed and said, "I love you, Momma."

"I love you too, baby. Get some sleep. I'll think on it."

It was a sure sign how tired he was that he had no idea what she was thinking on. He said "Okay" and hung up and went to lie down and watch Shane breathe. The rest he would work out later.

Chapter Six

THE DREAMS. Christ. Shane couldn't wake himself up, couldn't think, and couldn't fucking breathe. Galen was screaming and melting and shit, and at one point Vic was dressed like Carmen Miranda and his mom was there, wielding a cast-iron skillet and threatening to bean him with it. Shit.

Just.

Shit.

"Darlin'. Ease up. Ease up, you're dreaming." He wasn't sure when Galen stopped screaming and started petting him, but he liked the whole hat look better than the dripping skin melty thing.

"Dreaming." He liked dreaming. Except for the whole.... "Do alligators eat pineapples?"

Oh.

Pineapples.

Yum.

GALEN WATCHED SHANE CAREFULLY FOR A COUPLE of days, but he seemed pretty good. No ill effects save for a tiny hangover the next day.

Sometimes he was grateful for Shane's ability to bounce back.

And not only during sex.

In fact, he would bet the farm Shane was sick of him hovering, of poking and peering. He didn't want to say so.

Galen sat next to Shane on the couch. "You all right, darlin'?"

Shane looked over, grinned, hand sliding along his thigh. "Right as rain. Honest. It was just a little loopy. I'm cool."

"Oh, good." He should shut the hell up. Galen leaned in, arm going around Shane.

Shane snuggled in, all smiles and wandering fingers. "We should do something to celebrate my amazing allrightedness."

"We should." That made him grin back, made him relax for the first time in days. He leaned in even more, took a kiss. Shane met him halfway, kiss happy and eager, tongue pressing right into his lips.

He kissed Shane hard, showing all of his pent-up nerves, all of his need from the last few days of treating him like glass. He got a happy sound for his troubles, Shane climbing into his lap and rubbing against him.

They were really getting into the celebration when the damned doorbell rang, making them both jump.

Shane tilted his head, blinked. "We expecting company?"

"No." Galen lifted Shane up, set him aside. "Maybe it's Victor."

He headed for the door, dodging Shane's swat.

"You be nice about Victor, now. He was a good gator."

"He was." Well, well, well. He opened the door up, and there was his momma, plain as day, a big old picnic basket in one hand, a cooler in the other.

She smiled. "Hey, baby. Let me in. This shit is heavy."

"Len? Is that your momma?" Shane peeked around the door, smiling. "Well, hey, lady!"

"Hey, Shane. Since Galen is just gonna stand and stare at me, you can help. This is for you, anyway." She held out the picnic basket, pushed past Galen, and handed it to Shane.

It... wiggled.

Shane tilted his head and took the basket. "For me? Momma?"

Shane took a step back, eyes going wide as the basket whined.

"Well, open it up, boy." Momma handed Galen the cooler. "I brought you chess and meringue pies and a chicken dinner."

"Oooh... pie!" Shane sat on the floor, popped the top of the basket open, and... well, sort of made a peeping noise, but louder. "Oh. Oh, Len! *Look*!"

"What?" Galen bent, looked, and sure enough, there was some kind of dog, all floppy ears and wrinkly face. "Lord, Lord."

"Oh...." Shane looked like a kid—an incredibly muscled, studly, tanned kid—as he carefully lifted the puppy up and cradled it close. "Oh, damn. Look at you. Look at you." Those bright eyes gleamed up at Momma. "What's its name?"

"He doesn't have a name, honey. It's up to you. He's just been weaned. Can you believe he was abandoned with his littermates on the side of the *road*?"

Galen had to smile; his momma sounded so outraged, and Shane looked so damned cute.

"No...." Shane cuddled even harder, petting those long ears. "Poor puppy!"

"All the other ones were girls, and they got adopted. But Doctor Jameson was gonna have to put this little boy to sleep. I couldn't abide that, but I surely can't feed another dog."

Momma pushed past them, taking the cooler to the kitchen, leaving them with the... basset? Maybe.

"To sleep? But he's perfect...." Shane stood, headed right to him. "You want to hold him, Len?"

"No." Galen grinned. "He's for you, I bet. Momma knows I like bigger dogs." He backed off a step, knowing the pup ought to bond with Shane. "He's cute as hell, though."

"He *is*...." Shane loved on the pup, talking at it, the little fat tail wagging ninety to nothing.

Momma came back out, put an arm around Galen's waist. "Didn't I tell you that boy deserved a dog?"

Galen hooted. "You did. They'll go for long rides in the Jeep and take long naps."

Shane was busy taking the puppy out back, showing it the swamp, the yard, the bait shop. Lord.

Galen turned and hugged his momma tight. "Thank you."

She stroked his back, stood on tiptoe to kiss his cheek. "Y'all needed me to come visit and cook for you. And that boy needed a dog. Now get me some sheets for the guest room."

Galen nodded, his smile coming real and easy.

"Yes, ma'am."

Shane was up and bouncing, coffee brewing, puppy eating kibbles softened with warm milk. They had to take Momma to breakfast and buy stuff for supper and a puppy bed and toys and bones and a collar and maybe new sheets for the guest room, because Galen's momma had sort of got that look at them, and that always made Galen touchy.

Still, given that it was a surprise visit? The butt marks on random furniture were relatively few and far between, and the bathroom wasn't terrifying. The fridge had been, but him and Len had stayed up a little and dumped the worst of it.

The puppy finished his food, and Shane poured a cup of coffee, then scooped the sweet little turd up to go outside. "Come on, you little goober. Gotta do your business."

Galen came wandering out, blinking at him, looking rumpled and edible and grumpy as hell. "You're up early."

Oh. Oh, that voice was like whiskey poured on a scrape. All rough morning burn.

"The goober puppy was hungry and whining." He held up his coffee cup, offering, taking a good long look. Long and strong and *uhn*. All his.

Galen took the cup with a nod of thanks and downed the rest of the coffee in it. Those sloe eyes blinked at him, blurred and unfocused. "You gonna take him out?"

"Uh-huh. Wanna come sit on the porch with me?" He grinned, took a kiss. Fuck, Galen was something else.

"Yeah." Galen reeled him in, slow and easy, bending to make the kiss deep and hungry. It woulda gone on and on if Goober hadn't barked, making them both jump.

"Man, he's got a big bark for a little puppy." He headed out the back door, tugging Len along with him. "Gonna be a pretty day."

"We could spend some time out on the deck... soak up some sun." Galen came easily, hands moving on him randomly.

"Mmm... I like what the sun does to your skin." The pup went down to wander in the grass, and he leaned back against Len, relaxing under that touch.

"Hell, I like what the sun does for your everything, darlin'. Like the way it lights up the little hairs on your thighs, like the way it makes the muscles on your belly look." Galen stroked his belly, hands warm, firm.

Oh. Damn. He stretched up, damn near purring with it, lips tracing Len's jaw.

"Oh, y'all made coffee. Bless you." Momma's voice came

through the open kitchen window, breaking them apart. Len's momma was a progressive woman, but damn, you didn't want her watching through the curtain.

"Mornin', Momma." Shane tried not to groan, gave Galen a grin. Man, she could have slept another hour....

"Mornin', boys. Get a move on. I'm hungry, and you don't even have cereal."

Galen laughed, a puff of warm air on his neck. "We'll be good until she takes a nap. Come on, darlin'. Get the pup so we can crate him up."

"Crate? We have one? Will he like it?" They'd better get Momma decaf over breakfast....

"Uh." Galen got a look on his face. "We'll put him in the basket and bring him with us."

"Okay. Or we can lock him on the tile. It cleans easy...."

"Yeah. And I like to watch you clean."

Damn. If that was supposed to make him not want to do it in front of Galen's momma, it wasn't working. "Yeah. Bubbles." He blushed, rubbed against Galen a little as he went down to grab his puppy. "Goober! Come here, you. We gotta feed Momma."

The pup came tripping over its own ears, running right to him like he was the best thing going, panting and drooling.

"Oh. Oh, look at you...." He chuckled, scooped Goober up, and laughed. "Damn, that's something else. You see him, Len? He's something else."

"He is." Len looked like something else was both funny as hell and a little... odd. That look was fond but sorta bemused.

Shane handed Len the puppy, kissing Galen hard. "I'll go get newspapers and some towels."

Galen held the puppy gingerly, mouth opening and closing. He heard Galen's momma cackle as she opened the door for him. "Now, that's a sight."

Shane nodded happily. "They're fine together. Puppy's eyes are almost like Galen's."

"Oh, they are. Though I don't think that puppy has any thoughts of doing what Galen does to you, Shane honey." Oh, she was a wicked woman.

"Oh, Momma. Ew. That's just.... Ew. Galen, cover that puppy's ears before your momma scars his soul."

Galen laughed, low and husky. "She's got a point."

Momma chuckled. "Go on, Shane darlin'. Newspaper and towels. Those pancakes are waiting."

"Yes, Momma." He shook his head, blinking. Galen's momma was a force of nature.

She did love her pancakes too. He remembered that from last time. He could hear her and Galen talking, and Galen handed off the pup to go get dressed.

He put Goober in the towels. "Now, look. You go on the papers and sleep on the towels and don't make a fuss, and I'll bring you a toy."

"You're too cute, darlin'. Let's go get Momma pancakes, and maybe she'll let us fuck this afternoon."

"Decaf coffee, Galen. I'm serious." He grinned up, patting Goober and moving toward the door, Goober following right behind. "No. No, Goob. In the towels."

He picked up the puppy, got him settled, and headed for the door, Goober right on his heels.

Well, hell.

"Galen?"

"We'll train him to do all this stuff, Shane. For now, I say we fence him in." Galen got the big low chair from the entryway, one the pup couldn't get under or over, and put it in front of the little niche by the kitchen, plopping puppy, towels, and paper on the other side. "You go on before he starts crying for you."

"Crying?" Oh, poor Goober. "Just tell him when we'll be home. I'll get Momma settled in the Jeep."

"Will do." Galen gave him a thumbs-up, grinning at him.

"Thanks, Len." He grabbed his keys and wallet, then hurried out to the porch. "Come on, Momma. We're taking the Jeep."

"Oh, I like your Jeep, Shane. Honey, do you really like the dog? I don't want you to think you have to take him." She was looking at him, dark eyes just as serious as Galen's.

"Have to? Oh, Momma.... He's so pretty and soft, and we have to go buy him a bed of his own. And a collar. And bones. And other dog stuff."

"Oh, good. Galen told me you'd never had a dog, and I thought that was the worst thing I'd *ever* heard." She had this look, this momma look that meant all boys should have dogs. It was cute. Stubborn.

"We have a gator. Sometimes. He lives in the pool." He opened the door for her.

"A gator?" She climbed in daintily, looking ladylike as anything. "That's dangerous, honey."

"That's my Shane. He lives for danger." Galen hopped in. "Puppy taken care of."

"Thanks, Len." He started the engine. "Vic's not too dangerous, Momma. Not if you stay away from his teeth and give him the chickens real quick."

Momma laughed and laughed. "Only y'all would feed a gator off your back deck. Lord, Lord. Now let's go eat and shop."

"Yes, ma'am. Pancakes and PetSmart. Right away."

Hopefully the walk would tire her out enough for a long nap.

Chapter Seven

T HE HOUSE was spic-and-span. The puppy had a
bed, some bones, a whole box of toys, and enough
Beggin' Strips for a Great Dane.

When Momma went home, Galen breathed a sigh of
relief. Sure he missed her like he always did, but between her
and the puppy, he was getting a little grumpy.

Lord, that woman would clean anything if it sat still long
enough. And Shane was all about the puppy love. That pup
was gonna be so spoiled. He grinned to himself as he put the
last of the ingredients in his big pot for jambalaya. The place
smelled like tomatoes and hot pepper, and the smell of lemon
cleaner was slowly fading under it. That would have to cook
some.

Time to find Shane.

Galen washed up a bit and went looking, needing like
crazy.

Shane was on the floor, remote in one hand, dozing as
some shitty kung fu movie played. The pup was chewing on
the end of Shane's sock, tail wagging ninety to nothing.

He grinned. Damn, that was cute. But he wanted his piece of Shane too. Gently disengaging the pup, Galen gave him scritches all the way to his crate and wrapped him up in Shane's old sweatshirt. They'd found out that Goober wouldn't cry if he could smell Shane.

Then he went back to pounce on that fine ass.

He loved how Shane slept, ass in the air, head buried in pillows or one arm. Cute as fuck. Also? Easy access.

Hoo yeah. Galen stripped down. He didn't figure he needed all those clothes in the way. Then he knelt at Shane's feet and started working off the drooly socks.

Shane hummed, chuckled in his sleep, ass wiggling a bit. "Mmm.... Galen."

Well, at least he didn't say, "Mmm, Goober." That was a good thing. Galen worked his way up to sit level with Shane's hips, hands on that ass, squeezing.

Shane arched, pushed right into his touch, eyes blinking open. "Mmm... you done making magic in the kitchen?"

"I am. It has to cook for at least five hours." He grinned, massaging a little. "Whatever will we do, darlin'?"

"Oh, you're a smart man, Len. I bet.... Oh...." Shane arched, moaning low. "I bet you can think of something."

"You think?" Hell, yes. He needed to get to Shane's front, though. He tugged belt loops, getting Shane to turn over so he could get the button and zipper open. "I might could come up with something good."

Shane stretched out, hips rocking, wiggling, teasing him.

"Oh, darlin'." He slid one hand up Shane's belly, the other down into those open jeans. "Been missing this."

Shane hummed, rocked between his hands. "Feels good, Len. Like magic."

"Mmm-hmm." The shirt first, he decided. He wanted at those sensitive pierced nipples. He pushed the T-shirt off and pulled Shane up just a bit to get it over his head. "Damn. Pretty."

That tanned gold skin went all rosy, Shane's nipples tightening up into hard little points for him.

Fucking A. Galen pinched those pink nipples, pulling at the little gold rings. So hot.

Shane groaned, eyes going hot and needy, shoulders lifting up off the floor. "Len! Oh fuck."

"That's the idea, darlin'." God, that was amazing. He bent, took one little ring between his teeth, pulled hard. He heard Shane's feet drumming on the floor, heard the sweet, hungry cry as Shane bucked. One hand wrapped around the back of his neck, held him tight. He licked and sucked before moving over to the other nipple, sliding his hand back down into Shane's jeans to find his cock.

Oh, hell, yeah. Hot and hard, tip already wet—Shane was feeling it.

Feeling downright possessive after Momma's visit and all, Galen sucked one nipple until it was practically purple. His hand worked Shane good, thumb dipping into the slit. All sorts of words poured down over him—desperate and hungry, low and horny and perverted as all get-out. Shane humped against his hand, cock throbbing with it. He had to taste. Had to. Galen moved again, yanked Shane's jeans down around his knees, and bent to that hot prick, licked and sucked.

"Oh. Oh fuck. Len. Love." Shane's hands were in his hair, hips bucking up, driving up toward his mouth.

He hummed, loving the heat, the salt, the way Shane's cock rode against his tongue. Fuck, he loved to suck this man, loved the feel of it, the weight of it, the urgency. He pulled against Shane's balls as he hollowed his cheeks, just needing.

The cry that echoed right before Shane gave it up to him was pure desire, hotter than the August sun.

He sucked it all down, licked Shane clean before moving to straddle Shane's hips and taking a kiss. He rubbed and rubbed that sweet belly, cock hard as a rock.

"Mmm... what do you want, Len? Anything." Shane was a little blinky, the kisses sloppy.

"Just want you, darlin'. Need you so bad." He couldn't decide. Shane's mouth? His ass? The way he was feeling, he might come right there on that tight little belly. He pinched Shane's bruised nipple, relishing that gasp.

"Shit, love. 'M all yours." Shane squeezed his ass, tugged them closer together.

"Mine. Yeah...." Oh, fuck, yes. Galen rocked and rubbed, leaving a wet trail on the tiny hairs below Shane's belly button. "I ache, darlin'."

Those fingers on his ass slid inward, fingers tapping and teasing his hole. "Anything you want."

"Oh. Oh fuck. Touch me, Shane." Yeah, he was going crazy, humping like there was no tomorrow.

One hand slid around, worked his cock like a fucking pro while the fingers on his ass liked to drive him crazy. He couldn't hold it. When Shane pulled on his cock just that way and one finger slid right inside him, burning all the way, Galen lost it. He shot hard, wet heat spilling out on Shane's belly and chest.

"Oh shit, you're so fine." Shane was watching, eyes wide and bright, like he was the center of the fucking universe.

He bent and kissed Shane's swollen lips, feeling like everything had shifted back into place. "Just love you, is all."

Shane chuckled, tongue slipping out to taste. "Yeah. That's all."

He nuzzled, sniffed, the smell of them starting to mix with the jambalaya in the kitchen. "You want cornbread?"

"Mmm... yeah. I think there's cheesecake left over for after too."

"Oh. Cool." Not that he was inclined to move. Good thing they had a few hours on the food.

Shane nodded, lips soft and wicked sweet on his throat. Oh, hell, yeah. Good thing.

Chapter Eight

THE SUN was shining. The day was warm as anything, and Shane was out there in the sunshine and a pair of cutoffs, washing the Jeep with the kind of enthusiasm he usually reserved for the tub.

The pup was sound asleep in his little bed on the deck. There was turkey and sausage in the smoker Momma had gotten him for his birthday. Fuck, life was good.

Galen got his hat to keep the sun out of his eyes and started out to help Shane wash, but the sight of that little butt wiggling along to a Buffet song stopped him, made him tilt his head. Galen went back inside, got a tube of lube, and stripped off his jeans and shirt. At the last minute he put his boots back on, because, Lord knew, there would be mud, and headed back out, almost laughing at the way his cock bobbed in front of him.

But not quite, because when he slid right up behind Shane and pressed his cock against that ass just so? He wanted it to be a surprise.

Those cutoffs were soaked all through, the Jeep sparkling

and bubbly in the sunshine, Shane's skin gold and shining with the heat.

Hell, yes. He tiptoed right up behind Shane, moving close so there would be no spraying with the hose. Then he slid his arms around Shane's waist, resting his chin on Shane's shoulder.

"Hey, darlin'."

Shane jumped, gasped, ass pushing right back against his hard cock. "Oh! Hey!"

"You? Look edible, darlin'." He hooked his fingers in the front belt loops of Shane's cutoffs, tugging a bit. "Warm and wet and mine."

"Mmm... yours? You sure?" Shane was all laughter, eyes dancing.

The side of Shane's throat called to him, and Galen bit down on it. "Very sure, Shane."

Shane groaned, ass rubbing his cock, rocking, asking for it.

Galen wasn't much of a talker, really, but he had to tell Shane. He had to. "You were out here in the sun, darlin', just glowing, and I had to."

He unbuttoned Shane's cutoffs and pushed them down, let Shane feel him, naked and hot.

"Oh. Oh damn, Len." Shane's hands landed on the Jeep, slipping and sliding forward in the suds.

"Yeah. Had to have you." Perfect. Now Shane was all ready for him. Just like that. He grabbed Shane's hips, rubbing up on him.

Shane spread, ending up leaning over the Jeep. He could feel Shane's thighs, tight and hot against him. "Yours. Fuck, Len."

"Gonna, darlin'. Gonna fuck you good." He'd forgotten the little tube in his hand, but it was only a little squashed where he'd pressed it up against Shane's hip. Galen got it open, got his fingers slick, and slipped two into Shane's body, staring at where they joined up. "Fuck, you're gorgeous."

The breath huffed out of Shane in a moan. "Oh, that's.... More, yeah?"

"Yeah, Shane. More." He gave Shane more, fingers searching out the hot spot inside. The birds chirped at them, and soap bubbles popped on their skin, and he couldn't ask for a more perfect day.

Shane's head popped back when he pegged it, ass clenching around him tight as anything. "Oh fuck. Yes."

Galen still managed to slip one more finger in, stretching them out, stretching Shane. He wanted that ass open for him, ready, 'cause he was gonna ride it hard.

Shane stretched out over the hood, went right up on his toes.

Fuck. His cock jumped, his belly went tight, and Galen gave in to the urge that was riding him. He slipped his fingers free, lined his sun-and-Shane-warmed cock up, and he shoved right in, grunting at how tight Shane was, how fucking right.

"Yes." Shane bucked, muscles rippling and squeezing around him, holding him tight.

"Uh-huh." There. Right there. Galen pushed all the way in, hips against Shane's ass. He leaned down, hands sliding down Shane's arms, fingers twining with Shane's.

He fucking loved how they fit together, hand in fucking glove, Shane holding him tight. "Oh, hell, yeah. Love."

He moved, fast, hard jabs of his cock into Shane's body. He held on, loving the way Shane looked spread out for him, over the hood of the little Jeep, splayed and plugged. So fucking hot. Shane started shaking, shoulders rolling as they moved faster, the Jeep rocking back on its springs.

"Love. Shane. Oh, darlin', killing me." He rocked too, his hips snapping, his cock pushing so deep. He let go of one of

Shane's hands, reached up to pull and pinch one shining nipple ring.

"Len. Len." Shane groaned, riding him hard as spunk sprayed over the hood.

"God." Shane clamped down on him so tight, and Galen lost it, growling deep in his chest as he shot hard into Shane's body, banging him up against the hood.

"Mmm.... Damn. Damn, Len. That's something else."

He leaned, kissing Shane's cheek. "Couldn't resist you, darlin'."

"Good to know. I'll do your truck next."

"Hell, yes. And then you can scrub the deck." They'd kill themselves. But it was a beautiful day. And that was a helluva way to go.

Chapter Nine

"WE'RE GOING to Momma's for Thanksgiving. Is
that all right, darlin'?"

Shane looked up at him, squinting against the
watery sun. They'd had a big old blow the night
before, Tropical Storm Someone Fruity, and they were out
working at putting boards on the windows of the bait shop
where the glass had busted out. He'd not bother to replace
that until spring, when the worst of the season had blown out.

"Can we bring Goob?" Shane asked.

"You have to ask? Momma wants to know how he's doing.
I think she thinks of him as her grandkid now."

The cell phone clipped to his belt rang, and Galen reached
for it, but the way Shane's face fell made him let it ring. Then
the way those eyes lit up for him made him feel ten feet tall.

"You get time off from the business for Thanksgiving?"

He grinned. "Yeah. Frank and I are both taking the whole
week. No phone."

Shane bounced a little, that compact body flexing away,
making Galen pass over an admiring stare. "Cool! It's gonna
be fun, getting to go this year."

Yeah. Yeah, because last year he'd had to go by himself....

Galen forced that thought away and grinned wide, nodding before he reached over to goose Shane, just to hear him hoot and drop the hammer. "It'll be fun, all right," he said. "Wait until you taste Momma's pumpkin pie."

IT SMELLED LIKE TURKEY AND PECANS AND BREAD and fudge, and Shane thought he might die.

Of course, the guest room smelled like Galen and... something sorta fruity. Blackberry?

Blueberry?

Cranberry?

Weird candle-in-a-jar berry?

Something.

Shane leaned over, kissed Galen's cheek. They'd come in late-late last night and crashed like a pair of tired puppies. Sort of like Goob, and.... Man, Galen needed a puppy. "Happy Thanksgiving."

One big hand slid around his waist, just like Galen had been waiting for him and his kiss was a signal. The sleepy growl in Galen's voice told him Len hadn't been awake, really, but, well, that was how his Galen reacted to him. Immediate.

"Hey, darlin'. Happy Thanksgiving to you too."

"Mmm. Smells like your momma's been busy. Smells good." Sorta like what the TV said Thanksgiving ought to be like.

"It does." Galen took a long, deep breath. "Mmm. Pie. Rolls. Dressing. Just wait until she starts the turkey. The pups will be drooling."

"Yeah? Should I go help?" They didn't *do* Thanksgiving when he was little, and last year was.... Well. Not Thanksgiving.

"No. Nope. You should stay out of the way. By now Aunt Maura and Cousin Doola will be in there with her, and that's scary." Squinting past him at the clock, Galen chuckled. "In fact, we should stay in here until nine, when the parades start. We're expected to come out then and eat breakfast."

"Mmm.... Breakfast? Your folks don't mind that you and me are... in here?"

Breakfast.

Yum.

"Nope. Momma has stayed at our house, you know. And as for the aunts and uncles and cousins, well, this is Momma's house. Do we need to let the pup out, or is he gone already?" Len was *not* leaning to look. In fact he was... nibbling.

"I. Uh. Huh?" His nipples went hard and he rolled closer. God, Galen smelled good.

"The dog, darlin'. Does he get a free show, or are we alone?" That voice. God, he loved Len's voice, all sandpaper and *grrr*.

"Mmm. Momma let him out a while ago." She'd winked at him and smiled and shut the door.

"Oh, excellent." One big hand stayed on his waist. The other started sliding down his belly, fingers callused and rough. "We'd best get busy. It's eight thirty."

"Already?" He rolled over on top of Galen, straddling those lean hips. Fuck, they'd best get on it.

"Mmm." Stroking his back, Galen curled up to lick at one of Shane's nipples, teeth threatening. "You look happy."

"Uh-huh. I...." His toes curled, and he swallowed a moan. "I never did Thanksgiving before."

Those big black eyes stared into his, Len looking shocked as all get-out. "What, never?"

"No. My folks went out to a restaurant. I always worked." He'd sorta thought it was a myth.

"That's just wrong, darlin'. I tell you, you might be in for a shock, then." Those hands went right down his butt, squeezing.

"Is that bad?" Not the butt squeezing—that rocked. The shock part.

"No. I think it'll be good. I really do."

Oh, kisses. Kisses were good too. Len gave him one that was long and deep and hard. Shane stopped thinking about turkey and pie. Well, the whipped cream part sorta stuck around, because that mouth and his cock and whipped cream would be.... Damn.

"Mmm." There it was again. That hum. Galen cupped his cock, his balls, fingers squeezing him.

"Galen." He spread, hips starting to roll, pushing against Galen's hip, Galen's belly. "Want."

"Uh-huh. Me too. Want bad." Yeah, he felt Galen hard against him, right up on his thigh. Hot, wet, so hard and good. Hands, mouth, cock, everything about Galen felt good.

It was almost as good as being in their bed, almost, because this bed squeaked a little and Momma was right out there and *ew*.... A guy *didn't* want to think about anybody's momma while fucking.

They rocked, Galen pulling him down to get great friction, their skin slipping and sliding. Hoo yeah. They'd make it by nine, no problem.

He nipped Galen's bottom lip, tugging at it, loving Galen's little growl, the deep groan. His hand pushed down, wedging between them to get Galen's cock.

"Oh, darlin'. Yeah." Galen thrust right up into his hand, and suddenly both of them were stroking, straining, pulling.

Shane nodded, biting on Galen's shoulder to muffle his cry as Galen rubbed *right* there.

"Uhn." Grunting, Galen drove up into his hand again and again, hips pumping, wet heat spreading over Shane's hand just like that.

Oh. Hot. He. Oh. "Len."

Man, he hoped no one heard that sorta rhythmic squeaking noise.

"Come on, darlin'. Gimme." Greedy Galen.

"Uh-huh. Uh-huh. Oh. Damn." He arched as he shot, eyes rolling a little as the heat flowed through.

"Oh, Shane. Good. Happy day, indeed." Grinning, Galen hugged on him.

"Mmm-hmm. Happy day." Oh, he should bring Galen to Momma's for Thanksgiving every year.

"And we made it in time to wash up before we have to go out there," Galen said, popping his butt, laughing as he jumped.

"Bitch." He nuzzled a second, chuckling. "Man, I thought it was bad, to shoot so soon."

"Only under certain circumstances. When you're both there at the same time? Not a problem. Come on, darlin'. Momma will be knocking soon."

"Oh, man. We *so* need to wash." He rolled out of the bed and into the little washroom with the two doors, then peeked to make sure the hallway door was locked first. "You want a quick shower?"

"Yeah. Let's make some steam." Galen rolled up and padded after him, looking like a predator. It was hot. Oh. Oh, be good, Len. He'd get all het up again. Shane turned on the water, heavy on the hot.

He had to laugh, because a loud throat clearing out in the hall had Galen hopping in with him and scrubbing them both, getting a good foam. The touches weren't designed to get him revved, just to get him clean.

Galen's momma had some stinky damn soap. Slickery too. Sorta silky. Weird.

The water cut off as soon as he got rinsed, and Galen

wrapped him in a towel, kinda like a mummy, then hauled his ass out of the tub. "Jeans or sweats, darlin'?"

"Jeans. I don't want your people thinking I'm nasty."

"You haven't met them. Trust me, sweats would be fine." But Galen gave him a pair of jeans and a light sweatshirt, grinning big.

He shrugged them on. Yeah, well, still. He wanted to make Galen proud.

"C'mere, darlin'." Galen hauled him close for a kiss once they were both dressed. "You ready to go meet the family?"

"Yeah." He was. For real. "I love your momma."

"She's fond of you too." Laughing, Galen slid one hand into Shane's back pocket and guided him out into the hall, where they were promptly attacked by the pups.

"Beasts!" Shane laughed, scritching Goob as Momma's dogs tackled Galen full force.

Len romped with Momma's big black Lab, ending up on the floor with her licking his face. Someone poked Shane in the back, and he turned to see Galen's momma, laughing, her dark eyes so much like Len's it was weird.

"Good to see y'all are up. Go on and sit in the front room, and I'll have Doola bring out the biscuits and gravy."

"Good morning." He reached out and hugged her, kissed her cheek. "We've missed you." It wasn't bullshit either. Galen's momma was... something special.

Oh, she smiled at him so hard her eyes almost disappeared. "I've missed y'all too. When breakfast is done, come on in and wash some dishes for me. We'll chat."

"I can do that." Washing was one of his superpowers. "Did you notice Goob's all trained? He hardly ever chews on stuff anymore."

"I *did*. Now if I could just get these monsters to mind." She waved at Lila and Poppy, the shepherd twins, who were happily drooling on Galen's collar. "Come on and visit when you've eaten, honey."

She left him with a smile and a pat on the cheek, heading off, whistling a Christmas tune.

He looked over at Galen, shook his head. "Biscuits and gravy, huh? They as good as yours?"

"Who did I learn to cook them from, huh?" After hauling himself up, Galen came on and led him out to the front room, where there were already three guys sitting on the couches. Two of them had long, long legs, so they had to be related by blood. The other looked more round and short.

"Hey, y'all." He nodded around, gave everybody a grin. Shit, he'd never found a group of folks he couldn't get on with that he wasn't related to. "How's it going?"

One of the long-legged pair grunted, but the other grinned, nodding. Honestly, they could be twins. The little guy waved from his seat. "Hey there," he said. "You must be Shane. I'm Galen's cousin by marriage, Buford. Grab a plate, son. Parade's on, and food is on its way."

There were plates on the little table over by the hall, and silver and napkins.

Lord.

This was sorta like the first time he'd gone to Galen's house with all the pans and plates and shit like a real grown-up. Sorta like, not all the way like, because there wasn't biting or bruising or him riding Galen's cock like Galen was a prize pony....

Still.

Lord.

The tiniest woman he'd ever seen, with the pinkest hair he'd ever seen, came in, carrying this huge tray that Len took from her and set down before grabbing the lady to kiss her cheek.

"Morning, Cousin Doola. How's it going?"

"Galen!" Gracious, she had a voice like Minnie Mouse sucking a helium balloon. She was cute as hell. "Good to see you, honey. Did you bring... you *did*."

The little woman advanced on him, giggling up a storm. "Shane. You have to be Shane. It's nice to finally meet you, honey." She hugged tight for such a small thing, and she smelled like cranberries and baby powder. And sausage gravy.

"It's nice to be here. It all smells real good." He hugged right back. What the fuck kind of name was Doola? Then again, Galen wasn't the most common name ever, now, was it?

"Well, there's biscuits and gravy and eggs and grits and potatoes...." She babbled the whole while as she dragged him to the food, elbowing one of the tall ones out of the way as he tried to scoop up half the eggs in one go. Somewhere behind Shane, Galen was *laughing*.

"Y'all went all out...." He was gonna whack Galen for real. Man, he needed a cup of coffee.

"Now, Doola. Shane's not a morning person." Galen elbowed right in too, filling them a plate and somehow whisking him right away without being rude. "Let us sit a bit, and he promised to come wash dishes."

Doola nodded and bustled out, and he and Galen staked out this huge recliner, coffee appearing under his nose.

"Have I mentioned you're on Santa's good list, Mr. Frost?" He gave Galen a smile, a real one, drinking deep and letting the familiar heat and flavor settle him out.

"I thought I might be. It can get overwhelming even when you know them all. Wait until the kids start showing up." Galen stroked his belly a little, totally unselfconscious.

"I like kids okay." He just sort of melted, all of him. He wasn't going to admit it, but there'd been a part of him that had worried about how Galen would be, once folks were around.

"They like you too. Kind of like dogs." He got a grin

before Galen dug into breakfast, feeding him bites every now and then. A quick peek at the relations told him no one was even looking. Cool.

That made it that much easier, and by the time they were done eating, Shane had the guys and Doola relaxed and easy. It felt good.

"Okay, darlin'. You'd best go help Momma with the dishes or she'll pout. There'll be more coffee in there too." He got a serious look, a touch to one cheek. "Want me to come with?"

"I'm good. Momma and I do good." She understood how he needed Galen.

He headed into the kitchen, Goob following along, ears flapping. Dorky dog.

"Shane! Hey, honey. Come on over here. You feeling better now you've had some coffee?" Momma smiled at him, then kissed his cheek, her hug good and warm and right.

"I am." He squeezed her, kissed her back. "Happy Thanksgiving. Thank you for breakfast. It's so good to see you. We hit weather in Georgia, and I thought we'd never make it in."

It had been fun, though. Driving with Galen and Goob. They'd taken their time, goofed off, laughed, sang Christmas songs, eaten weird random crap. He'd loved every minute.

"Well, I'm glad you did. Without y'all to ease the craziness of all of these weird folks, I might go crazy." She set him up at the sink, tying an apron around his waist. Goob started biting at the strings right off. "So you're not missing anything with your folks?"

"My folks?" He blinked, shrugging a little. "Oh, Lord, no. They never did Thanksgiving, and uh.... Well.... They don't talk to me anymore. Haven't in ten years."

"Oh." She gave him this look. This sort of squinty-eyed, lips-pressed-together look, and for a minute, he thought she was mad at him. Then she said, "Well, they just don't know what they're missing. It's a good thing you got us now, isn't it, honey? Got family to be with."

"It is." He grabbed a plate, started scrubbing away. Well, of course it was good. Galen and Momma were his family now, just like he was one of theirs. "Everything smells good. Did you make pecan pie? Galen's been talking about it ever since we left home."

"I did. And pumpkin and chocolate pie too. I know you like the chocolate." Someone he didn't know appeared at his other elbow, grabbing the plate and drying it.

"Hey, there." He nodded over, kept scrubbing. "Oh. Chocolate pie is the best. Do you need anything from us? Like for groceries or anything?"

"No, honey." Her hip bumped his as she reached for a bag of apples. It was homey. Like when he and Len cooked and cleaned together, only with less groping and kissing and all. Uh. Yeah. "If y'all want to go buy a bill of groceries after everyone else leaves, we'll talk on it then."

"Okay." That was really sort of Len's thing anyway. He struggled hard enough at the club making numbers match up. His money he handed over. Well, after Galen found out it was all in a tin can and he'd never even had a checking account, anyway.

Goober barked, and Momma tossed him a piece of sausage, making the silly mutt wag and wag. It was all so normal, so nothing like anything he'd ever had, that it made him blink.

"Are you all right, honey?" Momma asked.

"Yeah. Yeah. It's just.... You know how you see something on the TV and you think it's made up and suddenly it's not and you get a second of missing out on all the years you thought it was a lie and it wasn't?"

"Oh." She sniffed, her eyes shiny. "Oh, honey." Momma

gave him another hug, standing there with her arms looped around him.

"Oh. Oh, I didn't mean to...." He panicked a little, patting. "I'm okay. It's okay."

Where the *hell* was Galen?

"It's okay, honey. I just...." She sniffed some more. "Well," she said, letting go. "Those dishes are piling up."

He nodded, smiling at her, plunging his arms back into the dishwater, glad for something to do. "What's your favorite Christmas song?"

"I like 'O Holy Night.' Did you know that Galen's is 'O Little Town of Bethlehem'?"

Shane chuckled, nodded. "He does a pretty good 'Go Tell It On the Mountain' too."

In fact, that was one of his favorite things, Galen singing at the top of his lungs, a touch tipsy, ass draped with tinsel. Not a Momma-appropriate memory, but a favorite, nonetheless.

"He *does*. I should drag y'all to church on Sunday and make him sing." She looked so happy at the thought.

"Oh, I don't think so" came Galen's voice from the doorway.

Shane grinned over, beaming at the peace in those dark eyes. Galen looked happy, settled. "I like 'We Three Kings' best. You could do that one."

"I'd just sing about that rubber cigar, and Momma would hurt me."

The guy next to him drying dishes hooted, and Momma laughed right out loud.

"Now *that* we could sell tickets to." He winked over, started washing mixing bowls.

"Yeah, yeah. Watch it or I'll take a dish towel to your butt." There was no heat in it, and Galen moved right in beside him, saying, "I'll take over, Cousin Hal. Thanks for all your help."

Oh, now this was nice. Easy. Good smelling. Man, Galen looked good in black—like better-than-average good.

Something about the whole sleeves rolled up to dry dishes, muscles flexing in the forearms was the perfect look for his Len. It wasn't until Galen nudged him that he realized he was just standing there, staring. And Momma was laughing still, moving around him, peeling this and popping more dishes in the sink. She did know how he needed Galen, she really did. She seemed to like him all the more for it.

Which was good, because if it pissed her off? They'd be fucked.

Not only that, he wouldn't have Goob.

"So what time is supper, Momma?" Galen asked, bumping hips with him in a totally different way than Momma had.

"Not until late, as we have to wait on Aunt Louise. About three. Why don't you boys go play? And by that I mean football or something," she added, eyes twinkling. He grinned, felt his cheeks go hot. Somehow he thought their brand of tackling might be a bit... graphic and naked for Momma.

"Oh, I bet we could get Dale and Don out for a quick touch game." Grabbing his arm, Galen started pulling him out of the kitchen. "When she lets us out of dishes, we go. 'Kay?"

"Okay...." He grinned, following along, shaking his head. "Who all's coming for supper? Lunch? Whatever?"

"Oh, I don't know. Sounds like most all of the local cousins and all. Maybe forty or so people." Well, Galen sounded like that was normal. Nothing to panic over. Nope. Damn. And also sort of wow.

"Cool. You got a lot of family."

"Well, Momma does. I just sort of tag along." He got a wink, a pat on the ass before Galen was waving at the two tall ones. "Y'all wanna play some football?"

"Hell, yeah. Come on, man. Let's go."

Shane chuckled as one of them hooted, bounced up. "Skins or shirts?"

They bundled him outside, arguing over something or other, and before Shane knew it, there were six more burly guys out there with them, all sorting into two teams. Luckily Galen claimed him for his team.

He leaned over, whispered into Galen's ear, "Man, we ought to be shirts, yeah? I got my rings."

Somehow he thought that would be sorta bad, not to mention hard as fuck to explain.

"Yeah, okay." He knew that look. That one. With the holes-in-a-blanket eyes. Ka-ching. He definitely needed his shirt now. "No, Dale. I call shirts, I told you. I'm the one drove from the Keys."

That was right. Hell, Galen looked at him like that again, he'd have to untuck his shirt to hide what was peeking.

"You just don't want us all to be stunned by your hairy-assed chest, Frosty." Man, that Dale guy best watch himself. Galen tackled *hard*.

"Nope. Just don't want to scare you with my muscles." Flexing, Galen grinned, then grabbed the ball. "We won the toss. Come on."

He got the ball, bent over, Galen's hands right there near his ass, waiting for the ball. Man. Man, football was a sexy fucking game.

Galen called the play, giving him his "Hike!" Then he got to rumble with Galen's cousins, and oh... oh, he couldn't remember ever seeing Galen look like *that*.

The game got a little more intense, each play feeling hotter, more focused. Goddamn. Just. Goddamn.

Watching Galen take down Dale... Dan... Don. Something. Watching that smooth leap and tackle? Wow. Hot. Hot, hot, hot.

Of course, he also got the added bonus of Galen growls

when two hundred and eighty thousand pounds of Louisiana redneck tackled him and smooshed his ass. Lord.

And also, oof.

"No damaging him," Galen hollered, hauling his... cousin? Something up off Shane, letting him breathe again. "Got it?"

The guy nodded, grinning, gap-toothed and looking so happy Shane had to grin. "None? Man, he's little. We could squash him!"

Another one snorted. "Shit, he's little, but he's built like a brick shithouse, you see?"

"All right, y'all. That's enough." One long arm wrapped around him, Galen pulling him close and sort of bristling. "Mine."

"Hoo-ee! Look at that! What would your momma say, you getting all bristly like a boar hog?"

Shane chuckled, shook his head. Man, they hadn't seen bristly yet. "Quit your jawing and grab the football. You spent more time playing, we wouldn't be up by fourteen."

That got Shane a round of laughs, and everyone settled back into play. Shane had seen this in movies. It was like a redneck Norman Rockwell painting; it really was. He figured one of two things would happen—someone would send the turkey flying out Momma's picture window or there would be a thing tonight involving beer, Christmas lights, and a plastic flamingo dressed like the baby Jesus.

They finally got called in to help with supper just about the time two carloads of people showed up. Lord, it was like clown cars, maybe fifty little kids pouring out.

It was easy, really, to go into work mode. He knew about crowds and dishes and getting people moving where they should be, and hell, the way some of them folks were drinking, he might as well be slinging suds. Momma was in her element too, kissing cheeks and patting heads and prying kids off

Galen's legs now and then. Len was surprisingly good with the little ones, though.

And the food.

Oh God.

By the time everybody was settled—perched on every chair in the house, kids draped over every available surface, including Galen—Shane was feeling the urge to take a deep breath, wash his face. He wandered up to the little bathroom and sat a minute on the edge of the tub. Goob was right there, curled together on the little wee pile of dirty clothes they were needing to wash. "Happy Thanksgiving, Goober puppy. It's something else, huh?"

Goob's shifted and snorted and sighed. Made him grin. Look at that beast. Shit.

He had about ten minutes alone when a knock came on the door. "Shane? Darlin'? You okay?"

"Yeah. Yeah. I'm fine." He stood up, went right to the door, feeling sort of like a moron. "Just saying hi to the pup."

"It's okay. I'm getting a little squirrely myself. I told Momma I needed a nap. She said she'd call me when it was time to see most everyone off." Galen took his hand, pulled him right up for a kiss.

Oh. Hey. He stepped in closer, hands sliding around Galen's neck, holding on tight as Galen's tongue thrust right in. That was what he wanted. Just that. Humming, Galen shoved him back into the bedroom, kicking the door closed behind them, hands hard on his hips. Warm, good, so strong, Galen loved all up on him.

"Mmm... happy Thanksgiving." He licked Galen's grin, tongue sliding over those lips. "Gonna tackle me, redneck?"

"I am. You've been so good, Shane. I'm proud of you. Time for your reward." Oh, he liked the sound of that. Liked the feel of Galen rubbing against him better.

He groaned, eyes rolling back into his head. Oh. Oh damn.

He tilted his hips, let his cock rub against Galen just so. There was something to be said for the way they fit together.

"Oh, darlin'. Love the way you fit," Galen said, echoing his thoughts. See? They were amazing. Fucking amazing.

"Yeah." He leaned back, letting Galen hold his weight, support him. "It's all good."

So much better than before.

Galen bent and kissed his throat, his ear, lips warm and soft, the ridge of Galen's teeth hard and good. It was impossible not to moan, lift his chin, and beg for more. God, he loved the family and food and ball and shit, but wasn't any of it Galen.

"Love." Those hands lifted, cupped his ass, pulled him up so Galen could just.... Oh. There. Right there.

"Uh-huh. Len." His fingers got tangled in Galen's hair, keeping that mouth on his skin.

"Wanna. So wanna, darlin'." Oh, man, even with everyone in the house... thank God their room was off by itself.

"Door's locked. I was good. Did dishes and everything."

"Good." Lifting him, Galen carried him to the bed, the springs making a terrible squeal as they bounced down on the mattress. Galen just laughed, nibbling him, spreading his legs to rub between. He chuckled, leaned up to do some nibbling of his own, give back what Galen was giving.

That got him a hum, a nice growly sound. Galen kissed him again, fucking his mouth with that hot tongue, taking his breath away. It got him to wrap around Galen, legs tugging Galen closer so their hips moved in time with that tongue.

They rocked and rocked, that old bed hardly keeping up with them. That long body pressed him down into the mattress, Galen's cock pressing against his pelvis.

He struggled to get Galen's jeans undone, get his own open. "Skin. Galen. Come on."

"Huh?" Black eyes looking drugged, but not in the bad

way like Shane had been once, Galen looked at him, blinking, finally nodding. "Right."

Len reared up, flinging clothes off. Sexy fucker. His sexy fucker. He reached up, got hold of Galen's nipples, and tugged.

"Uhn. Shane. Darlin'." Galen's hips snapped forward, hard cock sticking out of his jeans. "More."

His lips opened and he nodded, tugging again, harder, wanting that prick so bad he could taste it.

Galen groaned, struggling with Shane's clothes too, getting his shirt up under his arms and his jeans open, those hands sliding over him. "What do you want, darlin'? Tell me."

"Fuck my mouth, Len. Hungry for you." It was Thanksgiving after all, wasn't it? Time to indulge.

He got a look, those eyes on fire for him before Galen moved up to straddle his chest, cock at his lips. "You okay, darlin'? Is this okay?"

"Uh-huh." He lifted his head, mouth open, tongue sliding over the swollen tip of Len's cock.

"Oh fuck, Shane. Good." Muscles bulged as Len arched back above him, hands on his thighs. God, he could see cock, abs, chest... yeah.

It was possibly the hottest fucking thing he'd ever seen.

Ever.

Period.

The taste of Galen slid over his tongue, hot, wet, and salty bitter. Cock slipping right in, Galen started moving, grunting a little. He started sucking good and hard, pulling that flesh in and in, running his tongue over the tip and pushing in. He knew how much Galen loved that, loved the way he tongued the slit in the tip. It made Len crazy, made him buck hard. He did it again and again, trying to drive Galen crazy, make his lover arch and groan.

It worked. Len sat up again, hands on the headboard as he leaned in, fucking Shane's mouth like crazy.

Hell, yes.

He didn't even pay attention to his own cock, the way it leaked and ached. All he knew was that heat, driving into his lips, filling his mouth.

"Come on, darlin'. Just like that. Fuck, you feel good...."

That throaty growl told him Len was this close to losing it. So did the precome that slid down his tongue, wet and hot and so right. Just right. He pulled harder, demanding, fucking wanting it right now. Now. His.

Galen came, whole body arching up and back, cock throbbing hard between Shane's lips. Giving it all up, just like that. So fucking good. So hot. All his. Fuck. Fuck him, yes. He drank Galen down, humming around the flesh in his lips, purring.

Galen let him have it all, then pulled free, sliding down his body to kiss his swollen mouth. "Want in me, darlin'?"

Like he could find words to answer that question with. All he could do was nod and moan, cock slapping his belly. Galen reached for the ditty bag they'd left on the nightstand, then scooted up to straddle him again, this time his belly. Oh. Lube. And... yeah. Galen was gonna ride him. His eyes rolled, hips arching up. His cock slid along one of Galen's asscheeks. Damn. "So hot. Fuck. Want you."

"Uh-huh. Yeah. Okay." Panting, cheeks flushed above his little beard, Galen looked down at him and put one hand behind himself, getting himself ready. Jesus. Len didn't do that often. Not nearly often as Shane wished.

It was enough to make a man whimper, to make every muscle in his body tight and hard. He reached out, one hand sliding down Galen's chest, petting him.

"Feels... feels good, darlin'. Don't stop." He could feel

Galen's hand working, feel it rub against his prick as Galen's fingers moved in and out.

"Won't. Damn. You.... You just." He grinned, tugged Galen down for a kiss that said all the shit he didn't have words for.

"Mmm." Galen hummed into the kiss, letting it stretch good and long before sitting up, pulling his cock into position. "Ready?"

"Balls to bones." His hands settled on Galen's hips, mouth open as he watched.

Galen nodded, face tight and intent as he rose up and then pushed down, taking Shane in smoothly, so hot inside that it burned.

"Galen...." He arched up, eyes rolling in his head like dice, teeth just clicking together.

"Shane. Oh God." Len started moving on him, up and down, taking him in and out. Those heavy thighs bracketed his waist, squeezing.

"Love." He let his hands run over Galen's thighs, hips, petting away, entire body thrumming, aching as they moved back and forth.

"Uh-huh. Happy... happy Thanksgiving, darlin'. You did so good." Galen loved on him too, stroking his chest, pulling his nipple rings.

"I. Oh. Oh, sweet Lord." His shoulders rolled up, left the mattress, hips moving faster and harder.

"God, yeah." He could see Galen's cock rising again, hard and tight, bobbing in front of him. It made Len even tighter around him.

Look at that. Just. Oh, he was the luckiest son of a bitch ever. He wrapped one hand around Galen's cock, stroking in time, petting. That made Len's muscles all bunch up again, the flush staining that tanned skin, the squeeze and release of Galen's body maddening him.

"Gonna." Oh. Fuck. Gonna. Now. His head tossed and he panted, trying to hold on, to give Galen a good ride.

"S'okay, darlin'. Wanna see. M'close." Oh, his Len was a wonder, riding him like crazy, teeth caught on his lower lip, eyes heavy-lidded.

Oh, thank God. He stopped worrying it, started humping up furiously, hips and hands moving together. It only took a few thrusts before he was shooting, filling Galen up as he fucking melted away.

"Oh, oh fuck!" Shane opened his eyes, who knew how much longer later, just in time to see Galen shoot, great spurts that landed on his chest, his chin.

He managed to lift his hand up, wipe his chin and suck his finger clean. Mmm. Galen. Damn.

"Shane." Collapsing down on him, Galen laughed, the sound husky and deep. "Been needing this since, oh, football."

"Uh-huh. I like that. Football. With you." Right. Coherence. Go him.

"Me too." It didn't seem to matter to Len. He nuzzled and kissed and all, loving on him.

"Can we nap for real?" He was getting all baby-headed and dopey, sinking into the pillows with a happy sigh.

"We can. Momma won't expect us to say good-bye to anyone but, like, Doola. We'll see them all again in smaller doses during the weekend, yeah?" Galen let him slip out, pushed to one side to curl around him, big and hot and sort of covering him.

"Mmm-hmm. Yeah." He kissed Galen's jaw. "Happy turkey day, huh?"

"Yeah, darlin'," Galen agreed. "The happiest one of my life."

SHANE REMEMBERED HIS FOLKS' PHONE NUMBER, AND Saturday morning after Thanksgiving, he dialed it and hung up the phone as soon as it rang.

What was he doing? Shit. They didn't want to talk to him. They hadn't in a long, long time.

Still.

Seeing Galen's momma and people made him think that maybe he should try. Just say hi and howdy. Say happy holidays.

Say that he wasn't a big loser like they'd thought, and he was good at running the bar, and he and Galen were like a thing and stuff. Just say that sometimes he missed having people around who remembered him from more than a couple years ago, people who could tell stories about when he was little.

He picked up the phone one more time, looking around to make sure no one could hear, and dialed again.

"Hello?"

Oh. Mom. "Hey, Mom. It's Shane. I wanted to...." He got about that far before he realized he was talking to himself, that she'd hung up. "Say happy Thanksgiving." The last part he mumbled to himself, staring at the receiver.

"Shane, honey? You in here? I need a partner at cards, son."

He put the phone down, found a smile for Galen's momma.

"There you are. You okay?"

"Fine, Momma. Let's go play."

She wrapped her arms around his waist and nodded. "It's so good, having my boys home."

Shane nodded, kissed the top of Momma's head. Yeah. Yeah, it was good. Good to be with his family.

Chapter Ten

G ALEN COULDN'T sleep.

That wasn't too damned unusual, though it was better now he'd gotten used to having Shane. Still, he'd tried to snuggle up to that fine, fine ass and go back to sleep, and it hadn't worked. Neither had trying to wake Shane up. Shane was obviously out for the night. Galen tossed and turned for a good bit, but he finally gave it up and went on out to the living room to maybe have a beer and watch a movie. Try to forget that somehow they'd zoomed through Christmas and New Year's like shit through a goose, and now Shane was looking at fucking tourist season again, and he needed to finalize the shit for training camp for the Lightning boys and....

Shit.

He sat on the couch with a Blackened Voodoo and flipped channels, fucking amazed at how many infomercials there were on at 3:00 a.m.

"You 'kay, Len?" Shane stood in the doorway—naked and at half-mast, blinking hard, Goober running in circles around his feet.

He grinned over, loving how Shane looked when he was sleepy and warm and... damn, Goober looked desperate. Galen got up and let the silly dog out the back before coming back to find Shane still right there, still blinking. He put his arms around Shane's waist.

"I'm fine. I was just trying to decide what we need more. The Boot Camp Training video or the cooker thing that makes empanadas and shit."

"Boot Camp? Oh, blah. Empanadas are cool. Mmm... you're warm...."

Hello, nothing like a cuddly Shane to make a man feel good. "So are you. I couldn't sleep." He nuzzled in, his beard scraping Shane's cheek and neck. Damn. Yeah.

"Mmm...." Shane slid his hands around him, cock jumping a little. "I'll make your dreams sweet."

"Promise?" He kissed Shane's throat, crowding close. Fuck, he hated not being able to sleep.

"Uh-huh. Couple of orgasms? Then snuggling. Then sleep. Guaranteed."

"You do always come through for me, darlin'." They should probably let Goober in, though. Just in case. "Let me let Goob in, and you can go to work."

"Work? Uh-uh. Fucking isn't work. It's...." Shane grinned, shrugged. "You know."

"I know, darlin'. There ain't nothing in the world I'd rather do, long as it's with you." He popped Shane's ass and went to let the mutt in, watching the silly thing bounce all over.

"Come on, Goob. Back to bed." They had come to an agreement—after an unfortunate incident involving low-hanging balls and milk teeth—Goober had a spare bed in the guestroom.

Goob waddled right on in, and as soon as the door was closed on his big, sad eyes, Galen grabbed Shane and kissed him hard. Shane groaned, arms reaching up and holding on tight, cock snuggling right against him. So damned honest and responsive. Galen searched out all of Shane's flavors, thinking how they really ought to move into the bedroom. But the hall would do in a pinch.

Shane snuggled close, rocking and rubbing, sliding against him, cock starting to leave little wet kisses. Galen had to touch that sweet cock, had to feel it, and he reached between them, his fingers grazing the head. He dipped his finger against the slit, then raised it to his lips, licking it off before kissing Shane again.

"Mmm." Shane went up on tiptoe, nibbling on his lips, tasting him.

"Oh, darlin'." He just groaned, grabbing Shane around the waist and hauling him into the bedroom. They needed to be horizontal. Now.

Shane came easy, maybe even doing a little pushing himself now. Encouraging him into the bedroom, onto the bed. They sorta tumbled together, their teeth clacking for a moment before they got it right again, mouths opening and tongues thrusting. Shane groaned, one leg wrapping around Galen's, tugging them closer.

Yeah. Hell, yeah. He shifted, encouraging Shane down into the bed, hips rolling as he rubbed. Damn, he loved the way Shane felt, smooth and hot and good.

"Quick one now. Then slow. Then sleep. Fuck. Len."

"Yeah, darlin'. Yeah." He lined their cocks up, giving them friction. Shane's hand landed on his ass, fingers digging in, squeezing. Galen rocked, feeling the heat rising, knowing it wouldn't be long. Shane got to him like a brush fire, made him hotter than the hinges of hell.

"Fuck, love. Come on. Come on." Shane's heels drummed on the mattress, hips bucking.

That just... shit. That put Shane's cock right along his,

rubbed them right. His balls slapped against Shane and Galen groaned hard, shooting in short, sharp bursts.

"Sweet fuck, yes!" Shane arched, heat spreading over his belly, his hip.

"Mmm." Damn, didn't that make him purr like a big old cat. Galen nuzzled, waiting to catch his breath for round two.

Warm hands petted his back, fingers sliding easy. "That's it. That's right."

Warm, cuddly, and concerned Shane. Galen grinned. Yeah. He liked that. "Sorry I woke you up, darlin'." He wasn't. Not really, but it was only polite to say it.

Shane chuckled. "I'm not. Not even a little."

"Oh, good. 'Cause I'm not either. So, did you say something about slow and long?" Galen rolled off onto his back, hands behind his head.

"Mmm... long. I like long." Shane chuckled, moving to straddle Galen's hips, soft ball sac rubbing his prick.

"Yeah? So do I, darlin'. And I like how you look up there." Fuck, that was pretty. Galen stroked Shane's chest, going for that flat belly that fascinated him so much.

"Mm...." Shane's body went tight, little gold rings bobbing as those nipples hardened. "Gonna ride you hard, Len."

"Woo." He grinned up, reached up and tugged one of those little rings. "I'm waiting, darlin'."

Shane's head went back, mouth opening on a deep, low cry. Oh, hell, yes.

That still fascinated, still shook him to the core, how Shane had done that, gotten those hot little nipples pierced through and how sensitive they were. Galen tugged the other one, twisting it just a bit, watching Shane's reaction greedily.

"Len." Shane bucked, cock throbbing against Galen's for a second before Shane moved, ass teasing his prick.

"Shane." One hand dropped to Shane's hip, pulling him

down. The other stayed on Shane's chest, teasing those glinting rings. "Get the lube, darlin'."

"Uh-huh." Shane stretched and reached, gave him a view of that fine, fine body. "Shit, that's... damn."

"You know it. I want you so bad." It never ended. Even when he had Shane all a hundred ways from Sunday, and five minutes ago too. He still wanted that hot body around him, on him.

Shane grabbed the lube, slicked his cock, hand moving sure and steady, moving him from mostly interested to hard enough to fuck. "Mmm.... That's it."

"God, darlin'." He was just gonna explode. Galen stroked down to Shane's hip, holding him steady. "Love the way you feel."

"Want to ride you." Strong thighs straddled his hips, Shane leaning to grab the headboard.

He lined up right and tight, the head of his cock flush against Shane's hole. "You ready, Shane? Or you need some work first?"

"Always ready for you. Always." Shane shoved back, arching as he bore down.

His cock slid right in, and damned if Shane wasn't the hottest, sweetest thing he'd ever had. Ever. He'd known that for a bit now, but it still surprised him. He always fucked up long before now. Galen rolled his hips up, shoving in.

"Yeah...." That sound was something else, all deep and needy and sort of raw around the edges, Shane giving it all up for him.

He reached down, spread Shane even more, his fingers brushing that tight little hole stretched around him.

"Oh. Sweet fuck." Shane's eyes went wide, ass clenching his prick. "That's. Damn."

"Shane." His cock throbbed, making his eyes roll. His stomach muscles clenched too, rippling as he pushed.

"Uh-huh. Uh-huh. Love. Fuck." Shane bounced, riding him like he was the prize pony at the fair.

They went to town, not exactly slow and easy, but he'd last. He would. He'd make it good for Shane. The chain that he'd bought Shane to decorate those rings was swinging between Shane's nipples, each motion tugging those dark little bits of flesh. That damn near killed him. Galen reached for it, tugging it, watching how it made those nipples harder and harder.

"Len. Oh." Shane leaned down, groaning. "Harder. I need more."

"Yeah. Yeah, Shane." He moved harder and faster, his cock stabbing into Shane, his whole body going tight.

Shane jerked, went tight as a miser's pocketbook, and shot for him, not even requiring a touch to that heavy cock. Galen shot deep, gritting his teeth on a cry. He wanted that so damned bad.

Shane slumped down against him, breath huffing out in a whoosh.

"Oh, love. Yeah, darlin'." Oh fuck, that was like nothing else going. Nothing. Galen put his arms around Shane's back and held on tight.

"Think you can sleep okay?" Shane's lips were on his jaw.

"I think I'm gonna sleep like a baby." He grinned, nuzzling in. There was nothing worse than not being able to sleep, but with Shane as a blanket? He was going to have a good night after all.

Chapter Eleven

JESUS FUCKING Christ on a pink sparkly pogo stick. Shane felt like he'd been rode hard and put away wet, and he wasn't even put away yet.

Seriously.

He hadn't been home in forever, and he was fixin' to lose his ever-lovin' mind—between deposits and ordering, cleaning and paperwork, and add that to the fact that every fucking bartender in this entire frigging town had the plague, he was done. Just pure-D done.

"Hey, man, what's up?" One of the guys who had floated in on the tide came into the bar, all deep-tan and sun-streaked blond hair.

"Working."

"I swear to God, you work harder than any human being on earth." Mr. Blond-and-Whitened-Teeth plopped down on a barstool. "I thought you were the boss."

"The manager, and all that means is I work when no one else will and I still have to do the paperwork." Shane wiped down the bar. "What can I do you for?"

"You available?"

"Huh?" What? Everyone knew he was Len's. Everyone. "Oh, honey. I'm taken. Like bone deep taken. I mean, I ain't sure I remember what he looks like, but I know that if I ever get another four hours off in a row, I'll sure do my best to figure it out."

"That's too bad. I'll have a Bloody Mary, to start me off."

"I'm on it."

He'd just about plopped the celery into the glass when his cell phone rang. He actually winced. God, he knew it was going to be someone calling in. He knew it.

"You don't have to answer that, you know...."

Shane shook his head, but he knew better. He'd answer and he'd work, because that was what he did. "I'm the manager."

He grabbed the phone. "'Lo?"

"Hey, boss, it's Jake...."

GALEN HUMMED AS HE CLEANED, SHAKING IT TO some serious fiddle music. Goober looked at him like he was nuts, but the poor mutt really didn't appreciate a good bouncy bluegrass song.

He was waiting for Shane to get home. They'd kept Shane working for the last eighteen days, thanks to so many bartenders calling in with the flu. He'd been needing, and after tonight, Shane was supposed to have three off, so he had *plans* for that ass. He just had to keep himself, and Goob, occupied until Shane came home.

Goob heard Shane before Galen did, howling and beating those heavy paws against the door, ears flapping. Damn, that dog lived to see Shane, adored him.

Galen could relate.

He let Goober out. The dog could reunite with his master

out in the yard. There would be ball throwing and slobber. Then Shane was his.

He heard Shane's voice, tired but happy, Goob's bark getting a low laugh. "Where's Len? You been good for him, sweet baby? Lord, it feels like I've worked forever. *So* glad to be home."

"He was a doll. Come on, darlin'. I got a beer and some mac and cheese with your name on it."

"Oooh. Mac and cheese! For real? Have I mentioned I love you?" He got one of those grins, pure happy and all his. "Got four days off in a row. Aaron's pulling a swing and doing deposits."

"Thank the good Lord." Galen went over and took a kiss, smelling smoke and whiskey and Shane's sweat.

Shane pressed close, hands sliding around his waist and holding on.

"Mmm. Hey, darlin'." God, he loved the feel of Shane against him, loved the taste of Shane on his lips. He held Shane close, rubbing and swaying.

"Hey." Shane leaned in, looking at him, smiling. "Good to be home."

"Good to have you home, Shane." Kissing Shane's throat, Galen moved them to the kitchen table. "Why don't you eat, and we'll take a shower."

Shane nodded, digging right in. The man was easy to please—Galen still couldn't quite fathom that Shane hadn't ever seen mac and cheese that wasn't Day-Glo and from a box before he'd made some for them. His momma had been appalled when he'd said that, sending him all sorts of recipes. Hell, he was getting downright domesticated. "So, you have a good night?"

"Not bad. Long. Wanted to be here." Shane ate hearty. "Been a long few days, you know?"

"Yeah, darlin'. I thought if I came in, it would just make it worse." For him and for Shane, if they had to stare at each other over the bar, damn it.

"Yeah. I can see that. Still." Those eyes met his, all of the sudden hot and needy. "I'm home now."

"You are. I got plans, Shane." He did. Oh, Lord, he so did.

"Yeah?" Shane licked his lips, put the fork down. "I'm done eating, Len."

"Yeah." He got up, held out a hand. "Come on, darlin'. Let's get that shower. Then we'll have some fun."

They could have fun in the shower too, for sure.

Those warm fingers curled right into his, Shane pulling him close with a sharp tug then kissing him good and hard, making sure he felt it. Then Shane bounced off and hurried down the hall, clothes flying. "Come on, then."

Chuckling, he followed fast, slipping his own clothes off so he was nude when he reached the bathroom. Shane already had the water going, steam rising out of their shower. Galen stepped in with Shane, reaching for that hot, wet skin.

Shane grabbed the soap, started sliding it along Galen's ass, his back.

"Mmm. I'm supposed to be taking care of you." He moved even closer, cupped Shane's ass in his hands.

"Mmm-hmm." The hard bar of soap felt good, Shane rubbing it against him and working his muscles.

Shit, that felt fine. Gave him all sorts of ideas, but that was what the big dildo by the bed was for. He kissed Shane hard, tongue sliding between Shane's lips. He got a low moan, those lips parting for him like the Red Sea for Moses, just letting him right on in, Shane hard and hot against his hip.

Hell, yeah. Galen lifted Shane up on his toes, kissing that mouth for all he was worth, rubbing against Shane's belly. He heard the *thunk* of the soap hitting the tub, Shane's fingers holding him tight, tugging him close. They rocked together, so hot for each other. Never ceased to amaze him how hot they got. Like flash fire. Galen bent, lips sliding down Shane's chin and down his throat, sucking up a mark.

Shane's chin lifted, giving him more skin to mark, to bite. That skin called to him. It was a fucking addiction. Galen left a bruise on Shane's neck and a bite mark on one collarbone.

"Oh. Shit. 'S good, Len." Shane was moaning, rocking into him.

"Mmm-hmm." Oh, there. The ball of Shane's shoulder needed teeth marks. He bit, licked, and sucked until he had the perfect purple. "Soapy."

"Happens in the shower." He got a wicked grin, Shane's eyes laughing and heated.

"Yeah, yeah." Just for that he pinched Shane's ass. "You're cruising, darlin'."

"Promises, promises." Shane pushed a little, wiggled.

"Oh, you better believe it." Galen rinsed them off, rubbing all on Shane as he leaned to turn the water off. "Come on, darlin'. Need you."

Shane nodded, following, pinching and teasing and playing all the way. They got to the bedroom, and he swept Shane off his feet, tackling him on the bed, driving the breath out of him.

"Oh. Hey." Shane panted, stretched out all pretty underneath him.

"Hey. You ready to play, darlin'?" He held Shane down, reaching to the side table for the black leather straps. "I am."

"Oh, hell, yes. Been too fucking long. Too long." Yeah, it had been. Longer and longer between each time.

"Yeah, darlin'. Yeah." Fuck, Shane felt good under him, but he knew he could make them feel even better. Galen sat up, straddling Shane's waist, grabbed one of Shane's hands, and wrapped the strap around it. He lifted, slowly stretching Shane out, then tied that wrist to the bedpost.

Shane watched, tongue licking those sweet, swollen lips. "Oh."

Yeah, oh. Fuck, that made him hard. He paused to flick one of Shane's little nipple rings, watching it bounce for him.

That dark red skin went tight as a stone, just wrinkling around that shiny metal.

"Fucking love that, Shane." And didn't he have to taste, then? Yeah. Galen bent, licking and tugging the ring with his teeth.

"Uhn...." Shane bucked up, free hand sliding through his hair, holding his head.

That wasn't gonna do. Grabbing that hand, Galen sat up and pulled another strap around it to fasten it down too. God, Shane looked amazing in black leather, all splayed out and ready for him. He touched the wet nipple, the quivering belly. "Gonna make you fly."

"Oh damn. Want you." Shane rocked up toward his touch, muscles going tight and hard.

"Yeah. Soon, darlin'. I promise. Got a few other plans first." He knew how much Shane liked the dildo, not as much as he liked Galen, sure, but as a setup? It worked like a charm. He got it, got the lube, then sat back between Shane's thighs, his cock leaking against Shane's leg.

"Open up for me, Shane." Those muscled thighs parted, knees bent and pulled back, offering him everything. Lord. That made him moan. Galen got the dildo good and slick, along with his fingers, and pushed two of them against Shane's hole, holding the dildo ready.

"Shit." Shane was watching, panting, teeth sunk into that bottom lip.

"Hot. Shane. Darlin'." So hot inside. He got it going quick, knowing neither of them could take too much teasing, got Shane stretched just enough that the dildo would burn going in. Then he slid his fingers out and slid the warmed toy right in, watching Shane open around it.

"Oh, fuck, yes." Shane arched, balls drawing up tight. "Galen."

His fingers found the edge of that sensitive skin, barely touching, tracing the end of the dildo. He couldn't believe how that looked, what it did to him.

The headboard creaked as Shane tugged, body going taut.

"You just make me want things, darlin'. Such things." The plan. He had to get with the plan. Well, he was doing pretty damned well, but Galen wanted more. He reached for another strap; this one wasn't leather but a soft braided silk. It trailed over Shane's nipples as he dangled it.

"What do you think I'm gonna do with this one?"

Shane blinked, moaning low. "It's soft, feels good. Gonna drive me crazy?"

"You bet I am." Himself in the process too. He ran the end of the strap down Shane's belly, just over the straining cock.

"Oh. Oh." Shane bucked up, rolling.

"Makes your skin jump and twitch, doesn't it?" Shit, yeah. Galen wrapped it loosely around the base of Shane's shaft, pulling so it rubbed lightly as it slid free.

"Uhn." He got a nod, a gasp, Shane's legs shifting and sliding on the bed.

That? He had to do again. He wrapped, pulled, watched Shane's face as he did it over and over again.

"Fuck. Fuck. Len." Shane bucked up, whimpering low.

"What about here, darlin'?" The strap slipped down, rubbing over Shane's balls.

"Oh. Christ, love. Don't stop."

"Not gonna." Not by a long shot. He teased Shane with that damned strap until they were both shaking, both panting. Finally he reached for the dildo, jostling it. "You ready for me, Shane? Ready to let me in?"

"Please. Need it. Now." Shane twisted, damn near wild. "Now."

He shuddered, easing the dildo free, getting himself slick so he could push right in, taking Shane deep. He just... fuck.

"Len!" Shane's ass rippled around him, fluttering and squeezing and driving him crazy.

"Shane. Darlin'." He was gonna go off like a firecracker on the Fourth, and he wanted Shane with him. He wrapped that silk strap around Shane's prick and started stroking, moaning deep and low, feeling it vibrate through him. Shane started babbling, making promises and threats, filthy words pouring out as his lover worked him, met each stroke. He nodded, knowing exactly what Shane meant, feeling his balls pull up and his eyes roll back. "Shane! Fuck!"

He shouted as he shot, filling Shane deep and hard.

Shane followed right along, grunting and pulsing in his hand, making the silk hot and wet.

Galen slumped, landing half on and half off Shane's chest. "Oh. Darlin'."

"Uh-huh. Love." Shane nodded, heart pounding.

"That'll show you to work so much." He nuzzled, holding Shane close, laughter chuffing out of him.

"You know it. Missed you something fierce."

"You too. Missed you bad. You're gonna have to make it up to Goob too." Later. After they snuggled and maybe did that again.

"'Kay. Will. Promise." Shane nodded, kissed him.

"Just stay here a bit, though." First he wanted his share of Shane. And that? Well, hell. He'd never get enough of that.

Not in a whole lifetime.

THE PHONE RANG JUST WHEN GALEN WAS ABOUT TO get up and grab a cup of coffee. He and Shane had been busy beavers, and he was feeling good, so he went ahead and answered it. "Hello?"

"Len! You got a minute?"

He tried hard not to roll his eyes, even though the guy on the other end couldn't see him. He recognized the congenial North Carolina accent as one of Frank's cronies. One he didn't particularly trust.

"Hey, EW. What's up?" Galen headed out on the deck so he didn't wake Shane, who needed his sleep.

"I was wondering if you'd run some numbers with me. I got a meeting with the board at Duke Electric today, and I need some help."

Galen blinked. "Not sure that's in my area, E-Dub."

"It's a sponsorship, so it really is our purview. You have a knack, buddy."

"I have some plans today, man." He'd guaranteed his time, in fact.

Goober came waddling out and flopped in the sun, ears flying. That meant Shane was up and moving.

"It'll take five minutes."

Galen glanced into the kitchen window. Shane wasn't looking for him yet, so he sat at the patio table. "Five minutes, man. That's all I got."

"Thanks. I really appreciate it, Lenny."

He gritted his teeth. That drawn-out Lenny made him want to hit something. "Bring it on."

When Shane brought him a cup of coffee ten minutes later, he caught Shane's wrist and pulled his lover down to sit with him. They were just going over the same old thing over and over.

"Uh-huh. I think you got a handle on it, buddy." He winked at Shane. "No, I got to go. Right. Bye."

"I didn't mean to interrupt," Shane said, eyes shadowed by a gimme cap.

"I know. I was glad you came out. Boring."

"Mmm. It's good that you're in demand."

The phone rang again, and Galen checked the number. Nope. Not today. He turned off the ringer. "What do you want for breakfast?"

"Besides coffee?" Shane chuckled. "Something sweet?"

"Sounds great, darlin'. Let's do it." He stood and stretched, glad he'd kept his resolve and not spent his whole day doing business on the phone.

That smile on Shane's face made it all perfect. Now, if Goober would just stop farting.

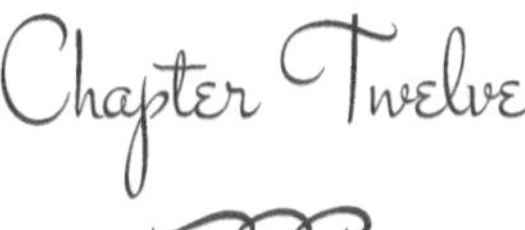

Chapter Twelve

MAN, GOOB could snore.

The pup was curled up under Shane's desk in the little bed Galen'd bought him, sawing logs while Shane got tomorrow's deposit ready, listening to the guys downstairs cleaning and singing and goofing off.

Still, snoring was way better than farting, and the sound was like home.

Not Galen-moaning home.

Or the home when Len called him "Darlin'."

Or even the way Galen sang while he was cooking.

Or....

Okay. Shit. He was getting a woody. He shifted in his chair, adjusted himself.

"You got Goob down there with a stick of butter, darlin'?" Wow. He'd conjured Galen out of thin air. Cool.

"He's dreaming about bacon and chew toys." Shane grinned up, licking his lips at the sight that filled his doorway. Boots, jeans, black shirt, black hat—the whole fucking package just for him. Damn.

And there was this... belt buckle. He couldn't remember

ever seeing it before, but man, it was shiny and big and sat just above Galen's....

"Are you listening, darlin'?"

"Huh?" Listening? To what? He'd been busy looking.

"Are you listening to me? I was asking if you were about done. I figure we wouldn't even wake the pup if I bent you over the desk and fucked you nice and hard."

Whoa. Growly, dark-devil-eyed Galen.

"Oh... I shoulda been listening." His hand found his cock, good and hard now, rubbed through the denim.

"Stop that." Galen grinned, pushing off the doorframe and coming right up to the desk, that buckle taunting him. "That's mine, Shane."

"Yours?" He reached out, fingers sliding on that tight fucking belly. So hot.

"Yeah. I want to touch it. Feel you. How about you get up around here and show me?" Galen took his hand, pulled him up, pulled him around the desk. Then he got a kiss that made his brains leak out his ears. Oh, sweet fuck. He wrapped his hand around Len's nape, petted the short, thick hair curling there.

"Mmm, yeah." Oh, the steel wool voice just made him melt. Galen gripped his butt and lifted, that buckle pressing into his belly.

"Fucking hot." He licked the edges of that neat, trim little mustache, hips jerking as Galen shivered.

"Yeah. Got to missing you, sitting at home. Thinking about you. Decided it was time to come get you." Galen tugged at his shirt, getting it up and off and floating off to the floor somewhere. Then those big hands were on his jeans, opening them right up so Galen could feel just how hard he was.

"Oh fuck. Was thinking about you. The way you sound."

He started unbuttoning Galen's shirt, fingers slipping in to stroke those tiny little nipples.

Galen moaned, the sound deep, almost hoarse. "Yeah? You like the way I sound, darlin'? I like the way you feel." Rough and callused, Galen's fingers closed around him, the flat of Galen's palm riding up and down his cock.

He groaned, eyes rolling, thighs spreading as his balls went tight. "Make me so fucking hard."

"I can tell, Shane. Love it. Let's get these off." Letting him go, Galen pushed at his jeans, the air brushing him seeming cold compared to Galen's heat. He wiggled, getting himself naked before reaching for that shiny buckle hiding that heavy prick from him. Galen let him, standing back a little, arms spread. "Come on, darlin'. Wanting to fuck you soon."

He nodded, groaning low, lips sliding on that exposed skin while his fingers opened belt and fly. Galen smelled so fucking fine, all sex and soap and man.

"Yeah. Oh yeah." Together, they got the belt off, the jeans down, and Galen stripped off that black shirt all by himself. "You have anything, darlin'? Or do I need to get you ready?"

"I got whiskey and lip balm...." He winked as Galen hooted, reaching for him. "Got to make a Galen drawer. You know—lube, breath mints, butt plug."

"There you go. Well, then, turn around here and bend over." Galen arranged him over the desk, face down, and he heard Galen's knees hit the floor behind him, felt Galen's breath on his ass. Then Galen's cheek rubbed him, hands spread him, just before Galen's tongue slid out to touch his hole.

He jerked, a deep sound sliding from him as his thighs went tight. "Len. Sweet fuck. So hot."

A rough noise was his only answer, sliding right up his spine as Galen licked and pushed, opening him up and getting him good and wet.

He rocked into it, nipples hard as fuck, little rings dragging on the desk. His cock was leaking, every motion making him throb.

Len slid two fingers inside him, scraping his last fucking nerve raw, stretching him. In, out, getting him good and open, that tongue just demanding. Finally Galen got up, rubbing all along him, chest hair scraping up his thighs, ass, and back. Galen's cock prodded him, wet and hot. "You ready?"

"Fuck, yes. Need it." He thrust back, demanding.

Bastard. Looking so fine. Sounding so good. Then teasing him with that prick. It was *good* to be him.

"Good. 'Cause I'm hurtin'." That was the end of the teasing, Galen sliding right in, splitting him with that thick cock, hot as all get-out. Hips against his ass, Galen pressed him down, hands sliding along his arms to spread them wide on the desk, so he gripped the edge. "Just like that until I say, darlin'."

Oh. Fuck him raw, he loved this man. "Bossy." He held on, all spread and stretched out, holding Galen tight, muscles buzzing with it.

"Needing." Galen started moving, just short, sharp thrusts, rocking him against the desk. They generated enough heat to warm up a third-world country, and Galen let him have it, grunting, talking to him, voice washing over him like a whiskey bath. The wood under him was slick, cool in contrast to the pure heat behind him, inside him. He could fucking feel everything—Galen's thighs, the pointed hipbones against his ass. Those lips against his shoulder, telling him things that made him ache, made him moan deep and low. Galen dropped one hand to his hip, the other sliding between him and the table to find his nipple, twisting the little ring.

"You got any idea how fucking hot you are, darlin'? How crazy you make me? Love you."

"Len. Oh, love. Been needing this. All of me." He lifted up on his toes, fingers going white-knuckled as he arched.

"Me too, Shane. So bad. Let go, darlin'." Galen pulled against his chest as his hands popped loose, yanking him up and back so that cock pushed up in him hard. Galen's other hand slid forward to wrap around his cock, squeezing.

"Galen!" He went all tight and white-hot, belly clenching as he shot, eyes rolling with it.

"Fuck...." Galen groaned, long and low, hips pumping. Wet heat filled him just a few seconds later, Galen's whole big body shaking behind him.

He looked up and back, trying to catch his breath, get himself a kiss. "Hey. Wow."

"Hey." Galen kissed him, open and sloppy. "That was worth gettin' all dressed up for."

"Uh-huh. You looked... damn. Ain't nothing like you anywhere else."

"Good thing too." Galen moved back, turned him for another kiss, laughing as Goob snored loud and long. "I sure thought it was more exciting than that, darlin'."

He chuckled. "Shit, Len. We don't want him getting enthused when there's dangling bits involved."

"Lord, no. Maybe he's just getting used to us."

"Maybe." He took himself another kiss. "Glad you came down, Len. Made my night."

"Let's get that deposit in, and I can take you home and make it again." Galen went for his jeans. "I'll even carry Goob."

"You're good to me." He leaned down, kissed the small of Galen's back.

Yeah. Good to him and just home.

Chapter Thirteen

D UDE.

   Kung fu theater.

   Popcorn.

Rain storm outside.

Beer.

Sleeping puppy.

Life? She was good.

Shane hooted as the big bad guy weirdo monk type fuckers tried to jump the good guy—Lee? Hwung? Something. You knew he was good, 'cause he kept getting his ass kicked and his teacher-dude died—and asses were kicked.

"Len! Man! You're *missing* it!"

"What? What the hell are you going on about, darlin'?"

"The good guy's gonna actually maybe win." He grinned over, grabbed some popcorn, trying to decide whether to eat it or toss it at Galen.

Oh.

Galen who was looking all showered and wet and....

Oh, yum.

Galen came right on out and grabbed some popcorn,

blocking his view a minute, but the towel-clad ass? Was just fine.

"Yeah? They always do eventually."

"Yeah, it's cool...." He reached out, hand sliding up along Galen's thigh.

"Sounds like a lot of wailing cats, darlin'." It did, kinda, when you weren't watching. Ooh, warm, right where Galen's thigh met his ass.

He slipped down onto the floor, tongue chasing the tiny drops of water caught on the dark, dark hair on Galen's leg. "Uh-huh...."

"Mmm." That was a happy, horny noise if he ever heard one. "Gonna teach me some kung fu, Shane?"

"'Kay." He wasn't really listening. Who would with all that skin waiting for his tongue? He licked up along to the crease where ass met thigh, fingers spreading those legs some.

Galen opened his stance right up, thigh muscles tight and strong under his hand, balls dangling between. The scent was all soap and man.

"Oh.... Oh, Len." He couldn't decide whether to spread those sweet, muscled cheeks or reach to stroke Len's balls, tug 'em a little.

"Mmm-hmm. Like that, darlin'? Sure I'm not interrupting the movie?" Oh, Len was teasing, ass swaying, that strong, strong back twisting. He settled on hefting that velvet-soft sac, rolling those balls while his teeth scraped the small of Galen's back. Fuck the movie.

"Uhn." That growly thing sent shivers right down his spine, and suddenly Galen's scent was stronger, hotter. He'd bet that sweet cock was hard and wet for him.

He slid his fingers up to check, and oh. Oh yeah. Thick and hot and hard as Chinese algebra—which was a dumb fucking saying, because they never, never, *never* did algebra in the damn movies and....

Oh, slick.

He got his fingertips wet, brought them around to draw a lazy circle around Len's hole.

"In me, darlin'. Want you. Please...." Man. Oh, man. Galen didn't ask pretty very often.

"Uh-huh. Wanna love on you." He spread Galen and started licking, started wetting that tight little hole, pressing inside, just enough to tease.

"Want you too. So bad. Was thinking about you in the shower, Shane. Waited for you, but you had popcorn." Len was kinda... babbling. It was cool. Made him feel.... Fuck, it made him feel damn fine—hard and hungry and all about being hot. He eased in deeper, working his jeans open with one hand.

They turned together, Len leaning down on the couch, the bend at the waist opening Len right up for him. He whimpered—couldn't help it, Len was so hot—and he surged up, tongue sliding along Len's spine. He got to the curve of one shoulder blade and bit down. Giving back a little of what Len'd given him.

"Fuck! Darlin'. Gonna drive me crazy." Every muscle in Len's big body tensed, and he could feel it. Feel Len fighting the need to turn around and give it to him good. It was sexy as hell.

"You can pay me back tonight. Right now, you get to be all mine." He bit again, toes curling right up. His cock nudged Len's hole, begging to be let in.

"Now." Pushing back, Len tried to rush him, tried to line him up. The hair on Len's thighs brushed him, that tight butt rubbing.

"Uh-uh. You let me love you, now." He waited for Galen to relax, fingers rubbing all along that muscled back, making sure Len knew he wasn't being a bitch, wanted to make it all right.

Gradually, Len relaxed under his hands, sighing happily and stretching, but not demanding. "Yeah, darlin'. Yeah. Love how you feel. How you do."

He smiled, tongue dragging here and there. "Good. So good for me."

When Galen groaned, shivered, he eased right in, sinking into Len's heat. The sheath of muscles closed around him, Len's body out to burn him right up. Galen's muscles jumped, twitched, sweat beading up in Len's skin.

He licked the sweat up, waiting to move 'til Len eased, that grip not so tight. "You ready?"

"Yeah. I am. Need you." Growl. Like sandpaper right over his nerves, that whiskey voice. So hot. "Come on, darlin'."

"Oh, good." He wrapped his fingers around Len's hips, started fucking with deep, long strokes. He pulled them together over and over, made the couch creak for them.

They moved so well, so easily, Len moaning for him, rocking back against him. They almost lost their balance when Len leaned up on one arm so he could use the other hand on his own cock, but they got right before they fell.

Shane shifted and moved until he found the perfect spot to send Len flying, Galen's low cry letting him know he hit it right. "Oh. Fuck, yeah. Right there."

God, if Len got any tighter, he might just die. Galen's moans came fast, low, so rough and deep. And the rhythmic movement of Len's arm and shoulder told him how close Len was as it got faster and faster.

He leaned down, pressed his lips to that dark mark he'd left, hips slamming. "C'mon. C'mon. Gimme."

"Fuck!" That shout rivaled all the weird cat noises on the TV, and Galen gave it up for him, coming like a freight train. And Len's body closed so tight around him that he saw stars. He emptied himself out, bucking furiously, buried in balls-deep as he shot. Sweet fuck.

Galen supported both of them, head down between his arms, legs starting to just shake. "God, darlin'. Love you."

"Love you. Damn, Len. I... I'd a come to the shower. You... you're way better than popcorn and kung fu."

Laughing, Galen folded at the knees and they went down. Galen snagging the discarded towel to clean them up. Turning, Galen put an arm around him and pulled him close for a kiss.

"Mmm... hey." Shane grinned, rubbed their noses together.

"Hey. You taste like butter." He loved that look in Len's eyes, all unfocused and dazed.

"Popcorn." He grinned, licked, listening to the squealy, twangy weird-ass music from the TV. "Lucky for you it's a double feature."

"Oh, so I get fucking and kung fu." They snuggled up, a little sticky, a lot warm and happy.

"Uh-huh. Life? Is good."

He stretched, fed Galen a bite of popcorn.

Real fucking good.

BEER?

Check.

Munchies? Yep.

Goober? Where the hell was the mutt?

"Shane! We've lost the dog. How can we go to the beach without the dog?"

"Lost Goob? No way. Did you look on the bed?" Shane wandered in, flip-flops and straw hat and sunglasses. "Goob! You wanna biscuit, baby?"

Damned if there wasn't a flop and a grunt and then the shuffle-shuffle of that little beast.

"He hides from me." Galen grinned, took a kiss as Goob waddled in. While Shane fed the little butt-wagger, Galen found his straw Stetson and his old white canvas sneakers. "You ready?"

"You know it." Shane bounced. The man loved the sun, the beach, the whole package, grinning at him, eyes dancing. "Let's hustle."

"Don't forget Goob's leash. Remember how he wandered off last time, hunting that wild corny dog." Darned hound sniffed so hard he wandered off a *mile* up the beach before they found him. Galen got the cooler and the snacks, and they headed out to the Jeep. Goddamn, it was a fine day.

Goob howled along with Shane to the radio, both of them happy as pigs in shit.

It was all Galen could do not to just laugh and laugh. Shane and that pup... well, his momma had been right. They were a match made in heaven. Didn't look like it was too crowded at the beach either, so maybe they could play some Frisbee, tease the pup.

They got all set up, Shane glistening in the sun, damn near glowing. The little radio got turned on, and he got a beer and a grin and a nice, nice view. A man could live for weeks on a look like that. Galen settled his cold beer on his crotch, knowing it was way too damned early to be getting a stiffie. Pulling his hat down, he wiggled down in his lounge chair, grooving on the waves and the sun and Shane humming.

"Man, I love being out here. 'S why I stayed, you know? Got down here and got all addicted and shit."

"Yeah. I didn't think too much beyond swamp when I came down. Reminded me of home. This was a bonus." But he'd gotten used to it. The water and sand and Shane over the hood of his Jeep and... Goob eating something nasty.

Shane turned over, legs spread, sweat drops slip-sliding

down his thin spine. "Yeah. You think Victor's found him a lady gator yet?"

"Oh, I imagine he has. He's a handsome bastard."

Victor. Lord, Lord. Galen chuckled, then wrapped his lips around his longneck and pulled.

Shane grinned, nodded. "He was something else. How many folks got them a backyard gator?"

"Yeah. I bet he'll be back someday." He would bet on it too. Free chickens and a pool with floaties. What more could a gator ask for?

"He will. Maybe with baby gators." Shane snorted, cackled. "Oh, man. That would be funny. Little baby Vics."

"Oh, sure. Goob would try to eat them. Besides, according to the Nature Channel, it's the momma gator who hangs around until they can go out on their own." Because if it was on Discovery, you knew it was true.

"No shit? I think they'd give Goob the runs." He got a grin, Shane shifting on the blanket. "And speaking of mommas, yours'd shit a pink Twinkie."

"You ain't just a woofing." He could damn near see his momma running around with a broom, beating little gator babies. The thought made him laugh right out loud, and he nudged Shane with his toes, sharing the visual.

Shane cackled, rolling over, hand sliding up along his thigh, little tease. Every inch that hand moved up his leg gave him another bit of elevation on his cock. Galen raised one leg to hide it just as a couple of kids came along to pet Goob and... good God, that pup's breath.

Shane sat up, gabbing with the kids, throwing a stick for Goob so they could watch the pup run and bounce, those ears like Dumbo's. Surely the mutt was gonna take off and fly one of these days. The kids distracted Shane enough that Galen could run his foot right along under Shane's butt and tickle as the kids ran off.

Shane jerked, hooted, asscheeks squeezing up as he wiggled. "Watch it. Gonna get sand in scary places."

"I like friction, darlin'. But not that much. Want some Cheetos?" Those orange things were just the ticket for a lazy day.

"Oh... hell, yes. We got Swiss Cake Rolls too?"

"We do. We'll have to eat those up or they'll melt." Little Debbie first. Then orange stuff. Goob came back, and he flipped the little mutt a Cheeto. There was nothing much better than chocolate and beer. Sex with Shane. Good whiskey. That was about it.

Oh, well, there was watching Shane eat those damned cake thingies. Damn. The chocolate got nibbled and licked, and then the cream filling got licked out.

"That's almost obscene, darlin'." He was so hard a cat couldn't scratch him. He wanted Shane's mouth in the worst way.

"Just almost?" Shane waggled his tongue, winked, then went back to teasing.

"Yeah. Now, if you deep-throated it? It would be something else." Little shit. He wiggled his toes just so....

He got himself a little peep, a squeak. "It's too short to count for anything, man. A big carrot? Cool. A big-assed cucumber? Worth begging for. But this? Nope."

"There's always the longnecks." Abandoning the chair, Galen crawled down on the blanket, stretching out on his belly. He'd lost his T-shirt when they arrived, and his cutoffs should be riding down just right. "Lotion me up, darlin'?"

Shane licked his lips, watching him, eyes suddenly hot. "I can so do that."

Shane straddled his ass, slicking up his hands.

"Oh." He growled, feeling Shane against him. Damn, this might backfire on him.

"Uh-huh...." Shane's hands landed on him, slip-sliding right up along his spine.

Lord. That was gonna melt him right into the sand. "Feels good."

"Sure does. Damn, you're fine, Len." Those hands knew where to touch him, how to touch him and make him melt.

"You think, darlin'?" Would he ever get tired of Shane admiring? He sure hoped not. Galen pushed back a little with his ass, rocking up.

"No, sir." Those fingers dragged right down his spine, a hint of sand making them scratch. "I know."

"We should either get in the water or go home, darlin'." No way could he just let this one subside.

"Whatever works for you, Len." Shane was in the same spot, cock hard and hot in the seam of his shorts.

The water meant they could tie Goober to the leg of the lounge chair and keep him occupied with Cheetos while they jacked each other under the water.... The Jeep meant picking everything up and waiting and.... Well, even salt water was better than that. He bucked Shane off and got the pup secure, then headed off at a good clip. "Last one in has to do the laundry, darlin'."

"Oh, fuck that."

That man could *move* when he had incentive. What Galen had on Shane in leg length, Shane more than made up in quickness, and damned if the banty little rooster didn't splash into the water right in front of him. Galen made up for it by dunking Shane right under, laughing like a loon.

Shane's hands eased into his trunks, fingers sliding up the leg of his shorts, sweet as fuck.

"Yeah, darlin'." He hauled Shane up, pushing into that hot hand, his own sliding into Shane's shorts to cup his ass.

"Mmm... you're something else." He got a wild, happy

grin, Shane hot and eager. It was just right, fading sun making Shane's skin glow.

"And you make me crazy." He wanted to eat Shane up, but there were still people around. So he settled for doing things where no one could see, sliding one hand around to cup Shane's cock.

"Mmm... damned sun needs to go down." Shane let the waves push them together.

"You know it. I want. Oh, darlin', the things I want." He was about to bust.

"Uh-huh. Dreamed last night about that time in the storm with the ropes, remember?"

"God, yeah." Even he could hear the growl in his voice. That had been a damned good storm. He got inside Shane's shorts, stroking that sweet cock nice and firm.

"Uhn." Shane's eyes went wide, teeth sinking into that bottom lip just like that. Wanting that bottom lip so bad he could taste it, Galen sank down in the water almost to his neck, pulling Shane down with him. There, out of sight of the beach, he could take a kiss.

"Oh. Oh, shit, yeah. Want." Shane got it, nodded and moved closer, diving into it.

Mmm. Yes. Heavens, yes. He stroked Shane's cock, sucking Shane's tongue like there was no tomorrow. As the sun went down, everyone else left the water, and it was like they were in their own private world.

Shane's hands weren't still, tugging here and pulling there and setting him on fire, right there in the water. He gasped, bucking, Shane's name hard on the heels of their last kiss, falling over into the next one. They licked and sucked and bit, both of them humping hard.

"Come on, come on." Shane arched, gave it right on up.

"Oh, damn." His whole body shook hard as Galen came, bucking and grunting. "Oh, darlin'."

"Yeah. Yeah, love." Shane nuzzled his chin, shaking with it. "So good."

"Gonna sink." And Goober was gonna shit orange for days if they let him eat the whole bag of Cheetos. "Wanna stop and get barbeque on the way home?"

"Ooh... yeah. Ernie over at Rib Kings owes us supper for me covering his tab that night his wallet got stole."

"Excellent." Hoo yeah. Coleslaw and cornbread too. "Come on, darlin'. Let's go rescue your mutt from the horror of Cheeto poop."

"Len. Gross." He got a wary look. "Is it gonna be as bad as the plastic rubber duckie pieces?"

"Might be worse. The ducks don't glow in the dark." He chuckled, hauling them up so water ran off them, heading inland just as Goob started howling for his human.

"Lord, he sure can sing, can't he?" He got a grin, a kiss. "We're coming, Goober! Chill out!"

Watching Shane slosh up to free his mutt, ass swinging, Galen decided there was no better way to spend a fine, sunny day in Florida than on the beach with Shane by his side and a cooler of beer.

Even if Goober *did* burp toxic orange all the way home.

Chapter Fourteen

L ORD, LORD. What a day.
      Night.
      Morning.
What-the-fuck-ever.

A group of punks had tried to break into the bar as they were closing up—all leather and chains and trying to be big badasses, waving a pistol around like they were gangsters. Now, that wasn't too terrible. There was a bat under the bar and a nice length of iron bar in the office, and they almost had fun running the little pricks off.

Until the cops came to arrest *him*, for fuck's sake.

Stupid little asshole pricks going to the hospital and saying he *beat* on them.

Which, he sorta did.

But still, they deserved it.

They'd walked in like they owned the place, strutting like weird leather daddy chickens. One of them shoved Terry Favors right into a little pod of ladies who were trying to decide whether to come on in and order or just leave.

Shane knew right then this wasn't gonna end well. He'd

made sure he knew where the bat was, since people tended to move it, but he flashed them a smile when they made their way to the bar.

"What'll it be, boys?"

"Who are you calling boys?"

Shane bit his tongue. "Figure of speech."

"We want shots."

"Sure enough. What kind?"

Thug number one grinned, a gold tooth glinting as he pulled the .33 out of his jacket. "The free kind, asshole."

"Oh, son, I don't think so. I don't serve free drinks to dickheads."

The front man blinked, then scowled. "What did you call me?"

"You heard me. Now get on out of here." He'd pulled out the bat, and his barback had come over with that piece of pipe, and Shane went over the bar like a pirate boarding a rival ship.

Then it had been all over but the cleanup. Until the cops.

He slipped out of the Jeep, heading to the house. Took all fucking night to take care of it too. Thank God for security cameras.

"Hey, darlin'. I was worried sick about you." There was Galen, turning on the porch light and heading out to grab him right up.

"Hey." He pushed right on into Galen's arms, sighing, relaxing. "What a fucking night."

"Figured it had to be bad, darlin', but I couldn't get away from the damned phone." That sports team Galen had done some investing in was sucking up his time. Sucking up enough time that Galen was on the goddamn phone when he was busy being arrested, even. Of course when Galen was kissing him like that? He kinda forgot all about it.

Kinda.

Almost.

Well, not really. Being arrested sorta sucked.

"Yeah. They fucking handcuffed and fingerprinted me and everything." Shane pushed into the kiss, hips rubbing, cuddling into Len's heat.

Galen gave him just what he wanted, kissing him so hard he saw spots in front of his eyes, the only indication of how much that whole police thing pissed him off the way Galen's hands tightened on his ass.

His groan echoed, pushing into Galen's mouth. He gave up being tired and a little pissed for wanting, for needing it.

Shoving him back, Galen ran him right into the hood of his Jeep, hands under his ass lifting him up. Galen muscled in between his thighs as they spread, rubbing back, bending him like he was made of Play-Doh.

"Oh fuck. Len." He spread wide, begging for it. The hood was still warm, the heat sliding up through his T-shirt, his jeans.

"That's the... fuck. That's the idea, darlin'." Teeth digging into his shoulder, Galen worked a hand between them and opened his jeans, wrapping a hand around him. "Been missing you. Worrying."

"Bastard kids. Aaron's got a broke wrist too. Made me so fucking mad." He couldn't stop looking, watching Galen's hand on his skin.

"Oh, man. You're gonna be busy as a...." *One-legged... oh.* That felt good, Galen's thumb right there, his mouth just so.

"Uhn. More. More, Len. I need." He'd worry more later. Tomorrow. Some time.

"I know, darlin'. I know." God, Len swarmed up him, opening his own jeans so they could rub, fingers plucking the rings in his nipples through his shirt. Kisses deep and drugging pulled at his lips, Len sucking his tongue right into that hot mouth.

Oh. Oh, that was what he wanted. Just like that. Right

there. He got his fingers all tangled in Galen's hair, holding on tight. Galen got them moving, rocking, the hood of the Jeep squeaking under them. Groaning, Len really went to town, leaving bruises on his throat, his shoulder.

His cries echoed, ringing through the air as his body rocked, worked to get closer to Galen.

"Come on, darlin'." Grabbing his thigh, Galen wrapped his leg up around Galen's hip, encouraging him. "Come on. You. So good."

He nodded, bumped his head against the hood. His balls drew up, hips snapping, and he shot hard.

"Oh. Oh fuck, Shane." Galen came maybe two seconds behind him, warmth and wetness spreading over him as Len jerked and moaned. "Oh, darlin'."

"Uh-huh." He sorta melted, panting. "Yeah."

They rested for a bit, Galen's forehead against his, sharing breath. As he was about to doze off right there, Goober set up a howl from inside the house, making both of them jump.

"Lord, that puppy sounds like a haint." He groaned, let Len tug him up, a little shaky in his boots. "You get all your business done?"

"I did. I'm all yours for the day, darlin'. Though I ought to let you say hi to your mutt."

Hitching up his jeans, Galen took Shane's hand as they wandered up to the house. Goob hit his legs like a hairy cannonball as Len opened the door.

"Oh, look who I found!" He got down and scritched Goob's ears. Man, that little tail wagged and wagged.

"He's been missing you too. But it's just as well he wasn't behind the bar tonight, huh?" Oh, Len got the cutest smile on his face when he watched him and Goober. Like a proud papa or something.

"Oh, he'd have bit those stupid motherfuckers hard.

'Course, I reckon I'll hear from that one boy's lawyer. He's all tore up." He sighed, nuzzled Goob a second.

"Well, you've got the tapes. And I got better lawyers, I bet." Len pulled him up for another kiss, heading on in, Goob tripping along behind. "You hungry?"

"I guess." He went to make coffee, pottering, finding a treat for Goob on the way. "What did you have for supper?"

"I just had a sandwich. I could eat. You want some bacon and eggs?" Len rubbed on him as they passed in the kitchen, went to the fridge and pulled shit out.

"Sure enough." He washed his hands, fingers working the couple scratches left by the cuffs. Assholes. Fucking made him ride to the goddamn police station in a goddamn black and white.

Even busy cracking eggs, Len didn't miss that, frowning over. "They didn't hurt you, did they? 'Cause I can always go kick some ass."

Right, 'cause Galen had all this spare ass-kickin' time.

"The stupid cuffs. Kids didn't get but one or two shots in. They were just posers." Scared him, though, seeing that pistol.

"Fuck, darlin'." Galen abandoned the eggs and came over, pulling him close. "Fuck."

"Yeah. Gonna have a talk about locking up after last call." He was starting to shake a little—tired, he guessed. Hungry.

"Yeah. Come on and sit down." He made it to the table before his knees gave out, the coffee starting to smell good. "You relax. You want some orange juice?"

His Len. Always looking out for him.

"No. Yes. I mean, I'm okay. Just...." His hands were jittering like they belonged to somebody else. Lord.

Squatting in front of him, Len grabbed his hands and held on warm and tight. "Let me get you some food, darlin'. It will help. Here, pet Goob a bit."

He nodded, the pup snuggling into his arms, all skunk-breath and floppy ears. "Sorry. I'm good. It was real quick. Well, except the waiting part."

"I know. But it gets to you when it all stops and you have time to think."

Before he could even blink a few times, there was bacon and eggs and orange juice, Galen sitting down with him and pushing him to eat, fussing a little. The food tasted good, but it was the orange juice that really set him to rights—all bright and sweet and shit. Okay. Okay, better. "Thanks, Len."

"No problem, darlin'." Yeah. Those black as fuck eyes said the same—*No problem, and I'm glad you're all right, and I love you.*

He nodded before reaching out to grab Len's hand and holding on. Squeezing.

Tugging, Len brought him over on Len's lap and held on as well, nuzzling against his neck. He could feel the day's growth of whiskers, feel the tension in Len's muscles ease.

Shane leaned in close, lips on Galen's head. "Gonna just stay right here."

"That sounds like the best idea in a long while, darlin'." Turning to kiss his neck, Galen stroked his back, humming. "It surely does."

He nodded, breathed in deep. It was good—the smells of bacon and coffee, oranges and Pine-Sol, Galen and him. Smelled like home.

Home and safe and sound.

Which was a hell of a lot better than the police station for sure.

GALEN SWORE BY ALL HE HELD HOLY THAT IF ONE more drunk motherfucker so much as touched him....

"So where are you off to after this, Mr. Frost?" the

bartender was a sweet little girl who kept pouring him iced tea without a mutter.

"Home. It's been damn near a month, and I need to...." He needed Shane, for fuck's sake. He needed touch and love and a certain tight-assed little bastard who was at home waiting for him. "Just get home."

"I get that. Where's—"

"Frost, Frank here told me you forgot to shave, man." Some son of a bitch clapped him on the back, sloshing his tea over his fingers. "Let me buy you a grown-up drink."

"Thank you. I have to drive home." Christ, he was tired of being here, feeling like a jackass yokel, like he was this stupid swampbaby that needed the suits to give him cash. Worse? He hated knowing that he needed these suits to give him money. "In fact, I was just on my way out. Y'all have fun."

"You're leaving?" Somehow Frank was right there at his elbow, hand on his arm.

"I am. I have to get home, man. It's been weeks." Too many weeks and his lover was waiting there like a promise. "I'm going to take a few days"—*weeks*—"off and get some sleep."

Frank rolled his eyes. "Go on, then. Our next big meetings will be in Dallas—your look will go over better there, huh?"

"I sure as shit hope so." See him, see him not lose his ever-loving shit. "See you. I'll call."

It took nothing to get his truck from valet and then get his happy ass on the road. This had been his last stop, and he was only a little over an hour from home. All he had to do was keep it between the navigational beacons and he was home free.

Or, given the time, bar free. Home would have to wait for Shane to get off work.

It seemed like forever and no time at all before he pulled into the parking lot, coming to light beside Shane's Jeep. He sat there for a second, listening to the quiet, just closing his eyes and having a moment.

Then he headed into the bar, searching for Shane, his eyes landing on his lover like Shane was made for him.

Popping the first three buttons on his stifling dress shirt, Galen let his jacket hang open, bellying right up to the bar and waiting for Shane to notice him. God, Shane looked good. Like home.

Those eyes landed on him, going from surprised to happy to hot as fuck as they traveled over him. Oh. Oh, man. That look did a man good.

Shane walked over as if drawn there. "Hey."

"Hey, darlin'. You having a good night?" Most everyone knew, but there was always a yahoo or two in the bar who might not take kindly to them doing what Galen really wanted to do, so he curled his fingers into his palms.

"Yeah." He got a smile, the black shirt clinging to every fucking one of Shane's muscles before disappearing into jeans that looked just like a second skin. He could see those nipple rings, clear as a bell. "Better now. You?"

"It was boring, darlin'. I had a lot of time to... think." A whole lot of time. Grinning, he leaned his elbows on the bar.

"Yeah?" Shane grabbed a glass and a bottle of Jack, poured him a double. "You thinking something good?" He could see Shane vibrating, those eyes like a touch.

"I am. I sat in that meeting and drank enough iced tea to make a man drown and thought of you...." Oh, the things he'd thought of. Galen shifted, his cock rising.

He just heard the moan, deep and quiet under the music. Oh yeah. Somebody was needing him.

"Good thoughts?" Shane asked.

"Uh-huh. Was thinking about putting your chain on you, maybe tying your hands up so your arms stand out all pretty...

maybe the plug. It kept me going. They all just got drunk, Shane." Bastards.

"They ain't worth thinking about, Len." Shane stepped closer, watching him like a rabbit watched a snake.

"Uh-huh." Galen sucked down his shot and motioned for Shane to pour him another, reaching out to stroke Shane's wrist as he poured.

Shane's hand shook, whiskey spilling over those square fingers. "Galen."

"Shhh." He waited, lightly holding Shane's wrist as he set the bottle aside before bending down over Shane's hand to lick the Jack right off it.

This time the cry wasn't quiet, just a little desperate, needy as Shane's fingers curled.

"Let's go upstairs. Please? I can put you in the office chair, leave marks all over you." God, he wanted that.

Shane nodded, fingers twining with his and tugging him toward the stairs, not even saying a word to the guys on the clock.

Galen raised his free hand to wave at Jake, who'd caught his eye and nodded, following Shane up. Once they were locked in the office, he took a kiss that tried hard to knock the top of his head off.

Shane was hard as diamond against his thigh, rubbing furiously, working away. No one had ever reacted to him like Shane did. No one.

Galen pressed Shane back against the door and dropped to his knees, the dress pants not nearly as good for that as an old pair of jeans, but Galen ignored the scrape, opening Shane's button and zipper, working that sweet cock out so he could touch and taste.

"Galen." Shane stared down at him, thighs rock-hard in denim, cock pushing out for him. Wet-tipped and dark, Shane smelled so good, so needy.

"Mmm-hmm. Want." Without waiting any longer, Galen sank his mouth down on that sweet cock, lips closing tight so he could suck.

Shane's hips rolled, that crack as Shane's head hit the wall enough to make him chuckle. He reached back into the thin denim around Shane's hips, fingers searching out Shane's balls to roll them gently. Shane was on fire, salt sliding onto his tongue, balls tight as all get-out.

Yeah. Oh yeah. Galen rode the feeling, sucking and licking, encouraging Shane to move, to roll his skinny hips. Then he pulled off for a second to rub his bearded cheek against Shane's wet cock. Unlike the business assholes? Shane liked his beard.

In fact, Shane whimpered, arched right up and shot, Galen's name ringing out.

Chuckling, Galen wiped at his cheek and neck, licking Shane while he shrugged out of his jacket. Grabbing Shane's hips, Galen got up, moving them to the office chair by the desk. Shane's tongue slid over his cheek, his jaw, cleaning him up, revving him up.

"Now, I think I said something about putting you in this chair and loving all over you, didn't I? Get naked, darlin'."

"Uh-huh...." Shane fumbled over his shirt buttons, mouth still moving on his skin.

Poor Shane didn't do multitasking well unless he was behind the bar. Galen helped, pushing Shane's open jeans down, squeezing a nice double handful of ass.

Shane groaned, teeth on his skin, low whimper tickling him. "Want to feel you everywhere."

"Gonna, Shane. Let's get this off...." The rest of Shane's clothes fell to the floor, and Galen pushed, letting him fall back into the chair, groaning at the picture Shane made, all spread, eyes heavy-lidded and lazy.

Shane hummed, fingers wrapped around that half-hard cock, stroking slow and easy.

"Uhn." Damn, that just…. Fuck. "Should I start at the top or the bottom, darlin'?"

"Top. Top. Kiss me."

"I can do that." Leaning on the arms of the chair, Galen took a kiss, only his mouth touching Shane, his tongue slipping out to taste.

Shane moaned, lips opening, tongue sliding out against his own.

Kissing Shane was one of the great pleasures of his life. It really was. He took that kiss deep and hard, finally touching, bracing on one hand and raising his other to cup the back of Shane's head. That got Shane to arching against him, hands sliding down his chest.

His clothes were in the way, the shirt and pants feeling hot and tight. Galen let go long enough to strip down, giving Shane a show, watching that hot little body the whole time. Shane kept jacking that pretty prick, one knee drawn up and back, letting him see.

"Oh, darlin'. What you do to me." His own cock tried to smack his belly when he let it loose, and Galen gave it a few good strokes, feeling fine.

"Mmm-hmm. You're something, and I want every inch of it."

"You're gonna get it. Soon as I mark you all over I'm gonna sit in that chair and you're gonna ride me." Then he'd take Shane home and tie him and plug him and just…. God.

"Yeah. Then we're going home to play, Len. I'll take tomorrow off. Tomorrow and Monday." Shane's tongue flicked out, wetting those lips.

"Oh. Yeah. I love that." Galen sauntered the few steps back to Shane, bent and bit Shane's shoulder. Shane jerked like he was surprised, like electricity passed right between them, the deep cry sweet as all fuck. That sound made his cock jerk right back, and Galen went looking for more, lips and tongue moving on Shane's upper arm. The muscles there were tight as fuck, the tanned skin just begging for him to bruise, to bite. Shane always took what he gave so beautifully. He left a mark on Shane's arm, sucking hard, loving on him. Shane stretched up, spreading out for him, giving it up. Decadent and so pretty, his Shane.

Where next? Shane's chest, maybe, right above the nipple, his tongue flicking the tiny ring below. Shane shifted, ass sliding on the leather chair. The leg caught on the chair arm spread wider, Shane groaning. Galen couldn't stop his hand from reaching, from sliding down Shane's chest and belly to grip Shane's cock, even as he pulled the nipple ring with his teeth. That dark flesh went tight and hard under his lips, Shane's cock jerking in his hand. Low babble started, nonsense words as Shane tugged his head closer, kept his mouth right there.

Galen licked, flipping the little ring back and forth before biting again, pulling. All the time his hand moved, stroked, his fingers sliding on Shane's cock. Shane's lips brushed his head, fingers traveling, searching, wanting. Felt good, so good, Shane's hand on his skin. All the time he'd been gone he'd thought of it, let it keep him from killing those smug jerks he was meeting with. Galen bit down on Shane's nipple harder, letting it sting.

"Uhn. Fuck, yeah." Shane's fingers liked to drive him crazy, pushing and rubbing good and hard. Sensation zinged up and down his spine as Shane touched him, shoulders to ass, then stroked his arms. Galen moved his mouth over to the other nipple, sucking up a hickey right above it.

"Oh." That skin flushed for him, sweet and rose, that blood reaching up for his lips.

"Mmm. So pretty." Bending deeper, Galen licked at Shane's belly, following the glory trail.

"Yours." Shane arched, thighs pretty and tensed, belly rippling.

"Mine," he agreed, rubbing his cheek there, letting his beard scrape that sensitive lower belly before dropping to his knees again to nibble on Shane's thighs, the hairs tickling his lips. Shane moaned, chuckled, twisting. Fuck, but that was a happy sound. Galen dug his chin in, giving Shane a little extra sensation, a touch of harsh to go with the soft. That got him a grunt, Shane pushing right back, demanding from him.

Gripping the backs of Shane's calves, Galen gave, his lips nudging the head of Shane's cock, his tongue coming out to taste again. His own prick ached.

"Mmm.... Want you to fuck me. Need it, yeah? To feel you."

"Yeah, darlin'. Yeah. Gonna." He got up, lifted Shane up out of the chair, patting that tight little ass. "Go get the lube."

Shane got to digging for a set of keys, unlocked that little top drawer that held their stash. Mmm. There was the little blue plug. Shane could wear it on the ride home.

"Get the plug too, Shane. Put it on the desk." He wanted Shane to know while he was fucking him, to know that he'd be holding it all in while they made the drive. Galen sprawled in the chair, touching himself, watching Shane.

"Bossy." Shane did it, though, licking those parted lips, walking over to straddle his thighs.

"You know it." He gripped Shane's ass, so tight and hot, his fingers digging into the muscle. "Yum. Come here and kiss me."

The hum vibrated his lips, soft and slinky and hot as fire. Then Shane's tongue slid in, taking his mouth and making him melt. Damn. Just damn. And Shane called him pushy. He let Shane take the kiss where he wanted, opening his mouth up for Shane to feel and taste, the kiss wet and hot. Shane moved and rocked and loved on him, got lost in him like no one *ever*.

The lube had fallen between them, so Galen grabbed it up and wrestled it open, getting some on his fingers so he could reach behind Shane and press at that hot little hole, kissing and nibbling Shane's mouth all the while. He loved how soft Shane's lips got when they'd been kissing a long time, loved how Shane's breath came faster and faster. Shane watched him, eyes focused and dazed all at once where they stared into him. Between that and Shane's skin, hot as hell against his chest, his thighs, his belly, his hands? Damn. Just, damn.

Two fingers slipped right inside, Shane open and easy for him, responding so well, so pretty. All Galen could do was moan and reach, thrusting his fingers in, curling them, trying to find that little gland. He knew when he found it, Shane whimpering right into his mouth.

"Mmm." He hummed into the kiss, letting Shane hear his pleasure too, hitting the little spot inside Shane's body over and over again.

Shane started rocking, hand sliding down, wrapping around his prick. That thumb knew where to press, how to make him lose his rhythm.

"Fuck, Shane. You'd best watch it or I'll be wanting inside before you're ready." Though, really, Shane was ready. Open.

"'M ready. Yours." Shane bit Len's bottom lip hard enough to sting.

"Get up here, then." Lifting Shane took nothing, making him feel fucking strong. Galen settled Shane over his cock, letting Shane position it just so before easing that hot body down on him.

Then he got to watch Shane's head go back, throat working as he sank deep-deep, burying himself right on in.

"Oh, Jesus. Shane. Darlin'." Hot around him, so hot and

tight, and Galen started rocking up, the chair sliding beneath him. "Love."

"Yeah. Yeah, Len." He got one of those smiles, wide and wild and a little shocked, like Shane couldn't believe he was real.

Moaning, he buried his face against Shane's neck, inhaling the hot scent of sex and man, licking the sweat off Shane's skin as they started to really get to it, his cock pushing in over and over. They found their rhythm, settled into it, both of them moving and bucking, working together. Loving together.

Just what he'd craved all day. He let his hands wander, sliding up Shane's back, one slipping around to pinch and pull those tight nipples.

"Mmm. More. More, now." Like he couldn't feel it in Shane's body, that ass clenching around him.

"Uh-huh." He pulled again, twisting one little ring until it had to hurt, his cock jerking inside Shane's body. Then he reached for Shane's prick, needing to come, needing Shane to come for him.

Shane gave it right up for him, heat spraying as those muscles fluttered around his prick.

Galen cried out, his body bucking under Shane's, so hot and hard as he came, his belly like a board.

"Uh-huh. Just. Just like that." Shane's head rolled.

He panted. Fuck, yes, like that. And he'd take Shane home and do it all over again. Galen chuckled, reaching for the plug. Shane nuzzled his throat, all close and melty.

"Mmm. Gonna make you move, darlin', so I can put the plug in."

Mmm.... That got him another squeeze, a shiver. Yeah. "'Kay, Len."

Shifting a little, Galen put one arm around Shane to lift him, his cock slipping free finally. He turned Shane on his lap, got the plug all lined up. "Ready?"

"Mmm-hmm." Shane arched, hips canting to take it in.

"Oh. Pretty." The plug slid in easily after what all they'd been up to, catching everything and holding it inside, making Galen moan at the sight. Shane shook a little, hips moving, rocking sweet and slow. Damn. Someone was on fire for him. Galen wasn't sure why, but he knew he was grateful for it, wanted it. He stroked Shane's belly, murmuring nonsense words.

"Take me home." Shane purred for him, belly tight.

"You know it." Chuckling, he moved, got Shane standing. "'Course we have to get dressed."

"Damn. Details, details." He got a wink, a shit-eating grin.

"Life is in the details." Like plugs, and chains, and those cuffs at home. He couldn't wait. "Let's get a move on, darlin'. I have a lot more thoughts to share with you. At home."

"I'm with you, Len. There's nothing I'd rather." He knew it was the truth too. Shane was his, through and through.

Better than a bunch of stuffy old businessmen any day.

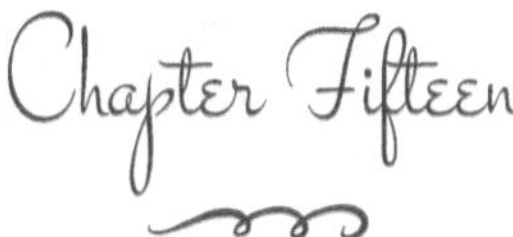

Chapter Fifteen

OKAY. So. Muffins?

Seriously harder to make than advertised.

The whole cracking eggs thing was nasty and fucked up, with the little bastards sort of shattering everywhere. But he dealt with that. After all, they *had* paper towels.

The chopping of the pecans was cool, although the frozen cranberries? Totally aerodynamic. Goob learned pretty quick how to catch them, though, so again, cool.

The real problem?

No one said when you put the mixer dealie in the bowl, the flour and shit sort of... exploded.

Or that, when the explosion happened and you jumped and dumped the cinnamon over onto the burner on the stove —which was only on because he wanted to make hot chocolate too, damn it.... No one said cinnamon caught fire.

Not big flames, of course.

Those happened when you whacked the cinnamon bottle with the pot holder.

Fucking muffins.

It was the smoke alarm that finally brought Len up from

the little workshop they'd built over the summer, Len sticking his head in the door. "You okay, Shane?"

"Uh. Yes?" He looked over, pot holder smoking in his hand, mixer whirring away.

Galen came all the way in and plucked the smoldering cloth off his hand, then turned on the faucet and dunked it in the sink. "Whatcha doin'?"

"Making muffins." He motioned over to the goo slowly climbing up the mixer doohickeys like the Blob. Wicked and also vaguely creepy. "I think."

Peering at the mix, Galen made an odd noise. "Maybe we should go to IHOP."

"I followed the recipe, Len. I did." He turned off the mixer, watching the goo sort of slink back into the bowl. "Man, this cooking shit? Harder than bartending."

"Yeah. Well, it's the whole solids thing. Not much of that in mixology." Len took the mixer away gently, then grabbed him and kissed him.

Oh. Oh, much nicer than cooking. He pushed up, tongue sliding right alongside Galen's and stroking. "Mmm... what was that for?"

"Because you didn't burn yourself or chop anything off with mixer blades, darlin'. I like you whole." Galen squeezed his ass.

He chuckled, rubbing right up against Galen, eyes rolling. "You know Goob likes cranberries. Those little things? Like buckshot."

"Yeah. They'll come out of him whole." He almost missed that one with the way Len was all over him, bending him back over the counter, but ew.

"That's disgust.... Oh...." Galen's teeth found a sweet spot, and things went hot and melty for a minute. "Yeah."

Soft kisses soothed the sting, but only for a bit, because Galen bit him again. Right *there*. "Hmm?"

One leg went up, wrapped around Galen's hip, tugging them together. "Again. Len."

"Yeah. Yeah, darlin'." Len bit again, making him tingle, making a mark pop up; he could damned well feel it.

He fucking loved that, loved Galen's hunger on him. "More."

"What do you want, darlin'? Ain't nothing I won't give for you, you know that." All the while Galen was nipping at him, hands squeezing.

"Anything you'll give me, Len. Just want you like nothing else." He gasped, groaned, rubbing them right together.

"Yeah?" Now there was a new note in Galen's voice, but he couldn't figure it, not with Galen reaching between them to rub his cock.

"Uh. Uh-huh. Oh. Len, s' good."

"It is. Been thinking." Len pushed Shane's sweats out of the way and grabbed him, hot-as-hell fingers wrapping around him and squeezing as Galen sucked up a mark on his shoulder.

"Thinking...." His head fell back, hit the cabinet, hands all tangled up in Len's thick hair. Fuck, yes. So good.

That short beard scraped his skin, Galen's teeth following, Galen's other hand coming up to pinch and pull his nipple rings. "About stuff we can do."

He was trying to follow along, honest, but those fingers, those teeth.

And his nipples.

Damn.

"Uh-huh."

Oh. Oh, man. Galen kinda... hoisted him, bending him back to suck and lick at his nipples, pulling the rings with his teeth. "Want to... oh, darlin'. You taste good."

Oh, this way his balls were rubbing against Len, nipples just on fucking fire. "Gonna come. Galen. Love."

"Go on, darlin'. Want to see and feel and...." Galen trailed off, biting him hard.

That was all she wrote. He grunted and his balls jerked, and he blew a gasket, coming so hard he saw stars.

"Oh fuck, Shane." Galen drew back, opened his jeans up and stroked his own cock maybe two or three times. The smell of Galen as he came couldn't be confused with anything else.

"Mmm. Oh. Man. Gotta cook more often."

"You nut." Galen grinned at him, looking down at the cabinet. "Oh Lord. We'd best clean up before Goob gets in here and thinks you spilled muffin mix."

"Gross!" He snorted and got down, started working on his mess. "Well, I tried to surprise you, man."

"And you have my unending admiration." Yeah, the way Galen was staring at his ass, he would bet that was true. But not for the muffins.

He snorted again, making sure to give a little wiggle, maybe even a bump and grind. "Perv."

Speaking of pervyness. Pervitude? Perviosity? "What were you thinking?"

"Huh?" The refrigerator opened and closed, and a beer dangled in front of his nose. "Oh. I was just... well. There was this thing I saw one time."

"Thanks for clearing that right on up." He chuckled, grabbed the beer. "Was it bigger than a bread box?"

Once his hand was free, Len swatted him with it. "No. Though from the look on the one guy's face, you would have thought it was bigger than anything."

"Yeah? Like a dildo?" Those were sort of okay. Less cool than the plugs, which always got them both going, and they had the one that vibrated and could make his eyes roll up in the back of his.... Oh, hell, yes.

"More organic." Which made him think of carrots and

cucumbers. Ew. But Len went on, "I was thinking more like putting my hand in you."

Galen's cheeks were red as anything, and he wouldn't quite look up.

"Like your hand-hand." He sort of blinked. He knew that, in theory, it could possibly maybe happen. They had most of the rubber hand he'd got Len for a present, after all. (Damn Goob and teething—that rubber thing had seen better days.) Still.... "Are you sure that's not a myth? Like mermaids or Godzilla?"

Now Len looked at him, and man. Wow. Molten. That look was hotter than the burning pot holder. "I'm sure."

"Oh." The whole cleaning thing sort of got forgotten, and he stepped forward. "You.... You ever done it? I mean, for real?"

"No. Not ever. That seemed like something that needed trust, and well...." Len snorted. "You saw who I used to hang with."

He growled some, nodded. Assholes. Lousy fuckers. He could get himself all riled up on Len's behalf.

"You, though...." Galen touched his cheek, fingers still damp. "You, I could see it with."

"I...." He looked at Galen's hand, right up close. He'd never even consider it with anyone else. Ever. "How would you pick which one to use?"

"I'd use my right hand, darlin'. It's my dominant hand, so I'd have more control. Not ever gonna hurt you." Galen leaned down, kissed him hard. "Not ever."

Oh.

He opened right up, want making a hot little ball in his belly. He'd do damn near anything to keep that look in Len's eyes. Even shit that could possibly seriously wig a man out.

Galen kissed him until he couldn't breathe at all, rubbing

against him, reminding him they were both still half in, half out of their clothes.

Oh, man, he was getting hard again. Len playing was a huge turn on, no matter which way it went. Made him ache inside.

"Oh damn, Shane. Can you just see it? Me stretching you? Getting you ready? Holding you?" Len was hard against him again, cock rising fast, so hot.

He groaned, images flashing through his head, teeth nipping Galen's earlobe. "Couldn't do it with anybody but you. Couldn't let somebody in so deep. Only... only you, Len."

"Love you, darlin'. I... oh. Fuck." Galen yanked at his sweats, pulling them down before pushing him back up on the counter again, this time so he was sitting right on it. Then Galen bent and put that sweet mouth on him, sucking the head of his cock.

"Galen!" He whacked his head against the cabinet again, but this time he didn't care. He just needed that mouth sucking him, working him, hotter than the hinges of hell.

There was no answer but the wet sound of Len's mouth on him, the feel of Len's hands spreading his thighs so wide they ached. That mouth worked him, lips sealed tight around him as Galen went all the way down to his curls. He gripped the edge of the counter, hips rocking in short, hard little bursts.

Rough and wet, Galen's tongue rubbed the underside of his cock, lips pulling against him all the way up. Those hands slid down, lifted his balls, Galen's fingers sliding across his hole.

"Gonna... gonna be your hand." He jerked, coming just like that, at the thought.

Galen swallowed right down, cheek resting against his

thigh for a minute before Galen shoved up against him, letting him taste himself on those swollen lips.

"Yeah, darlin'. Mine. Fuck. I need."

"Yours. Come on. Come on, now." He shifted forward, spreading wide, offering.

"Oh, Shane. Damn." Galen lunged, taking just enough time to slick up with some spit before pushing into him, not waiting for anything. The burn was so damned good, harsh, but good. They banged together, grinding and grunting, the cabinet biting into his ass and making everything bigger, huge.

He could hear Len's knees hitting the cabinet under him, could feel every thrust travel up his spine. Galen's skin shone with sweat, a drop of it rolling down the side of Len's face to land on Shane's belly.

"Fuck. Fuck, love you. Feel you everywhere." Their teeth clicked when they kissed, Shane's eyes rolling with the heat.

Galen grunted into his mouth, hips moving sharp and hard, that cock swelling inside him. "Darlin'! Gonna. Fuck."

Yeah. That was that. Galen shot deep inside him, filling him right up.

Shane held on, breathing, petting, watching Galen as they came back to Earth.

"Oh God, Shane. You're something else."

"Gotta...." He grinned, chuckled. "Gotta make up for the whole not-cooking thing somehow."

"You more than make up for it, darlin'. Trust me. How about I make pancakes?" Galen smiled at him, looking sated, those eyes so dark.

"Mmm...." Galen's pancakes rocked. And syrup? Added bonus. "I'll keep you company and make coffee."

Galen hooted. "That I know you can make.... You think the muffin mix would make good dog biscuits?"

"Maybe. Goob likes the cranberries. Ooh. Precut-up pecans for your pancakey convenience."

"Mmm." Kissing him again before easing away, Galen nodded. "I can use those. And you? You think about it, yeah?"

"Yeah." He nodded back, met Galen's eyes. "Yeah, Len."

"Good." He got one more kiss before Galen moved away to toss his muffins and start on pancakes. He probably wouldn't think about anything else for a while.

Except maybe the cranberry stuck to his ass.

GALEN CAME HOME FROM THE GROCERY WITH BEER and ham salad and some of those fancy chocolate chip muffins. It'd been a few days, but Shane would be craving them again, and Lord knew, he didn't want the guy to lose a finger in the mixer.

He got the groceries put away, got them both a muffin and some milk, and went looking for Shane.

"Hey, darlin'? I got you something."

"Huh? Oh. Uh. Bathtub. Be right out." Oh, he so knew that husky, low tone of voice. Someone was polishing his morning—midafternoon—wood.

Like he was gonna let Shane finish without him at least watching. Goob was out, so Galen set the muffins and drinks down on the coffee table and went on in to the bathroom and leaned in the doorway.

"Hey, you."

"Hey." The bubbles covered up the evidence, but the water was rocking, Shane flushed. "How... mmm... how're you?"

"I'm good." He hooked his fingers in his belt loops, looking down at Shane from under his hat, which he hadn't had a hand to take off. "Lookin' good."

Shane groaned, looked him up and down. "You are. Damn. Was thinking about you."

"Yeah?" Popping the top button of his jeans, Galen spread his stance, letting Shane see the bulge rising in his jeans. "What were you thinking, darlin'?"

"Yeah. Thinking about... stuff. Fuck, you're fine."

"What kind of stuff?" He knew Shane loved it when he got growly, so he let his voice get all deep and low.

Oh, look at the way Shane arched for him. Luscious. "About... about the stuff we were talking about the other day. About how it made you look."

"You liked that, huh?" Fuck, he knew Shane had been thinking about it. Just knew it. He had to lower his zipper too, give himself more room. "I want to, Shane. Want to see your face when I do."

Shane nodded, eyes on his prick, on his belly, chest flushed dark. "Yeah. Yeah, Len. I want it."

He loved the way Shane's nipple rings glinted with soap, loved the way he could read Shane's thoughts by the color of that fine-grained skin. Right now those thoughts must be pretty damned hot. Galen pulled his cock all the way out, stroking it a bit.

"Oh. Want." One of Shane's hands slid up, tweaked one nipple, tugged the pretty little ring.

Hell, yes. But he was gonna tease them both more first. It had been a while since they played, and right now? He was enjoying the watching. He pushed his jeans all the way down, bent to pull both them and his boots off before unbuttoning his shirt and getting rid of it too. The hat he kept. "Want what, Shane?"

Shane's chuckle was a little rough, breathless. "You. Shit, Len. I want you."

"You got it, darlin'." He wandered over to the tub, putting a hint of extra swagger in it. "All of me."

One hot, wet hand reached out for him, wrapped right around his cock.

"Uhn." His breath left his lungs with a whoosh, and Galen arched, pushing into Shane's hand. "Oh damn."

"Uh-huh...." Shane sat up, stroking him, lips parted, just watching.

His cock throbbed, his balls drawing up as Shane's fingers stroked over the tip, dipping into the slit. Fuck, that was good. He reached out, trying to touch Shane's face or throat, anything he could get to.

"Look at you...." Shane moved, lips moving over his fingers, his knuckles, dragging over them.

"Rather look at you." Still, it made him look down, made him look at his cock in Shane's hand. His stomach tightened, his asscheeks tight as he thrust.

Shane bucked, water splashing, and those lips wrapped around his thumb, sucking hard.

"Shane. Darlin'. Gonna. Oh." Yeah, just like that. Hell, Shane had started way before him, and he was the one gonna come, so fast.

Shane made a deep, low sound around his thumb, eyes rolling, hand making waves in the water. Galen made his own share of noise, groans tearing from him as he came right into Shane's hand, his whole body shaking.

"Damn. Hey." Shane leaned, licked his cock clean, sliding in the water.

"Hey." He grinned, waiting for Shane to finish up before kneeling beside the tub for a kiss. "I got muffins. And a hellacious amount of lube."

Shane's cheeks went bright pink. "Yeah? I... I like muffins."

"I know. I got you chocolate chip walnut." He poked. "So you were thinking on it?"

"I was. Yeah. Reckoned we could try it. No reason we couldn't stop if it didn't work." Shane met his eyes, the look hot, hungry.

"You know it. Anything that doesn't feel right, we can stop." That had always been their policy, and so far Shane had never stopped him. He felt heat rise in his own cheeks, his nipples going hard again. "I just... I want to try."

"Uh-huh. I keep thinking about you. Your hand. Yeah."

"When?" Damn, he knew he was pushing, but he wanted.... "We got milk and muffins out there."

"I got today and tomorrow off, Len...."

"Tonight, then, darlin'. Tonight." God. He couldn't wait.

"Yeah." Shane nodded, licked his lips, kissed him. "Tonight."

"I'll make it good for you, darlin'." He would, so good that it blew both of their minds.

"Well, duh." The look he got made him grin, made him proud. There wasn't an ounce of doubt there.

He kissed Shane, hard. "Cool. Come on, darlin'. Let's go have muffins before the milk gets warm." He wanted to build the anticipation, make sure they were both good to go tonight.

"Mmm. Chocolate muffins." Shane stood up, water sliding down his skin.

Galen stood too. "Yeah. Just for you. No sharing with Goob." Not after the last muffin mess. Ick.

"No. Because cranberries? Not fun." He got a wink, a grin.

Galen laughed. "Not for him. But they sure make good bait."

Shane cackled, whapped him with the towel, good and hard.

"Oh, you'll pay for that, Shane." He tweaked one nipple, pulling at the ring. God, he loved doing everything with this man, laughing right up there at the top.

"Promises, promises." Shane headed out, focusing in on those muffins, towel wrapped around that fine ass.

God, he couldn't wait for tonight. That ass? Was just begging for it.

He couldn't stop staring at Galen's hands.

On the remote.

Petting the dog.

Holding his coffee cup.

Scratching one arm.

Shane was a little worried. After all, he couldn't stop staring now—what the hell was he supposed to do tomorrow?

Tomorrow when they'd.

He'd.

That hand had.

Damn.

Of course, he didn't have to work tomorrow, and if he couldn't stop staring, well, he reckoned Galen would forgive him.

Either that or Galen wouldn't be able to stop staring at his ass and they'd be even up.

Galen made sure there was lube and lots of it, along with a good bottle of whiskey, some towels and washcloths, and candles and shit for atmosphere.

He felt like a dork.

But, damn, he wanted it to be good. Right. Something special to remember, not a disaster. Shane was still in the bathroom, showering, kinda shaky after the... well. After they'd cleaned him out good. That was the safest way to do it, and Shane had been mostly okay with it, and it was all ready.

Fuck. He sounded like Shane. In his head. He needed to

just get on with it. He got the fluffiest bath sheet thing they had (bright purple with pink flamingos, bought for Shane's last birthday) and went to get Shane out of the shower.

"Come on, darlin'. We're ready."

"Yeah." The water turned off and Shane stepped out, pushing right into him and the towel, face lifting for a kiss. He kissed back, feeling like both of them needed the reassurance, the steadying. This was supposed to be hot, good, and it would be, but he hadn't ever played on this level. Not even with Shane.

The kiss went on and on, Shane relaxing into it, starting to moan, to rub against him. Oh yeah, that was it. Perfect. Fucking A. Galen grabbed Shane's butt, squeezing, lifting him a little so Galen could start them back into the bedroom. He wanted Shane spread out on their bed.

Shane came easy, soft sound pushed into his lips, almost vibrating. "Like those brown candles. Smell like you, sorta."

"Yeah? I like the kinda off-white ones." They smelled like vanilla and musk. He grinned. Sappy. They sank down on the bed, and he stretched Shane out, licking those swollen lips, loving the feel of that body beneath his.

"So long as we don't buy the pink rosy-posey ones? We're good." Shane's lips chased his tongue, eyes gone all hot and wanting.

"Nope. Nothing but manly for us." His tongue fit in Shane's mouth so good, so easy, and he pulled at each of Shane's nipple rings, tugging at them hard enough to sting.

"Uhn." Shane arched, following his hand, hips pushing up against his.

"Yeah, darlin'." He reached down, stroked that sweet cock he loved so damned much, licking the drops Shane already had there off his fingers. "So hot."

"Yeah. Been wanting and wanting." Shane's tongue licked his lips.

"Me too." Maybe he should take the edge off for Shane, relax him even more. Grinning, Galen bent to lick at Shane's nipples, pulling Shane's cock hard.

"Oh!" Shane's head went back, hips pumping up into his hand.

"Hot. So hot." He stroked and pulled, watching Shane wiggle and squirm, watching that skin go dark red, chest, belly, and thighs.

"Uh-huh. Gonna, Len. I. Oh fuck. Love." Shane's heels dug into the mattress, giving Galen everything.

"Now, darlin'. Now, please." He wanted that, needed to see. Shane answered him with a sweet cry, heat spraying over his fingers. "Just like that." He licked his hand clean, bent to kiss Shane lightly on the lips. "So fucking hot, darlin'."

Shane hummed, all relaxed and blinking. "Melted my brains, Len."

"Just your brain?" He grabbed the lube while Shane was still out of it, because the size of the tube might freak Shane out. He wanted to get Shane while he was melted and blinky. Galen grinned. Yeah, take advantage of that relaxation.

Shane chuckled, stretched out, looking like the cat that got the cream. "Brains and bones, Len. All of me."

"Mmm. Liquid Shane. I could market it, make a fortune." His fingers were good and wet, so he pressed two against Shane's hole, using his other hand to spread those legs wider. His own need was still strong, still there, but he wanted this so bad.

"Mmm...." Shane let him in, easy as pie, the look on that face pure happy, not worried at all. "S'good."

"Yeah. Hot and tight." Shane's body fit him like no one else's ever had. He moved his fingers in and out, jonesing on the look on Shane's face, loving the little noises he got.

It didn't take long before Shane was moving with him, hips pushing and rocking, riding him. Eager.

Hell. That was amazing. His fingers kept on moving, and he watched the hot flush that traveled up Shane's chest, watched the nipple rings glint in the light. The third finger slid in as smoothly as he eased it in, trying to make it natural and good.

Shane bent his knees, heels digging into the mattress. That made Shane's belly ripple, go tight as he moved. "Mmm.... Len."

"Pretty, pretty, Shane. You look fucking decadent." Erotic, addictive. He could eat Shane up. They stayed with three fingers for a bit, stretching Shane out, nice and easy.

"Just love this." Shane rolled up a little, stole a kiss.

"Love you." Yeah. He was amazed at how easily the fourth finger slid in after he squirted more lube out and he rubbed it around, how Shane took him. Just took him in.

"Mmm... full." Oh, that groan was fine, eyes drooping, lips parted.

He stroked Shane's belly with his free hand, feeling muscles quiver. His own belly was so tight, his breath catching in his chest. "You feel... oh fuck, Shane. Amazing."

He got a nod, a soft groan. Shane reaching up for the headboard.

He stopped moving the fingers inside Shane, petting with his other hand. "Breathe, darlin'. You gotta breathe and just ride it."

"Breathe. I can do that." The joke was soft, shaky.

"You can, darlin'." He leaned in, careful not to move his arm, and kissed Shane's chin. "You're so hot. Wanna move so bad. But I'm not gonna hurt you."

"No, you won't. Gonna...." Shane's eyes met his, dazed and hot. "Gonna hold me in your hand."

"Yeah. I am." The tight muscles around his hand loosened, Shane relaxing for him just like that, and Galen drew a deep breath, making sure he was slick, so wet he could fold his thumb under and slide right in with it too. Shane clamped down on him for a moment. Then like he was meant to be there, Shane opened and let him in, and he slid all the way in, the widest part of his hand pushing through.

A deep, low sound ripped out of Shane, pure, raw sensation. He could feel those muscles around him, rippling and fluttering, trying to adjust to him, his hand. To his wrist, when it finally stopped, Shane's body snapping down around him. Galen shook, and he controlled himself ruthlessly. This was no time to lose it. Fuck, Shane felt like nothing else. It couldn't be more intimate if he held Shane's beating heart in his hand.

"Galen." Shane's eyes were huge, wild, searching his. "I feel.... Oh."

God. Galen nodded, swallowing hard. His heart beat so hard he could barely hear anything else. "Yeah, darlin'. You do. I'm holding you. God."

He got a nod, and Shane reached down, fingers touching that flat belly, almost like Shane was feeling for his hand. "Yours. Love."

"Love you, darlin'." Galen finally moved, opening and closing his fingers, watching Shane's face for any sign of distress. His other hand moved almost on its own, grabbing Shane's fingers and holding on tight.

"Oh. Oh, Len. That." Shane started panting, sheened with sweat. "So big."

"Good?" He knew it was good for him, knew it was probably good for Shane from that look, but he wanted to hear it.

"Uh-huh...." Shane spread, panting for him. "Please."

Fuck, yes. Galen moved again, slow and gentle, fingers flexing even as he bent to kiss Shane. The touch of their lips was soft, sweet, totally at odds with the primal feel of what they were doing. It made Galen whimper. Shane's fingers stroked his face, holding him, petting. Little sounds slipped into his lips, random and gentle, Shane giving them up for him.

He kissed harder, his hand moving in even more, slipping and sliding. Galen panted, resting his forehead against Shane's. "Darlin'."

"Uh-huh...." Shane shuddered, heart pounding and, oh Christ, Len could feel it around his hand.

"Shane. Jesus, Shane." His lower lip stung something fierce, and Galen realized he was biting it, hard. His hips wanted to move, his cock hard as stone, but he stayed still, so still, all but his hand inside Shane's body. That he started moving rhythmically in time to Shane's heartbeat.

Those low sounds grew a little louder, Shane starting to move, so careful, so hot. Galen lost track of time, lost track of everything; the only thing in his whole fucking world was Shane. He brought his free hand down, touched Shane's cock, barely stroking over the slit.

That made Shane jerk, ripple around him. "Again, Len. Please."

Anything. He'd do anything to hear that voice sound that way. He stroked Shane again, fingers closing around that hard prick, and he finally found his own voice too, words spilling out. Rough words, filthy words and love words. Heat poured over his fingers, Shane's cock spilling and spilling and staying hard for him. Those cries filled the air, sweeter than Tupelo honey and twice as precious.

"Oh God, Shane. God." Galen shook, his own cock jerking without ever being touched as he shot, holding his damned arm still by will alone.

"Never. Never gonna not feel this. In me." Shane's head tossed; he panted. "So fucking big."

"I know, darlin'. I know." Galen watched Shane, tried to catch his breath. "Love."

"Uh-huh." Shane whimpered, legs moving restlessly, hips moving in tiny jerks.

He couldn't ever put into words how Shane looked, how Shane felt. He wasn't good at shit like that. But Galen knew he'd never forget it as long as he lived. He stroked Shane's belly and hip, just touching. Every touch made Shane purr, made him shift and moan, made that pretty, hard prick jerk.

Nothing had ever looked better. Galen shifted enough that he could bend, could take the tip of Shane's prick into his mouth, licking and sucking. Oh, sweet fuck. This time he felt Shane's orgasm, felt the muscles go tight around his hand, rippling, squeezing, going hot before Shane's cock swelled, poured into his lips.

Galen took it all, opening up and sucking Shane down, not letting that sweet cock go until it started to soften. Then he looked up, meeting Shane's eyes.

Dazed, sated, blinking so slow. "Love, yeah?"

"Yeah, darlin'."

Galen smiled, watching, waiting for Shane to relax enough that he could slick up some more and slide out. And damned if he wasn't reluctant to do it, to let go. He did, though, finally, before Shane fell asleep on him. He wanted them both cleaned up before that, and he got the towels and the washcloths and… yeah. Fucking amazing, his Shane.

Shane got settled, curling into his arms, pressed against him with a little moan, fingers drawing random patterns on his skin.

"Thank you, darlin'." He nuzzled into Shane's neck, holding tight. He'd gotten more than he'd even dreamed.

Shane hummed, sighed, the sound sweet, sleepy. "Yours, Len. In me."

He nodded. Shane always got right to the simple heart of things. He was a part of Shane now.

He'd held Shane in the palm of his hand.
That man was his. Period.

Chapter Sixteen

"GODDAMMIT, FRANK, I don't want to come to Miami. I don't care...." Galen sighed when Frank, his investment advisor, went off the deep end again. Fuck this shit. He was going to sell the fucking shares at this rate.

"No." He nudged Goober away from his trash can with his bare toes. He should never have thrown the ice cream wrapper in there. "No, I don't care what Mr. Elias says. I don't have the time."

That was a bald-faced lie. He had the time. Shane didn't. Shane had been busy as fuck at the bar with Will down, and the girl, hell, she hadn't been around long enough to remember her name, with her quitting. And he wasn't about to leave Shane for another week right after being gone.

Oh, wow. His eyes widened, and he completely forgot the phone as the man himself came in from washing the Jeep, thin cotton pants showing off everything, all wet and transparent. Galen motioned, trying to get Shane to come on over.

"Huh? What was that, Frank?"

Shane wandered his way, all loose-limbed and fine, smelling of suds and sunshine.

Oh yeah. He wrapped a hand in the waistband of Shane's pants and pulled, leaning to rub his face against Shane's belly, sniffing deep.

Shane hummed, making offers that were *way* more appealing than whatever shit Frank was saying.

"Gotta go, Frank. Time to go open the bait shop."

The bait shop didn't even open on Sunday, but Frank didn't need to know that. Galen hit End on the portable handset and put both arms around Shane's waist, really pushing in, tongue coming out to taste.

"Uhn. Love. Damn." Shane's fingers tangled in his hair, tugging. Sweet sounds filled the air, happy and horny.

"Mmm-hmm." Yeah. His sounds weren't so sweet. More growly. But they were heartfelt all the same. He nudged the little trail of hair on Shane's belly with his chin. "Taste good."

"Feels good." Shane moved, rocking just a little. "We gotta unplug the phone, lock the doors, and make the world leave us be."

"Oh." Now that struck him as a fantastic fucking idea. He nodded, rubbing his cheek on Shane's ribs. "Yeah. Okay, we can do that."

"Yeah?" He got a grin, slow and sexy and pleased as fuck. "I'll call the club, tell 'em I'm sick. You lock the doors."

"Then you turn off the phone." A last kiss to Shane's belly button and he was up, locked all the doors and windows and turned the fans on. God, a whole day with Shane with no interruptions... it had been too damned long.

Shane made his phone call, then turned the phone off and the cell phones, turned the machine down. "There." That one word was pure satisfaction.

"Got the doors." Grinning, he went right back to Shane, his very own lodestone, and got grabby. "Couch or bed?"

"Bed. Gives us room to play." Shane took his hand, started tugging.

"You're just full of good ideas, darlin'." He went easily, chasing that sweet ass he could see moving under thin cotton. In fact, he was close enough to cop himself a feel, thumb sliding along the crease.

Shane squeezed, trapping his thumb for a second, laugh echoing. "Watch it now."

"I am. That's half the problem. You're tempting as hell." Chuckling, he crowded Shane the last few feet, forcing him down on the bed.

Shane bounced, arching back against him. "You gonna make me fly, Len?"

"I am, darlin'." Hell, yeah. The pants gave easily under his hands, sliding down Shane's thighs to bare that tight ass, and Galen bent to bite into one cheek, then licked to ease the sting.

That low cry made his balls tight, the way it gentled into a groan, almost a plea.

Thumbs digging into Shane's muscles, Galen spread Shane wide, mouthing his way to Shane's hole, poking at it, getting it good and wet. He loved those sounds, loved the way Shane wiggled and arched.

The bed creaked, Shane moving like he was fucking dancing, body tight, begging.

"God, Shane." He pressed deeper, feeling Shane's heat, letting his finger slide in, opening Shane up.

"Uh-huh. More." Oh, demanding thing.

"Spoiled." Grinning wildly, he nudged two fingers in, easing the way with his own moisture, tongue flicking. Shane tasted like heat, earthy and good.

"Yeah. Yours. All yours." That voice was low and deep, a little thready, a lot breathless.

"Mine." His own voice? Purely satisfied. Possessive. Lord, what Shane brought out in him. He lifted up, propping Shane up on the bed more, and climbed up behind, reaching for the lube. Time to really take advantage of having Shane home with him.

"Uh-huh. Fuck me. Want you." Shane leaned, teeth scraping the sensitive skin of his upper arm as he stretched.

"Yeah, darlin'." A quick dose of lube on his fingers got Shane open and ready the rest of the way, ready for him to slide his cock right on in, pushing until his hips sat hard on Shane's ass. "Fuck. Tight."

Shane rippled, squeezed him good and hard, that ass gripping him tight.

Uhn. Moving was about the only thing he could do, because thinking and speaking were out. He started rocking, hips running back and forth, hands sliding up and down Shane's back. God, that skin.

Shane crawled up along the headboard, meeting his thrusts, slamming back hard.

Bending, Galen stretched out along Shane's body, biting at the back of Shane's neck. He reached around, searching out those pierced nipples, twisted them with each thrust.

"Oh!" Yes. Yes. He loved the way he could feel that, the way Shane bore down, shook inside with each twist. Harder and harder he moved, thrusting in, giving them some serious friction. He closed his eyes and rode it, loving on Shane with all he had.

"Galen...." Shane moved back and up, ending in his lap, his cock shifting as they came together, skin slapping.

"Shane!" Oh. They teetered as he struggled for balance, but then he got it right, got them set. Which was when he reached for Shane's cock and started pulling.

"Yeah. Yeah, just like that. Sweet fuck." The low babble filled the air, Shane hot enough to burn him.

He was gonna bust. That was all there was to it. Split wide open and ooze all down the bed. Galen bit down hard on

Shane's shoulder, sucking up a mark, claiming. That did it too. Shane grunted and squeezed, heat pouring right out over his hand, just like that.

God almighty. Galen managed one, two more thrusts before he was coming like a freight train, his eyes rolling in his head. Shane was like nothing else, ever.

"Mmm-hmm... better than the fucking phone any day."

"Hell, yes, darlin'. Though we should have locked the bedroom door too." Because damned if Goober wasn't sitting there looking at them. And kinda... wagging.

Shane started laughing, the happy sound making that pup wag harder. "Oh. Oh shit."

"Yeah." Grinning, he let them topple over, flopping on the bed and reaching down for Goober. "C'mere, mutt."

Shane chuckled, hand sliding on him, just loving. "He deserves a friend, Len. And you ought to have a Goob too. Well, not a 'Goob,' because they'd get confused and it would be weird, but a puppy."

"I do *not* need a puppy." Though he guessed he could call his momma and see if she knew anyone who had something. A Doberman. Or a Rottie.

"Uh-huh." Goob clambered over to get to Shane, drooly little shit.

"What? I don't." Galen grinned, watching those ears flap as Shane scratched behind them. Okay, okay, maybe it would be nice to have a his-sized dog to wrestle with.

"Yep. Something big enough to scare Vic off if he tries to eat Goob." Shane grinned up at him, that look wicked as all fuck.

"You're a shit, you know?" He grinned back, pinching Shane's nipple. "Yeah, yeah. I'll look into it."

"I'm your shit and you love me." Shane grinned, then got this serious look on his face. "We ought to think on a vacation after tourist season, Len. Go somewhere, stay here, I don't care. But we should."

"Okay, darlin'." He scooted close, moving Goob to one side. "You had enough?"

"Yeah, kinda? I mean, I know I'm supposed to be all ladder-climby and shit, but I didn't mind bartending, and this working ninety hours a week shit sucks. I love that club, but it ain't you. You remember New Orleans? Or Vermont? Just us? I need me some of that."

Yeah. Oh yeah. He remembered. And damn, even when Shane had been home lately Galen'd been on the fucking phone. "Then we'll plan something. Something... oh. Maybe something tropical this time. Aruba. Barbados."

"Mmm.... Anywhere. I like to go and see stuff with you." Shane's fingers slid over his arm, down his chest, petting him.

"I like taking you places." Everything was new through Shane's eyes. Different. "Love you, darlin'."

He cuddled close, just... being.

"Yeah." Shane nodded, kissed his chin. "Yeah, love."

They'd work the vacation out later. Right now he'd settle for a quiet night in.

Chapter Seventeen

ORK WAS starting to get to him. Galen sat behind the counter at the bait shop, a diagram laid out in front of him, his shiny new laptop humming along with the radio. Damn, but he hated that he had to get out of the house to get anything done, but Shane was... constant temptation.

The little bell above the door jingled, Old Man Taylor limping in, his little blue heeler romping right in behind. "Well, well, Frost," the old man muttered. "Was wondering if you'd packed up and gone to Yankeeland again."

"Nah. Just been busy." Great, now he was getting guilt from the locals. "This is a hobby. You know that."

"Well, some of us fish for a hobby and need you to be open, son." The grizzled old fart grinned before reaching around the counter and grabbing a bottle of Coke out of the cooler Galen kept there. He plopped down and crossed his feet at the ankles. "So what all are you doing?"

"Oh, been making calls on investors and advertisers. Did you know the average non-NFL team has to have an average of fifteen sponsors to stay out of the red?"

"Sounds boring as hell, son."

That stung, but only because it had a ring of truth to it. Galen sighed, taking off his hat and rubbing his head before scrubbing at his beard a little. "Well, it's mainly a favor to an old friend. Really," he added at Taylor's skeptical look.

"Sure, son. Sure. Just remember that you're semiretired. You get to my age without enjoying that and you'll regret it."

Galen nodded, staring at the bright screen of his laptop. "I'll keep that in mind, old man. I surely will."

GALEN SANG ALONG WITH THE RADIO, HIS VOICE morning-rough and harsh. Man, he needed to stop going to the bar on Saturday nights; the smoke killed him these days. But he missed Shane. A lot, thanks to the fucking work schedules they'd been keeping. So he went.

He poured the champagne into the orange juice, then flipped the pancakes on the plate. He'd gotten up early enough to make brunch in bed for Shane. About noon, in other words. Galen flipped a sausage link to a very hopeful Goober before shoving him out into his run, then headed into the bedroom, just a'humming away.

Shane was sprawled out in the sheets, one arm above his head, the other lying against his belly, thumb slowly rubbing the long, hard cock.

The tray bobbled in his hands, and Galen set it down on the dresser with a thump, staring.

"Jesus, darlin'. You trying to make me dump hot food on myself?"

"Nope." Shane didn't even open his eyes, just licked his lips and moaned. "Was dreaming about you, Len, about us."

That thumb circled the tip of Shane's cock, spreading the drops there, Shane's thighs going tight.

Galen grunted, leaning back on the dresser on his braced arms, watching. "Oh God, darlin'."

"Mmm-hmm. Love that. Love how you sound." Shane moaned a little, hand starting to move, Shane jacking himself off, not holding back a bit.

"What...." Galen cleared his throat, trying not to growl. "What sound?" Fuck, Shane was gonna kill him.

"The way you say darlin', the way you rumble. The sound you make when you're wanting, when you're watching me ride you, watching me all filled up."

Oh fuck. Look at those thighs spread. Galen clenched his hands on the dresser to keep his knees from buckling. "Love how you look, darlin'. All the time. But like this... oh fuck."

"Uh-huh. Want you. Want all sorts of things." That free hand dropped, tugging the chain, making those pretty, shiny rings in those nipples shift.

"Yeah? Tell me what, darlin'." Was that his voice? Sounded like he'd been on a three-day whiskey binge. Galen realized he was rocking, his cock showing against his boxer briefs.

"You, in me. In here or outside in the rain, spread and all hungry. Fuck, Len. Love." Shane drew his knees up, hips pushing up, driving that cock into his fist.

He could smell how close Shane was, could feel it vibrate all the way across the floor. Prying one hand off the dresser, Galen rubbed himself through his shorts, moaning as he kept his eyes peeled, wanting to see.

"All wet with the rain, filled. Fuck. Fuck, yeah." Shane reached down, rolled those tight balls, and cried out, spunk spraying.

Galen almost fell right over. Instead, he wobbled to the bed, growling as he landed next to Shane, skinning off his shorts. He rubbed against Shane's thighs, all sorts of curses falling out of him.

Shane moaned, turned toward him, nodding, hot and damp and smelling of sex.

"Darlin'. Need. Touch me." He grabbed Shane's wet hand, tugging it down to wrap around his cock. He couldn't last long, not the way it was zinging up his spine to his brain.

"Uh-huh. Mine. Love. Come on. Want," Shane babbled, hand working him like nothing else, just jacking him straight to heaven.

Galen grunted, back arching as he shot like nobody's business, his cock throbbing he came so hard. His groan shook him all the way down to his toes.

Shane made a happy little sound, nuzzling and cuddling into him. "Mornin'."

"Morning, darlin'." He grinned, licking Shane's throat and rumbling. "I made brunch. Mimosa Sunday."

"Oh. Mimosas." Shane petted his hair, humming low. "Smells good."

"Mmm-hmm. So do you." Galen breathed deep. Shane smelled like them, like come and sweat and their bed and salt. He could fucking get off on that smell for years. "I even made sausage."

"Too fucking cool." A man could live forever on that sound, happy and satisfied and his.

He kissed Shane's neck, his shoulder. "Lemme go get it. We can eat and snuggle."

"Mmm... I'll grab it. You cooked." Shane hopped up after mopping them both up a little, bouncing and flopping and grinning. "Ooh... strawberries!"

"Uh-huh." Rolling to his back, Galen tucked his hands behind his head and watched Shane saunter back over. "You do a man good, darlin'."

Shane settled down next to him, snuggling right in, offering him a berry. "Just one man, yeah? Just one."

"Just this one, for sure." The growl was back. No sharing for him. Shane was his. Period.

Shane nodded, hand hot on his belly. "Don't see us sharing anytime soon."

"Nope."

He gave a satisfied grunt and offered Shane a link of sausage. "Even if we do let Goober sleep with us sometimes."

Shane chuckled, nibbling on his fingertips. "Goob's good for footwarming, so long as he doesn't lick."

"Or fart." Lord, that dog could bust some nasty stink bombs. "So, I figure we need a plan for the day."

"Plans are good. I can hang with plans." He got another bite, this time of cantaloupe.

"Good. Here's my idea. We eat. We shower. We maybe fuck some more. We eat and drink some beer in front of the TV…. How am I doing so far?"

Shane tilted his head, nodded, those eyes just twinkling. "So far, I'm liking the plan. Go on."

"Oh, somewhere in there we play with Goob. And maybe give massages if it doesn't seem like work." He grinned back, happy in his bones.

"Mmm-hmm. Maybe a nice lazy blow job during commercials."

Chapter Eighteen

HE'D BEEN thinking on it a lot. Like a lot a lot. Watching Galen get all frowny and bitchy and testy and, well, grumpier than a dog with mangy balls, which was not only gross, but damned grumpy too. Shane didn't know what the fuck was up—maybe Goober ate one of Len's house shoes; maybe there was weird money shit; maybe the state of professional football made the man's butt itch. Galen could be complicated and shit.

It didn't really matter. Shane figured it was his job to fix things before someone took a tire iron to Galen's head and fucked up the man's part.

He put the massage oils and the furry glove and the lube on the bedside table, then grabbed the little wrist-tie dealies. "Galen? Can you c'mere?"

If loving the man into goo didn't work? Shane reckoned he'd have to call Len's momma.

Len really didn't want him bringing Momma into this.

"What?" That frown was right there as Galen came into the room, bending Galen's little mustache all down.

"I need a favor, sorta. Can you get naked?"

"Can I get...." Galen looked at him, squinty. "Why?"

"'Cause you're in a shitty mood and I want to make it better." He held up the ties. "Just trust me, 'kay?"

Galen looked at the ties, looked at him, and he could see it in Len's face, the stuff that Len would never say. But finally Galen nodded and started unbuttoning his shirt. "Okay, darlin'. We'll play it your way."

He went over, kissed Galen's jaw. "Thanks."

Then he started helping and touching and kissing, making things as least weird as he could.

They got Galen naked, got that big body all bare for him. Galen's chest rose and fell, that belly tight and hot under his fingers.

"Come on and lay down, yeah?" He wouldn't tie Galen to the bed, just tie those hands together so Galen could worry about feeling good.

"Okay." Galen went with him, stretching out on the bed, looking docile as Victor in the kiddie pool. 'Course, Len had teeth and was about as quick as Victor too.

He stripped down, settling beside Galen and cuddling, kissing one wrist before slipping the black leather around it.

Oh, okay. That?

Sorta hot.

Maybe more than sorta.

"This cool?"

"Yeah." Galen tensed up but relaxed nice and easy against him after a few seconds. "Yeah, it's cool."

"If it stops being, you say." Like he wouldn't know. Still, Shane figured he should say something about it out loud. He brought Galen's other hand up, twined the leather around, nice and simple. Damn, that was pretty, all dark against Galen's tan.

"I will, darlin'. You know that." Those dark eyes watched him, really intense, like the first night they'd met.

He nodded, moving to straddle Galen's hips, fingers sliding down the muscled arms, touching, feeling. Galen was like a little furnace under him, and it was all he could do not to rub. "Oh damn. I love touching you, Len."

"Mmm." Arching under him, Galen smiled. "Love it when you do, darlin'."

Those bound hands moved, stopped short, and, oh, that was pretty.

"You just feel, Len. That's all you gotta do. I'll love you right." He leaned down, tongue slip-sliding over one of Galen's dark little nipples.

"Oh, fuck. Shane. Good." He could tell it was, the way Galen moved under him, the way Galen's whiskey voice went all growly. He hummed and nodded, lips surrounding the whole little nipple, tongue working the tip. His hands were on Galen's belly, Galen's hips.

Galen hummed back, legs shifting restlessly, cock rubbing against him. There was nothing on earth like that long prick.

He let his lips drag over to the other nipple, giving it a little of the good loving while his hands cupped Galen's balls. They fit nice in his hand—soft and hot and covered in dark hairs that tickled his palm.

"Shane!" Galen bucked for him, every muscle in that big body shaking. "Oh, darlin'."

"All yours, yeah?" He smiled and worked his way down, lips mapping that six-pack, fingers rolling Galen's balls. "Smell so good, Len. So fucking good."

"Love the way you feel. Love the way you look loving me." Galen shifted, trying to get closer, bound hands curling up against Len's chest.

"You're just feeling, now. Let me... I wanna make it right inside you." He settled so his cheek was on Galen's belly, tongue exploring the tip of Galen's cock, fingers moving to love on the soft skin inside Galen's thigh.

"Always do, darlin." Spreading for him, Galen rubbed, cock hot against him.

"Good." He smiled, leaving soft, sucking kisses on that hot, taut flesh, tasting that salt and wet. Shit, he liked this, being able to just chill out, feel and look and not have to get all distracted and insane. Well, okay—he fucking loved the distracted and insane, but this was still rocking cool.

Len liked it too. Yeah, Shane could tell. Galen's muscles quivered under his fingers and his lips, and Len's cock throbbed against his mouth. He scooted down a little more, took more in, sucking easy. Galen spread, and Shane's hand slid down one thigh, petting away.

Galen growled, that low, sexy sound he loved so. "Tease."

"Not. I'm loving on you." He grinned wider, tongue flicking that fascinating, sensitive ridge at the tip of Len's cock.

"Oh God, darlin'." Galen rocked into him, pushing into his mouth. He could smell Galen, the scent stronger now.

Oh yeah. That was it. Shane let his hand slide back up, fingers tapping along that wrinkled, hot skin behind Galen's balls. Galen panted, rising up, letting him have all the room he needed. Yeah. That skin was hot, good under his hands. He hummed, feeling the vibrations move through Galen's cock. Oh, now. That? Cool. He hummed louder, just to see what Galen would do.

Galen grunted, head coming up off the bed, those eyes wide and dark as Galen looked right at him and came, hot and wet in his mouth.

Oh, man, did that make him feel thirty feet tall or what? He licked and nuzzled, cleaning Galen up, loving with all he was.

"Damn. Shane." Len looked dazed, eyes cloudy, a quiet smile playing under the short-cropped beard.

There was his smile. "Yeah, you taste good, Len. Damn good."

"You think so?" Galen relaxed back on the bed. "What else are you gonna do to me, darlin'?"

"Think I'm gonna get you all riled up again and then take you for a ride. Got all night, though, so I ain't in a hurry."

"Got me at your mercy, huh?" Those bound hands waggled at him. "S'okay, darlin'. I think I like your plan."

He chuckled, pushed up and kissed Galen good and hard. "It's all about you, Galen. About you and me."

"Kiss me again, Shane." Galen strained, lips swollen and hot, the look in Len's eyes even hotter.

Shane nodded, fingers holding Len's head, petting as one kiss became two became three. Galen kissed him back, tongue sliding into his mouth and pulling back, teasing him.

Oh, now. That was cheating. He thrust harder, giving Galen all he had. Moaning, Galen opened for him, head arching back on his neck, taking the kiss in deep. He started rubbing, cock sliding on Galen's belly. He fucking needed, so bad, and the kisses just made it worse. Better. Whatever.

"Love. Oh God, Shane. Yeah." Rubbing right back, Galen purred for him, growled for him, just twisting like a big old cat under him.

"Wanna make love to you, yeah? Need to feel you all around me. Let me in?"

"Yes. Darlin'. Want you." Galen just... oh damn, he put his hands up over his head and offered everything right up.

"Oh...." He scooted down, spread Galen's legs, and reached for the slick stuff. His heart was pounding, cock throbbing in time. "Galen...."

"Come on, darlin'. Come on." That hot six-pack was tight, Galen's cock firming again, rising for him, balls tight and high. Damn, his Len was like nothing else, ever.

He slicked and stretched Len, not playing around, not teasing. Teasing was for later, when his cock wasn't so fucking hard. Then he slicked himself and settled between Galen's thighs.

"Now. Yeah?" Galen opened his thighs wide, hips rolling up.

"Now. Yeah." He met Galen's eyes, smiled and pushed in, easy as pie. "Love...."

Hot, tight, Galen opened for him, stretched around him, so good. He got noises, growly, deep noises that told him Galen needed him, loved him.

He bent down, lips surrounding one of Galen's nipples, sucking hard.

"Fuck!" That little bit of flesh swelled for him, going red and hot. Galen's cock rubbed his belly, wet on his skin.

Oh yeah. He pulled harder, rocking and moaning and loving it, loving what he was making Galen feel.

"Love. Love you...." It came out on a moan, Len panting for him, gasping for him, whole body begging.

"Yeah. Len. Need you bad." He leaned up, hips rocking nice and hard.

He felt Len clamp down on him, felt every shudder, every gasp, all the way through Len's body. Galen shot hard again, without him even touching that pretty cock, simply came for him. Just like that.

He reached down, hand shaking, and slid his fingers through the hot come. All it took was licking his fingers clean and he shot, shaking and pushing deep into Len's body.

"Good, Shane." Galen twisted. "Need to touch you."

He nodded, unfastening those fine fucking hands. "Please."

Galen stroked his back, one hand staying on his ass, cupping it, the other coming up to sit on the back of his neck, rubbing lightly.

Shane hummed, nuzzled Galen's throat. "Better now?"

"Yeah, darlin'. You melted away the bad mood for sure."

"Good." He listened to Galen's heart beating, sure and steady as fuck, all good.

"You're always good for what ails me, Shane. Sorry I've been a butthead." Galen kissed Shane's cheek, his throat.

"Just glad I helped." He grinned, took himself a long kiss. "'Sides, you're a cute butthead."

Len popped him, but it was halfhearted. Galen? Looked about as relaxed as Victor after a bath.

And now he looked a lot less toothy.

Chapter Nineteen

"Hey, man. What's up?"

Shane looked over the bar, grinning at Wade's familiar buzz cut. "Hey, bud. Ain't much up. It's dead in here. You want a beer?"

He didn't really even wait for Wade's nod to draw a Sam Adams. Christ, the man was more than a regular; he was a friend. "I'm surprised your man isn't here."

"Yeah." Shane shrugged. "He's real busy. Making money, though."

Not that it seemed to be worth it, really. Galen sure didn't look happier. Course, Shane couldn't bitch, really, with pulling extra shifts, but still.

"Money's good." Wade winked over, and Shane laughed, nodding.

Yeah. Yeah, it was, and Galen worked hard. Real hard.

Him and Wade chattered until Will showed, bullshitting and joshing, laughing some. "Okay, man. I'm off the clock."

"You want to sit and have a few?"

Shane tilted his head, looked at his watch. "Sure. Galen's won't be home yet, I don't think."

"Hoo-boy!" Wade laughed. "Pour me and your boss a round, Will."

They settled in a booth with a couple other guys, doing shooters, watching the ballgame, goofing off. Will set the jukebox to playing—rockabilly blaring, making Shane bounce in his seat.

"Wanna dance, y'all?" The new guy—all dark and tall and pretty and named Sam or Stu or Steve—grinned over, standing up and holding out his hand. "Come on, we'll have the dance floor to ourselves."

Shane sort of blinked over to Wade, who nodded. "You need to move sometimes. No harm in it."

"Oh. Yeah. Yeah, I fucking *love* dancing." They started moving, and Sam/Stu/Steve was good at it, moving them together, the booze *just* making the lights swirling and sparkly and shit.

They danced and danced, and other guys got up and joined them, and fuck, he was having fun. Only thing to make it better would be if Galen was there. That would make it perfect. Mmm.... Len.

A slow song started, the new guy pulling him close, dancing him around nice and easy. "Mmm... 's nice. Thanks, man."

The guy's chin rested on his temple—the dude needed a shave and possibly to use less aftershave, because damn. "Anytime, Shane. You dance like a dream. You get lonely? You call."

Right. He just wanted to dance. He got lonely-lonely, he'd go home and get Goob to show him how to do that pitiful basset hound eye thing. Len would be fucked.

THE DAMNED PHONE HAD RUNG OFF THE HOOK. Galen had thrown the fucker across the room and gotten his hat and his good boots and headed to the bar to get Shane. He didn't care who all was there to back up the bar. Shane was gonna either go out with him or go home with him, and they wouldn't replace the phone until tomorrow.

Or maybe the next day.

He parked his truck out behind the bar, next to Shane's Jeep, and headed on in. Looking for Shane behind the bar first, he didn't find him. The music was loud, the drinks and laughter flowing, and Galen shook his head. The place was twice what it had been. He went on up to the office but found it dark and empty.

Damn.

He went back down. The Jeep was there, so Shane had to be. Galen scanned the crowd. Where the hell was he?

When Galen found him, he damn near dropped his teeth. Some tall motherfucker had Shane, waltzing his lover around in lazy circles, chin right down against Shane's face.

Galen stared. And he stared some more, his hands clenching into fists. It was all he could do not to just go rip the guy away from Shane and beat him to a fucking pulp, but he'd gotten Shane fired once. He blinked.

Nope. They were still dancing cheek to cheek. Or chin to cheek. Or whatever.

Galen turned on his bootheel and started for the door. No. No way was he gonna sit there and watch Shane dancing what should be his dance with some yahoo. Goddammit. He'd trusted the man. Again.

"Frost!" One of the regulars stopped him three feet from the door. "Dancing's good tonight. You should go get Shane."

His muscles all tensed up, and he nodded. Yeah. Yeah, he should go get Shane. Damn it. Turning, he headed to the dance floor, intent on getting his own back.

Shane got turned again, those pretty eyes landing on him

and lighting up. Not going wide, not upset or ashamed. No. Lit up fucking happy. "Len!"

Tall, dark, and ugly got left empty armed, Shane heading over with a grin.

There was no way he could summon a smile. Hell, he couldn't even get rid of the scowl. "Hey."

"You have a bad night, man? You want a drink? I'll pour." Shane's hand slid up his arm. "I'm glad you're here."

"Are you?" He jerked his chin toward the dance floor, where the tall guy had found someone new. "Who is he?"

"Uh.... Sam? Steve? Stu?" Shane shrugged. "I don't remember. Some guy."

"Some guy." His chest eased a bit. Not much. But a little. Galen blew out a breath, grabbing Shane's hand. "I could use a Jack, straight up."

"Okay, sure." Shane held his hand, squeezing, winding them through the crowd. "You want it down here or in the office?"

"Office. I. We. I need to talk to you, darlin'." Fuck, he was an idiot.

"Sure, Len." Shane grabbed a bottle on the way past the bar. "You have a shitty day?"

"Yeah. Yeah, I did. And then...." He waited until they were in the stairwell, the door shut behind them before grabbing Shane and kissing him. Hard. Shane opened right up for him, the flavor of whiskey barely there. Hell yes, that was what he needed. Shane smelled all wrong, and Galen rubbed all up on him like a cat spreading his scent.

A low moan pushed into his lips, Shane reaching up and holding on tight.

His hand closed over Shane's hip, slipping down to pull Shane's thigh up so it wrapped around his leg, giving him access, friction. He rubbed, their cocks rasping together through their jeans.

"Mmm...." Shane sucked on his tongue, happy, horny little noises sounding, cock starting to fill for him.

Fuck. Fuck, that was good. Galen shivered, pressing even closer, his other hand cupping Shane's ass. "Need you, darlin'."

"Mmm-hmm. Come to the office, love." Of course, Shane wasn't moving toward the office, just pressing and rubbing against him.

"Okay." He could move, though, if it meant getting more of Shane. Like skin. Galen stumbled back, hauling Shane with him, then staggered up the stairs.

Shane's hand found his ass, squeezed. "Oh. Oh, been missing you all night. Thought you were busy."

"I was. I missed you." Squashing the thought that Shane could have come home and looked for him, he shoved them inside the office and locked the door, then dragged Shane right to the couch.

Shane sort of bounced, the whiskey bottle rolling away. Those clever fingers went right for his shirt buttons, working them open.

"Yeah, darlin'. Yeah." He kissed Shane so hard, his lips swelling right up, his cock swelling too.

"Need you. Please, Len." His shirt damn near tore, Shane yanking it down.

"So good." Always so good. He pulled at Shane's jeans until the button popped open, yanked the zipper down and shoved his hand in. Oh Christ.

Shane nodded, spreading, cock jumping into his touch. Shane's head went back, and Galen bent to suck up a mark, needing to claim and feeling like an ass for it. Good thing he was too far gone to care. It didn't hurt that Shane went wild, moaning and holding his mouth close, cock jerking and throbbing in his fingers.

Stroking Shane's prick, Galen licked where he'd marked,

tongue pressing down, adding to the burn. Damn. His. Shane was his.

"Oh. Oh, Len. Yeah. Yeah." Shane groaned, throat working. Shane's fingers scraped along his spine, zinging.

"Shane. Darlin'." He arched, pushing down against Shane's thigh, feeling his orgasm rising along his spine already.

"Want. Want you. Love you." Shane's eyes caught his, so honest, so fucking *real*.

"I can't. Shane, I can't wait." He didn't think he could even get his jeans open. Instead he just slid down off the couch and lifted Shane's cock to his mouth, sucking that sweet prick in, apologizing the only way he knew how for even doubting. Shane cried out, shaking hard, come filling Galen's mouth almost at the first touch of his tongue.

Galen licked him clean, savoring the flavor unique to his Shane before reaching down to rub himself through his jeans, grunting, breathing deep and harsh as he came in his pants like a fucking teenager.

Shane sat up, reached for him. "'Mere. C'mere, Len."

"Mmm-hmm." He went, letting Shane fold around him, nuzzling in on Shane's throat and breathing deep. Now Shane smelled right. Like them.

"Yeah. Hey. Oh. Loving you's better than dancing."

He rested his forehead on Shane's. "Darlin', I got a favor to ask."

"Sure, Len. What?" He got a kiss, Shane's nose rubbing against his.

"No more slow dancing with anyone but me. That hurt to see." He knew it wasn't meant to. He could tell Shane hadn't even thought on it. It was his deal. But that would be a start.

"Oh." Oh God. Shane's face fell. "Oh, Galen. I didn't mean to. Honest. I won't. I just was wanting to dance, to move. I won't. I promise."

Oh God. Look what he'd done. Feeling like the biggest

fucking heel ever, he kissed Shane's mouth to hush him up. "I know, darlin'. And if I'm not around, it's my own fault if you dance your ass off with someone else. Just... save the slow ones for me."

"Every one. Promise." Shane kissed the corner of his mouth. "I kept wishing you were here. Or home. Somewhere where there was music and no phone."

"I killed the phone." And the cell phone wasn't charged. There was no phone. Period.

"Yeah?" Shane grinned, eyes dancing. "Tell me you didn't kill the radio."

"I didn't." Relieved, he kissed Shane again, deeper. "We could dance."

"We could. We could stop and get doughnuts on the way home and let the guys close up." Shane stroked his jaw. "Unless you want to go downstairs and dance. So long as it's us, I'm happy."

"No, I need to go. Uh. Change. Drive-through dough-nuts?" His jeans? Swampy. Nasty, man. Nasty.

"Oh. Yeah. I hear you. I'll get you a handkerchief." Shane scooted up, tossed him a cloth, bouncing, then grabbed the phone. "Hey, guys? Close up. I'm going home. Huh? Nope. Gonna go home with Galen. I'll leave the Jeep."

Galen grabbed Shane before he could bounce off to the door and kissed him so hard they both gasped for air when Galen let him go. He grinned, helping Shane do up his jeans, wiping his own down before he was ready to go. Then he put an arm around Shane's waist.

"Come on, darlin'. Let's go home. I'll show you what a slow dance is all about."

"You got it, Len. 'S all I really want."

And that? He could live with. He'd have to deal with the crazy jealousy at some point. For right now he'd settle for knowing Shane had saved the last dance for him.

Shane heard Galen banging before he ever woke up, pans and plates slamming and clattering and all.

Must be time to wake up, huh?

He groaned a little, grinned as he blinked at the clock.

Man.

Nine thirty.

Galen was *early*.

Another crash and bang and Shane was up and tugging on a pair of jeans, hopping into them on his way into the kitchen. "Mornin'."

He got a grunt, and something went sailing into the sink, Len not even looking at him. That tanned back looked good rising out of a pair of loose sweats, though.

"I'll make coffee." He headed over, fingers brushing against Galen's hip. "You feed Goob?"

"Not yet. He was sleepin'." Damn. Just about that time something caught fire, and Galen cursed viciously. "Goddammit, Shane, get the fuck out of my way."

Okay. He could do that.

He grabbed a beer out of the fridge and headed out to the deck, whistling for Goob, then plopped into a deck chair.

It wasn't too bad out here, really. He could nap.

Until, oh... Tuesday.

He could hear Galen flapping about in the kitchen like a chicken with its head cut off, and then in two or three scratches of Goob's ears, Galen was at the door, growling.

"You were gonna make coffee. Pancakes and shit are almost ready."

"Sure." He finished his beer and stood, doing his best not to sigh. He was obviously fucked, and not in that fun spanky way.

Coffee. Water. Filter. See him. See him make with the coffee.

The way Galen vibrated told him the man was waiting for him to ask. Galen was like that. No fucking way was he gonna, though. That only led to ow.

There was this weird thing that happened where you went to sleep okay and woke up in trouble that was deeply fucked. Shane figured Galen either had nightmares or invented shit instead of sleeping. Probably the second, because not sleeping made people grumpy as hell.

Galen took the cup of coffee he offered and handed him a plate of singed pancakes and burnt bacon. Those dark-dark eyes dared him to say a word.

Good thing Goob liked crispy.

He read the back of the syrup bottle, twice. Man, corn was in everything.

The smacking of a plate on the table made him jump, and Len sat down, stabbing at the food. Those eyes kept landing on him, and Len kept muttering, but he couldn't make out about what. He kinda wished he could. Kinda didn't.

After choking down about half, he took a deep breath. "Thanks for breakfast." *Morning, Galen. What the fuck is your problem?*

"Oh, no problem, darlin'. I just about burned the damned kitchen down."

Okay, wait. Hadn't they had a good night last night? Hadn't they come and come? What, had Galen slept wrong and bent his dick?

Christ, it was too fucking early to try to figure shit out. With his fucking luck, he'd pretended to dance in his sleep and offended Galen all over. "I'll do dishes."

"Damn it, Shane. Who the fuck was that guy?" It snapped out like Vic's jaws closing on a chicken, all teeth and whomp.

Shit. Like he remembered the dude's name now. "Some friend of Wade's."

"You know how I feel about other guys touching you."

Man, he thought they'd covered that last night. And passed it. Buried it. Something.

"I said I was sorry last night." He'd been bored, more than anything, tired of watching all the guys dancing and playing and laughing and shit.

"You coulda called me." Len was scowling at him, something creeping into that expression. Something like hurt.

"You said you were busy." Fuck, he should go back to work. He was good at that. "I said I won't do it again."

"It just. I don't like it, darlin'." Len always knew when he was being unreasonable, and damned if Galen didn't sigh and rub one hand over his head. "Sorry. You want me to try again with the pancakes?"

"No. I'm cool." He stood up and started the water for dishes, wishing he'd put on a shirt and shit. Lord, it was only ten.

"Shane...." Galen slid right up behind him, hands on his bare waist. "I said I was sorry. I know I'm being an ass. I hate the idea of me not giving you what you need."

"I just wanted to fucking dance, man. I was having a good time."

Eyes flashing and lips pressing together, Galen nodded. "Yeah. Your idea of fun and mine are different."

Oh, now. That was just.... Goddamn.

"I. Yeah. I guess." Shane shrugged, headed for the bedroom. Okay. Shower. Clothes.

"Shane...." Len followed him, poking at it like a sore tooth. "I just. Damn it, after what happened with that one night and the Mickey they slipped you. And I walked in, and you were with that guy, and I wanted to beat him to the floor."

"You act like I was blowing him or something." Shane

turned around, meeting Galen's eyes, and finally asked the thing he'd been wondering about since that last big fight after Galen'd so much as called him a slut at the bar. "You really think I'd do that to you? Really?"

"No." The answer was immediate and gratifying. "I'm a jealous bastard, Shane. You know damned well I used to live in the kind of circles people would do that in. It's not you I don't trust."

"Then who? 'Cause it seems to me that either you think I'm stupid and don't know how to say no, loose enough not to want to say no, or—" Shit, what was a guy who couldn't say no? "—a... victim or something."

Len stared at him a minute, while Goob wandered to his bowl and then back to Shane's feet to drool some. Then Galen shrugged. "I don't think you're stupid or loose, Shane. Go on, take a shower or whatever."

Len turned on his heel and headed back to the kitchen, whistling for the dog.

Not stupid or loose, but not enough to hold his own, it looked like.

Shane grabbed a towel and a pair of jeans. By ten thirty, he was heading back out to the bar to do something he was good at.

GALEN LOOKED AT THE PHONE THAT HADN'T TURNED out to be near as broke as he'd thought, trying to decide whether he wanted to toss it across the room and really crack it or answer it. The caller ID told him it wasn't Shane, so he tossed it, grunting as it landed on the couch and not against the wall.

Goob trotted after him when he went to get a beer, then struggled across the yard with him when he went to open the bait shop for a bit. He hadn't done that in too long, he figured, if Goob was sneezing that way at the dust.

He was acting like an ass, and he knew it. He hated it when Shane went off like that too, all bruised and tight-looking.

Cleaning the counters and sweeping the floors used up some of his pent-up grumpy, and Galen finally sighed, whistling at Goob, who came running, a rubber frog dangling from his mouth.

"You think we ought to go get Shane a pizza, babe? Huh?" He scritched those long ears and watched Goober dance. That silly mutt was a go-puppy.

They got in his truck and headed into town. His cell was still plugged into the lighter, so he grabbed it up, called Roma's, and ordered Shane's favorite Hawaiian pizza and a deep dish supreme for the bar. By the time he crossed the bridge into town, it was ready, and he sailed into the bar bearing food and puppy, which ought to go a long way toward Shane forgiving him.

The bar was damn near empty, the boys at the bar hooting when they saw Goob. "Galen! Dude! You here for the boss? He's upstairs working on the books and shit."

"Yeah. Here. Gimme a slice of the deep dish, and I'll leave the rest." He pulled out a piece, and a longneck with a lid, and headed upstairs, smiling all around.

Goob galumphed up the stairs, ears flopping madly, the low howl filling the air when the hound found the office door closed.

"Goob? Goober, is that you?" The door opened, Shane's face appearing.

Goober slobbered all over Shane's feet, and Galen held up the box of thin crust with pineapple and ham. "Hey, darlin'."

"Hey. Come on in." Shane held the door open, nodded to him once, the look unsure, uncomfortable. "Smells good."

"S'your favorite. I got the guys a deep dish...." Damn him and his fucking pride. Galen moved in, bent to kiss Shane hello. "Sorry, darlin'. I really am."

Shane kissed him back, fingers squeezing his wrist once. "'S cool, man. I should've known better."

"No. Not your fault, okay? A man should be able to have a fuckin' dance." Okay, see him? He could be all progressive and shit. He could. "I just. I get all caveman. Wanna eat?"

"Sure." Shane swept the magazines and newspapers off the low table by the little office couch. "I'll go down and get some napkins and stuff."

"What? I brought plates. Come on, darlin'. Sit with me. Look at your dog. He brought you a present." That silly frog was still in Goob's mouth.

Shane looked. Then that stiff, cold look disappeared, Shane's laugh ringing out. "Oh, look at you and your nasty slimy frog. Lord." Shane plopped down beside him, hooting as Goob wagged and chewed.

"He wanted to bring it so bad. Fought me when I tried to take it away." Galen set the pizza out, got it on plates, gave Shane a beer....

"He ate the squeaker out of it. He'll be sad when it's chewed to nothing." Shane's thigh rubbed against his, throat working as the beer went down.

"We'll have to get him something else. Maybe a flamingo." The beer was history. Maybe they had some iced tea in Shane's little fridge. "You get lots done?"

"Yeah. I did paperwork stuff. Nothing exciting. You?" Shane groaned over the pizza.

"I cleaned up the bait shop a little." That had been kinda fun. "And I bought pizza."

"It's good pizza." Shane stole a bit of pepperoni off Galen's slice.

"It is." The sauce had a nice spicy aftertaste. "Roma's is good."

"I don't like fighting with you."

He glanced over, looking at Shane's kinda bewildered expression. "I know, darlin'. I don't like fighting with you either. I just have a protective bone. And it's not because I think you can't take care of yourself, okay?"

"Okay. I'm not going to cheat on you, Len. I don't want anybody like that but you."

"Good." He cupped Shane's cheek so he could bend and kiss the man silly.

He wasn't sure what it said that Shane opened right on up, let him in and let him take what he needed. Galen decided to take it as a good thing, decided to trust, and he pulled Shane half into his lap, the pizza box sliding away across the table.

Shane ended up straddling him, leaning against his belly, hands framing him face. "Hey."

"Hey, darlin'." Grinning, he rubbed noses with Shane, then kissed him hard, loving up on him. He cupped Shane's butt and rubbed them together, groaning at how good it felt.

"Your pizza's getting cold." Like Shane gave a shit.

"That's why you have the oven downstairs...." That felt like heaven, his own sweet Shane on top of him, rubbing like a madman, both of them groaning. "We'll get to it."

"Uh-huh." Shane's hands framed his face, eyes burning down. "I don't want nobody but you. You hear me?"

"I hear. Promise." Galen couldn't mistake the look in those eyes, couldn't help but believe. "My bartender, huh?"

"Yours, all of me." Shane shook him just a little. "Nobody else gets what you do."

"Kiss me, darlin'." He'd said he was okay last night, but now he was just getting there, Shane's vehemence as convincing as it was adorable.

The kiss damn near blew the top of his head off, all the

shit Shane'd worked himself up with building to a head. They rocked, both of them panting when they broke for air, both of them touching all over. He yanked Shane's shirt off over the man's head, thumbs going right to those pierced nipples to rub. Shane reached down, popped his fly, fingers wrapping around his cock, rubbing him through his briefs.

"Uhn. Shane. Darlin'." Arching, he rubbed right up into the touch, wanting it more and more. Shane got to him like no one else ever had.

"Uh-huh. Mine." Shane's thumb dragged hard over the tip of his cock.

"Yours, lover." Everything Shane wanted. All of it. Galen reached down and pulled his underwear to the side, shoving Shane's hand where he wanted it.

"Yeah." Shane nodded and started working him, eyes never leaving his, staring right into him.

God. His other hand shook, pulling at Shane's jeans, trying to get them together so he could rub their cocks along one another. They needed this. He did. All of it. He fished Shane's cock out, their shafts rubbing together, sliding just right. Shane's lips parted, cheeks going all pink.

"Like that, huh? I know I do. God, yeah." There. Good friction. Just fucking right friction. Galen moaned and started humping hard, really going at it.

"Yeah, Len. Need it." Shane leaned down, nuzzling right into his neck, and started sucking up a mark.

Fuck. Fuck a goddamned duck. Galen moaned, arching and bucking, his head falling back. Like his neck was directly connected to his cock, he felt that touch zing all the way to the end.

Shane moaned, bit a little, made him feel it, all the way to the bone.

"Shit, darlin'. Gonna make me." He was gonna explode. Damn, oh damn, his cock fucking *ached*.

Another bite and he was right there, Shane bucking along with him.

He came until his eyes crossed and his balls hurt, and in the end he was grinning like a mad fool, nuzzling right into Shane's neck and breathing deep. "Smell like pineapple."

"I'm not wearing a grass skirt and doing the hula for you, Len. No matter how nice you ask."

"We'll get Vic to do it. Goob can play the ukulele." At his name, Goob came romping over, dropping the slimy rubber frog right on Shane's leg.

"Oh. Dude. Icky frogness." The thing went flying, Shane laughing good and hard, easing the last little bit of worry in him.

"He just wants to contribute." Leaning, he snagged a piece of ham off the pizza and let Goob lick it off his fingers. "So, you gonna get me a drink when we get back down to the bar?"

"I am. Then I'm gonna let you dance with me for a couple before you take me home."

"That I can do, darlin'." He kissed Shane's cheek, his chin and mouth. "That I can definitely do."

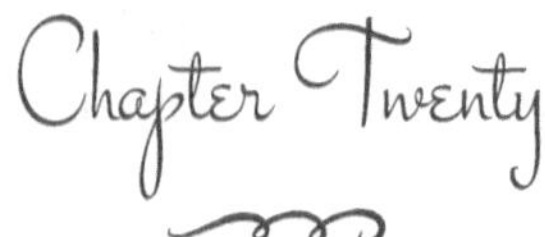

Chapter Twenty

G ALEN SUCKED in his gut and looked in the mirror, turning side to side. Then he let it out, frowning at his reflection. In. Out. In. Out. Maybe he needed to go to the gym.

"Shane? Darlin'? Tell me the truth. Am I getting porky?"

"Huh?" Shane looked up from the newspaper, head tilting sort of like Goober when faced with a chew toy.

He wandered away from the mirror and flopped down on the couch next to Shane, frowning as his belly kinda... spilled. "Am I getting wide?"

"You are not." Shane shook his head, rolled his eyes. Of course, Mr. On-His-Feet-Eighty-Hours-a-Week was all lean muscles.

"You sure?" Because he was feeling the tight when he moved, knew it was time to get doing some exercise. Fuck, he sounded like a girl.

"You wanting to go up and work out at the gym or something, Len? I mean, you aren't getting out like you like to."

Jesus. He *was* getting fat. "Well, I was thinking I need to do something. Maybe get some weights and shit for the house."

"Yeah? We could go dancing a couple nights a week.... That's like moving and getting out and stuff."

"Yeah." And after the whole dancing-with-someone-else thing, he wasn't about to let Shane go without too long. "We could do that, darlin'."

He got a grin, happy and wicked as all fuck. "There's lots of fun shit we can do, you know. Bowling. Swimming. Fucking. Badminton."

"Oh, I like the fucking." Badminton, not so much. Swimming might be fun. Bowling he always fucked up by overthrowing.

"Did you like playing ball?" The newspaper got set aside, Shane's full attention on him now.

"I did. Mostly." He grinned, sorta leaning into Shane. "The physical shit I never minded. It was always the politics."

"Politics? Like who got to play what?" Shane reached for him, touching, loving on him.

"And when and all. And there was always the pecking order among the players." That he didn't miss at all, and with a kinda blinding flash of duh, he realized that 90 percent of his trouble was that his wheeling and dealing lately was just like that. "I think I ought to quit my new job and go back to owning a bait shop."

"Yeah?" Shane nuzzled his temple. "You were happier then, before. You slept better."

Rubbing Shane's back, he leaned against the cushions and nodded, pondering that. "I did. But then, you were home more."

"Yeah." Shane sighed, cheek coming to rest on his shoulder, fingers moving restlessly on his belly.

Turning, he kissed Shane's forehead. Damn, they sounded like a couple of lovelorn critters. They needed to get off their asses and do. "How much longer before you can go on vacation?"

"I'm hoping the day manager agrees to cover me next month for a couple weeks."

"Good. We should go." He'd get buff before then. Maybe he'd hire an assistant. He let his fingers dance over Shane's ribs.

Shane nodded, chuckling. "We should. Just you and me. No phones."

"Mmm. No phone. No bar. No worries. Sounds good, darlin'. We could even drop Goob off with Momma."

"Oh, Goob would like that." Oh, man. That was something, Shane being willing to let the pup stay with someone.

That was about all he could stand of the touchy-feely talking too, without bubbling over. Galen turned and pressed Shane back against the couch, kissed him square on the mouth.

Shane's eyes went wide for a second; then those lips opened right up.

Oh hell, yes. That he understood. That he *got*. Galen kissed Shane good and deep, tongue sliding in to taste.

Shane fought him for control of the kiss, tongue stroking against his own.

Galen turned and pulled and lifted and... there. He got Shane up on his lap, straddling him. He bit down on Shane's lip as he pulled back for air, squeezing that tight little ass.

Shane rocked and rubbed, already filling those jeans. "You wantin'?"

"Mmm-hmm. Always." He squeezed again, pulling Shane down against his own crotch, letting him feel. "Always, darlin'."

He got one of those deep, rough sounds, one that let him know Shane would give him any fucking thing he asked for.

Those jeans had to go. Galen reached for the zipper, got

Shane out and into his hand. He stroked, loving on Shane so good.

"Len. Damn." Shane curled over his hand, fingers reaching for his belt. All the while, that tight little ass was bouncing on his thighs.

"Yeah, darlin'. You look fucking hot." Felt fucking hot too. He loved the way Shane felt against his palm, against his legs. He sucked in his gut, letting Shane get his belt open.

"Gonna let me ride you?" He could see the hint of that chain, tugging Shane's nipples, making them tight.

Pushing at Shane's shirt so he could get to it, tug it, he nodded. "Yeah, darlin'. Nothing better."

Shane stripped the shirt off, gold shining against the tanned skin. "Want to touch?" Then the little tease leaned back, belly stretched out.

Lord. Growling, Galen stroked up along Shane's chest, pulled at that little chain he'd gotten Shane two Christmases ago, watching those nipples turn red and hard for him. Shane's prick leaked, hot little drops that slid down, slicking his fingers.

Galen tugged at the chain with his other hand, letting Shane's cock go for a minute to taste, licking it clean before easing down again, lifting cock and balls and squeezing. When they were like this, he didn't think about what he looked like. He just thought about Shane.

Shane grunted, thighs spreading. "Want. Damn. Damn, Len."

"What do you want, darlin'?" Galen grinned, cheeks stretching with the wildness of it. He knew, oh hell, yes, he knew. But he wanted to hear it.

"More. You. Want you to make me scream." Shane's eyes were bright, sparking, daring him to give it up.

"Uh-huh." Fuck. Fuck, yes. He could do that. Galen

tugged the chain running between the little rings hard, watching muscles shiver and pop, feeling it in Shane's cock.

He loved that groan, that grunt, the way those little nipples went tight and hard and dark. Shane's hands went to them, rubbing the skin pierced by those pretty gold rings.

"No." Galen slapped them away. "Mine, darlin'." He bent and bit one, tugged the ring with his teeth, dragged through it with his tongue.

"Len." Shane's shoulders hunched up, rolled some, cock jumping under his touch, leaking like a sieve.

That was the prettiest thing. The other nipple got the same treatment, and all the while he pulled and pushed, stroked and cradled. Shane's skin burned for him, throbbing and heated under his tongue. Filthy words poured down over him, pleas and curses and promises. God, he loved it when Shane lost it like that, started babbling. All those bartender words that no one would expect from that pretty mouth. He bit down, feeling the shudder.

"Fuck. Fuck. More. Galen. More." Shane started humping up, trying to fuck his hand.

Gently, more gently than it probably seemed, he held Shane down, pressing that sweet ass against the couch. He wanted more, wanted to see marks on that skin, see the flush spread all the way from neck to pubes.

That flat belly rippled, muscles calling to him, begging to be marked. Fuck, the things Shane made him need. He scored that skin with his short nails, leaving little red marks. Yeah. Sweet.

Shane twisted, groaning low, damn near throwing him off the sofa. "Fuck."

"Going to soon, darlin'. I promise. I just want...." He growled. He wanted every fucking reaction. His fingers slipped down below Shane's balls, pressing the strip of skin behind.

"Anything." Shane rippled, one leg bending, propped on the back of the sofa. "Anything."

A low moan left him, and Galen bent, sucked Shane's cock in. Oh yeah. He loved that taste. Pure sex. One hand tangled in his hair, the other kept working those rings, the chain between, Shane caught up in the sensations. This time he let the grabby hands go. He had his prize, and he worked it, loving on Shane, tongue working the big vein.

"Gonna. Yeah. Love." Yeah, he could feel it, taste the drops pouring faster and faster into his lips.

"Mmm-hmm." Oh Jesus. He just encouraged it, rolling those heavy, tight balls, groaning around Shane's flesh. Shane shot, filling his mouth, cock deep as it throbbed.

Oh yeah. He still had it. Galen licked Shane clean, swirling his tongue into the slit to get the last drops. Then he moved up to take a kiss, slipping against Shane's thigh. Those hands landed on his ass, tugging them tight together, sliding his prick against the hot, sweat-slick skin.

"Want you, darlin'. So bad." He pulled back a little, rubbed down between Shane's thighs. His cock felt like stone.

"Yours. Yours." Shane grabbed his cock, rubbing the tip against that tight little hole. Fuck. Fuck.

"Shane. Darlin'. You sure?" They hadn't done anything to stretch.... When Shane nodded, he lost it, pressing hard into Shane's body.

The grunt pressed into his shoulder; then Shane's teeth sank in when he stilled. "Don't fucking stop. Take me."

"Shane." His voice sounded like ground glass, and Galen gave up the talking, just moving in and out, hips plunging.

Shane took him, took everything, and demanded more from him. He bit hard into Shane's neck, cock throbbing, so close. On the edge.

Shane's ass clenched, gripping him, "Yours. Galen. Yours."

"Mine...." Galen shot, his breath catching in his chest as he pumped into Shane over and over.

He settled down into warm, solid arms, Shane rocking, humming, fingers petting him. He nuzzled Shane's neck, loving the scent of sweat and man and warm leather from the couch. He didn't even mind that Goober was sitting over by the door, watching him.

"So, vacation soon."

"Mmm-hmm. No phones. No bars."

"Nothing but us and a bed and some good food. Maybe some whiskey." Yeah. Oh, hell, yeah, that sounded good.

He'd better get that weight set and get ripped before they went. He didn't want to go on vacation with a potbelly.

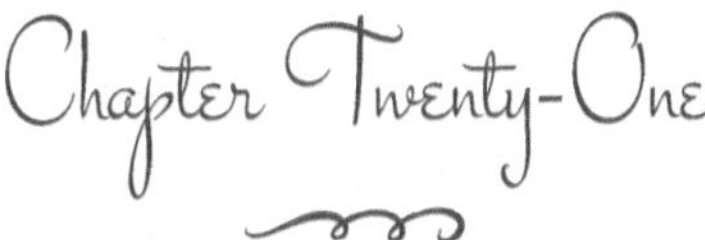

Chapter Twenty-One

T HERE WERE certain unavoidable weirdnesses in life. The way women could talk with lip goop on. The fact that people ate squid. Vic's ability to eat a whole chicken in a single gulp.

Then there was the way Galen got when he thought maybe someone was looking too hard at Shane's ass.

Or nipples.

Or anything.

Damn.

Shane shook his head, watched Galen glower and growl at some little redheaded boy who'd dared to ask him out. Galen did that whole looming-and-glowering thing really well. It was like he got taller and his shoulders got wider or something. Like it reminded you that Galen had been a semipro at football.

Not to mention the stubborn chin. Damn.

Of course, it was kinda sexy.

Okay, really sexy.

Glancing over, Galen caught his eye and immediately quit

making the kid piss his pants, coming over to him instead. "Hey, you."

"Hey." He couldn't help the grin, the slow, burning look. "You having fun?"

"I am now. Did you want to dance, darlin'?" Galen knew how he loved to dance, he surely did.

"Oh, hell, yes. Any day. Anytime. Yes." He moved right into Galen's arms, all about nodding and pushing close.

"Mmm. I like your shirt, Shane. It's not quite see-through."

It was. And it was just thin enough to feel the heat of Galen's hand on the small of his back, like a brand.

"I like how it makes you look at me." Like he was a bowl of chocolate ice cream and Galen was a starving man.

"Yeah. I like it a lot. Your nipple rings show," Galen said, rubbing right up on his chest as they swayed to the music.

"Mmm-hmm." He loved this, the way their hips settled together, the way they matched. They needed to do it more often, for sure. The music changed, going slower, kinda growly, suiting Galen to a T, really giving him some good dancing. Galen gave it right up for him.

"Oh. Oh, man." He leaned, lips on Galen's throat, cock filling right on up.

"Oh yeah, darlin'. I just love it when you get all melty." He could feel Galen's breath on his cheek, hot and damp.

"Dancing with you's like pure heaven." Pure, kinky, slinky sexy.

"Yeah? It's like being at home in bed, only with music."

And with strangers watching, but that was okay, right?

"Mmm. We're a little less naked here. Which is good, the way you growl."

"I don't growl. I just... you're mine, darlin'," Galen said, pulling him closer and growling right next to his ear. He'd bet someone had been looking too close.

"I am. Balls to bones." Like anyone else *anywhere* could be Galen.

"Good." One big hand cupped his ass, pulling him up, rubbing them together. "Good thing I'm not a jealous man, huh?"

"Absolutely. Might make life dangerous." He chuckled, nipped Galen's throat.

"Oh, do that again." Now he could feel Galen's answering hardness, pushing at him through their jeans.

Oh, hell, yeah. He bit again, letting his teeth sink in harder, deeper.

That fuzzy beard that Galen had grown in rubbed his cheek and his nose as Galen arched into the touch of his mouth, humming deep and low. The music picked up again, but they didn't, just swaying slow and easy.

It didn't get any better. Well, okay. It could get hotter.

Kinkier.

Way more naked.

But this still rocked his world.

Especially since he knew Galen would never, ever do this with anyone else. The man would rather sit at the back of the bar with a beer he'd opened, those long legs sprawled out, hips tilted just so, attitude pouring off... kinda like when they'd met.

"Why me?" He tilted his head, lips on Galen's earlobe. "There were other men at the club that first night. Why'd you pick me?"

"You had this thing, darlin'. This way about you. When that old man reached out and tweaked you, I wanted to take him down. That's when I knew." Galen pinched his butt, making him jump.

His chuckle was a little breathy, and he pressed closer. "Oh, man. I guess I got something to thank him for, then."

"Uh-huh. And he has you to thank for still having his

head." Breathing hard, Galen rubbed him, loved on him. "We might... we might need to go home."

"Uh-huh. Home. Bed. Naked."

Before somebody looked too hard and Galen got grumpy.

"Or you know, the Jeep and the beach."

Oh. Oh, they hadn't done that in an age. "Oh...." He just damn near died. "Weatherman said there might be a squall tonight."

"Let's go, then, darlin'. I've got a hankering to tie you to the roll bar." That wasn't a hankering in Galen's pants. That was a big old need.

"Mmm-hmm. You. Me. Rope. Rain."

Him and Galen.

Pure heaven and he hadn't even had to ask for it.

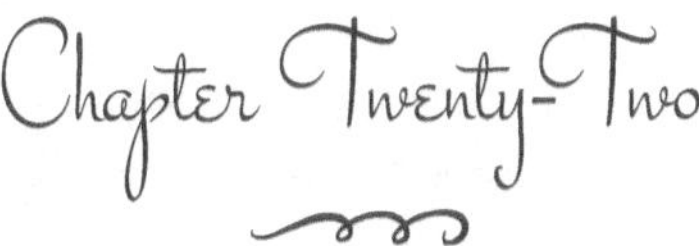

Chapter Twenty-Two

SHANE SCREECHED into the driveway, gravel flying. Galen Frost was going to get his ass kicked so hard he'd be shitting from between his shoulder blades.

It was bad enough no one could *ever* get through on the fucking house phone or Galen's cell, because Mr. Gee-I-Own-A-Fucking-Football-Thing Frost was always on it. Or that they never went out anymore, because somebody not him was always flying here and there doing football shit.

But being stood up?

While Tommy and Rick and them watched and laughed and pointed and offered to get him a real date? Somebody that showed up. Somebody that paid attention. Somebody that wanted him for more than a hard fuck on the stops home. Somebody that.... Yeah.

Fuck that.

He tore the door open, snarling. If the man wasn't dead, he was going to kill him.

There was no one in the kitchen. Or on the leather couch in the front room. Or even in Galen's office. In fact the phone was off the hook.

Oh shit. Maybe Galen was sick. Or attacked by an ax murderer. Or Vic. "Goober? Where's Len?"

Goob came wagging over, whuffling sleepily at his feet. Then the silly mutt waddled right off down the hall toward the bedroom, tail fanning back and forth.

He headed back toward the bedroom, trying not to wig out. Well, there was no blood. That sort of limited the whole ax murderer idea.

He got to the bedroom, and the lamp by the bed was on, the low light shining on the clothes laid out on the bed. Charcoal gray pants, the ones that showed Galen's ass off so good, and a thin, crazy-patterned shirt that gave him just the slightest hint of chest hair, sat there, along with Galen's good boots and hat.

Okay....

"Galen? Galen? Where the fuck are you?" There was a sinking feeling in the pit of his belly that damn near hurt, and the fear was metallic and sharp in the back of his throat.

He heard a tiny splash from the adjoining bathroom, Goober woofing and looking at him, ears flopping. Shane hit the bathroom door at a run, the image of his Galen fallen in the tub sudden and sickening.

Galen was in the tub all right—head back on the fancy rolled edge, arms dangling over the side. His lower lip maybe an inch from the water. He was snoring.

Oh.

Shane stood there for a second, heart just pounding, and then he flicked the toggle that let the water out before turning on his heel and heading out.

He heard a snort, a splash, a thud, and a yelp, Galen crying out sharply. Then nothing but Goob whining at his heels.

Fuck. Asshole. "Are you okay?"

"Shane?" Damn, Len sounded drugged, a little slurred, and a lot wet and gurgly.

"Yeah. Are you okay?" He didn't want to be fucking nice and go help.

"Uh." There was more splashing and squeaking, and finally a very damp and bedraggled Galen appeared in the doorway. "Oh shit, darlin'. I fell asleep."

"Yeah. You gotta be careful about that. You could drown." He tossed Galen a towel from the top of the laundry basket. "You feed Goober yet?"

"Yes?" Galen sighed, rubbing his hand across his short-cropped hair. "I don't know, darlin'. I think I did, but he always acts hungry."

"'Kay." He'd just feed the pup again. And not yell. See him not yell? He was so not yelling.

Stomping. Slamming down bowls. Possibly growling.

But not yelling.

Go fucking him.

"You're gonna explode, Shane. Come on. Let me have it." Galen spread his hands, shoulders slumping a little. "I deserve it."

He just shrugged, grabbed himself a beer, the air from the fridge cooling his skin. What fun would that be? Galen was tired, and they could go out whenever, maybe the next time Galen was home. It wasn't like he was fucking going anywhere anytime soon. Hell, he wasn't ever gonna get to be any better than he was right now; he knew it. "I'm gonna go change into some shorts."

"What time is it?" Galen had followed him out, staying just close enough, but not quite touching.

"Little after midnight." He hung up his good shirt, grabbed his shorts. He'd gotten off at seven, showered over at Rick's. Met Tommy over at the restaurant at eight.

"Oh.... I.... Damn."

That hangdog look was gonna make him kick something.

He didn't know what to say, so he just sort of didn't. He hung up the phone and sort of wandered.

"Darlin'." Galen finally stopped him by slipping up behind him, wrapping those long arms tight around him.

"This isn't gonna make me less pissed at you."

"What will?" A clean-as-a-whistle chin rubbed his shoulder. Galen only got that smooth when he shaved twice.

"I don't know. Tommy offered to get me a date." One that showed up, even.

Galen stiffened, but just as Shane was about to get all don't you even dare, Galen nodded. "Yeah. I can see that. I'm sorry."

"You needed your sleep. We can go out whenever." He finished his beer, watched Goob drag one of Galen's flip-flops down the hall. "You hungry?"

"No, but I could make you something." Galen backed off, letting him go, one hand sliding down his arm.

"Nah." Shane took a deep breath and blew it out. "I'm wanting Swiss Cake Rolls and another beer." Nothing like comfort food.

"We've got beer. No Swiss Cake Rolls. Maybe Moon Pies...." No. Galen didn't get to sound kinda lost and worried. Not tonight.

"Man, I'm batting a thousand tonight." He rubbed the back of his neck. Man, this being pissed thing sucked. "You want a beer?"

"Yeah." That smile was wry, Galen's upper lip curling. "You want me to make brownies?"

"No. I want you to stop acting all worried and start working on seriously sucking up."

That got him a sharp bark of laughter, Galen coming right on up and pulling him close, big hands on his hips. "Want me to kiss and make up?"

"I'm not ready to make up yet. But kissing's a start, yeah."

At least there, he knew Galen wasn't off thinking about football and phone calls and trips and stuff.

Well, he was pretty sure, anyway.

"I can do that." Bending, Galen set their lips together, kissed hard, pressing his mouth open to taste inside.

Oh. Oh, better.

He shoved back, letting out some of the frustration, some of the aggravation from the last few hours. Days.

Months.

What-the-fuck-ever.

Fuck, his Galen smelled good.

Felt good too, when Len grabbed his ass and lifted, pulling him right up against that hard, wide body. That kiss had his breath whooshing out, had him pressing close. He bit down on Galen's lip, fingers digging down into those shoulders. Bastard. Falling asleep on him. Standing him up. Moaning, Galen pushed him back, the world spinning until they hit a wall, until Galen could get leverage by working one thigh between his. Then he had something to press against.

Oh, hell, yes. Yes. Just there. It ached all through him, balls to bones. "More. Want more, damn it."

"Whatever you want, darlin'. However you want it." His skin stung as Galen bent to bite his neck, teeth sharp and hard.

"I want you. Fucking miss being yours."

"Shane." Galen looked at him for a minute, just stared, before bending and putting a shoulder against his belly, hoisting him up. Oh, Len hadn't hauled him to bed in too long.

He curled around Galen's shoulder, got his mouth on the first bit of skin he could find and started licking and sucking.

"Uhn. Shane. Need." They made it to the bedroom, but only just. He went flying, hitting the bed maybe a second and a half before Galen hit him, shoving him down and kissing him so hard he saw stars.

Fuck, yes. That's what he'd been wanting—more than dancing, than going out, than fucking *anything*.

Galen rubbed on him, licking him, kissing him, soft sounds coming from that wide chest. Like growls.

"More. Galen. I want." His skin felt tight, too small everywhere Galen's touch wasn't, and he arched up toward that heat, getting all the contact he could.

"Yeah, yeah, darlin'. I want in you." Oh, that raw whiskey voice shivered his spine.

He nodded, spreading wide as he could, begging Galen to fill him up. "Now."

"Just let me get...." Len scrabbled around, finally cursing and pulling back, lifting his hips up, setting that hot mouth to Shane's hole.

"Galen!" He arched, hands slamming against the headboard and holding on tight as that hot tongue touched him, pressed inside him. In and out, Len touched him, pushed him, opened him up. Got him wet. Goddamn that mouth. He couldn't breathe, couldn't stop crying out and twisting and begging for it. Bastard. Making him need. "Please!"

Slipping back up between his legs, Len pushed Shane's knees up over Len's wide shoulders, cock slipping against his hole. Then Galen was inside him, hot and hard and feeling better than anything had in so long.

Oh. Oh fuck, yes. He nodded as they found a rhythm, something that was just them and them alone.

Galen stared down at him, serious as a heart attack, eyes hot as those hips rocked steadily back and forth. Len had that laser focus, right on him, like he hadn't in a month of Sundays. It was what he'd been aching for, missing, and he'd almost forgotten. Forgotten what it was like to be trapped in those eyes.

"Shane...." He thought maybe Len was feeling it too, the

way his voice cracked. Sweat dripped off Len's chest, landing on his skin as they rocked harder and harder.

Shane nodded, gasped, heart pounding furiously. Yes. Yes, just like that. Just like.

Galen stretched him so wide, pressing down until his thighs screamed, reaching between them to touch his cock, fingers rough against the tip. "Love."

"Fuck, yes. Yours. Yours, Galen." Words poured out of him, all the bullshit he'd been trying to say about loving and needing and wanting and hurting pushing right into the air between them.

"Mine. Shane. God." He could see the way that upper lip curled, the way the grimace wrinkled up Galen's face, and he knew Len was close. So close. That thick cock swelled in him, egging him on. His hole burned and his entire body rippled, hips jerking up as he shot, spraying between them. The headboard groaned, his arm muscles burning, clenched so tight.

"Oh. Oh fuck, yeah." That was it. Galen shot deep inside, bucking and shaking.

Everything got still, both of them panting and sweating and fucking staring at each other like they hadn't seen each other in months.

Then Galen bent and kissed his mouth, the kiss feeling like something soft, something that ached a little.

The breath that pressed into his mouth kinda loosened his fingers from the headboard, let him reach down and grab hold of Galen.

"Mmm." The low growl worked right down into his bones. "Love you, darlin'."

"Yeah. Yeah, Len." More than just anything.

Galen rubbed noses with him. "We need that vacation."

"Yeah. Real bad." He kissed Galen's chin, sighing.

"As soon as you can clear your schedule. Okay?"

"I'll call the big boss in the morning and tell him it's serious."

"You bet." They rested foreheads together. "I mean it."

"You gonna deal with the plans and shit?"

"I am. I've gotten good at that crap." Galen grinned, the chuckle rueful.

"Yeah." He grinned back, tongue touching the corner of Galen's mouth.

Galen licked back, tongue meeting his, lips opening for him.

"Mmm...." He sorta purred, beginning to rock, loving the way their skin slid together.

"Mmm-hmm. Oh, darlin'." Galen rocked back, hot and damp against him.

"Yeah. Feels good." One kiss slid into another and another as his nipples went tight, thighs rubbing against Galen's hips.

"So pretty. God, Shane. How could I forget that?" Galen knelt up, shifting inside him, hands sliding along his torso. His nipple rings got special attention, Len twisting them.

"Oh. Oh, Len." He stretched, fingers petting Galen's hands. "Make me ache."

"Good." Starting up a rhythm again, Galen moved in him, on him, touching him all over. God, his Len was hot when he got that squinty-eyed look. Just pure sex. Shane let himself watch that belly rippling, hair tight and dark. Those hot fucking eyes watching him. That mouth....

That mouth.

"Kiss me."

"Yeah." So strong. Muscles flexing, Galen put one arm under his back and lifted him, pulled him up for a kiss that curled his toes. And changed the angle of Galen inside him pretty damned fast. The sound he made would be embarrassing if it hadn't felt so damned good. He held on, gripping

Galen's strong shoulders, hips bucking so Galen's cock pegged his gland over and over.

"Fuck! Shane." The kiss grew teeth, Galen giving it up good, pushing into his mouth. The kiss fucked his mouth like Len took his ass, over and over. Fuck. Fuck. Everything in him clenched, focused only on moving between mouth and cock. Len grunted, shifting him just a little... there. Right there. Now they could both move, both thrust. And every move rubbed him raw.

"Yeah." Fuck, they smelled hot. Pure sex.

Good, so good. They weren't gonna last maybe a half a minute more, not the way they were going. When Len ground against his sweet spot that one last time, Shane lost it, falling like a ton of bricks, coating Galen's belly with come. Galen roared for him, that whiskey-burned voice all growl, and shot inside him, filling him right up.

"Better?" Galen asked while they rested, forehead against his.

"No. But I'm willing to think on it." He grinned. "You might have to go to the grocery."

Galen laughed, the motion shaking them all over. "I can do that, darlin'. Hell, it's the least I can do."

Hell, yes. That was the very least the silly man could do for standing him up.

Chapter Twenty-Three

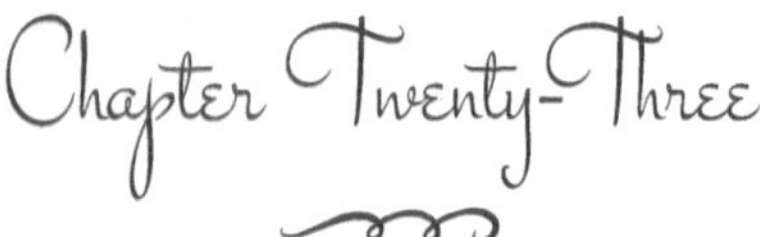

ONTRARY TO popular belief, Shane knew his way around a hammer.

Well, okay. There were only two ends, and it wasn't brain surgery, but.... He chuckled at himself as he pulled another roofing nail out and set a shingle. He could patch the roof while Galen was out and about doing... whatever fucking weirdness Galen did that was for the football.

The late-September sun was beating down, baking his bones, and the music coming up from the porch was good and....

"Goob! Goob, you better not have eaten the cord again. You're going to fry your nose off and short something out, and Galen'll bitch!"

"Goober is sunning by the hot tub. Like you should be." Galen's voice floated up to him.

"Oh!" He slid down a little, leaned over, and blinked down. Mmm. Black hat. He approved. "*I* am fixing the roof. See me be useful?"

"I see that. Now get your ass down here where I can see it.

Maybe touch it." Galen sounded pretty darned happy. The...
thing, whatever, must have gone well.

He hooted, crab walked over to the ladder, and shimmied
down to land damn near in Galen's arms. "Careful, man, I'm
dusty."

Dusty and sweaty and wearing an old Western shirt he'd
torn the arms off of and a pair of jeans so old they could probably register to vote.

"Well, hello there, darlin'." Galen gave him a kiss, fuzzy
little beard scraping his cheeks.

"Mmm... hey." He reached out, fingers hooking in Galen's
belt loops, tugging those tight hips closer.

"Mmm. You smell like sun and Shane. I like it." Oh, he
liked Galen liking it, if it was gonna get his neck bitten like
that. He lifted his chin, throat working as he got another bite
and another. Damn. Those teeth. Licking at the bites, Galen
rubbed his big hands up and down Shane's bare arms, making
him shiver. "So, darlin', what else can you be handy at today?"

"I'm all about hands." Mouths. Cocks. Galen's cock. *Uhn.*

"Uh-huh. I like your hand, darlin'." Galen grinned against
his mouth, kissed him so hard he heard bells or something, his
ears ringing.

Man, wrapping around Galen and rubbing was the only
thing to do, so he got to it, pushing in close and humping one
muscled thigh. That heavier beard drove him crazy, the texture
different than the usual stubble, the feel soft and electric.
Galen grabbed Shane's ass and lifted, pulled, gave them
friction.

The sun made his spine all loose and melty, the need made
his muscles tight. It was... too fucking cool.

Galen kissed all down his neck, making goose bumps
shiver up, then bent and bit right into his upper arm where the
shirt cut off, leaving a big old mark.

"Shit!" Electricity shot straight down his arm, the bicep going tight as a boar's backside. "Galen!"

"Mmm-hmm. Taste good, Shane. Good." Moving down maybe a half inch, Galen pressed his lips to Shane's skin and sucked. Hard. So hard he could feel the bruise start to rise under Galen's tongue.

His eyes rolled, chest and belly and thighs like rocks. "Don't stop."

"Not gonna. Promise." Oh no, Galen wasn't stopping. He was lifting Shane's arm, going right for the tender skin on the inside of his elbow.

There was that second where time just stopped still, where his heart stopped beating as he waited for Galen to hit that hot spot, for those teeth to sink in.

Then the sting traveled all the way up his arm to explode in his brain as Galen bit hard, the rough texture of Galen's teeth almost more than he could stand on his thin skin.

Shane sorta... babbled, brain shorting out as his cock throbbed, hurting it was so fucking hard.

Galen knew it. He always knew, darn his hide. That mouth kept moving, lips closing over the pulse point in his wrist as Galen shifted him so his cock rubbed against one firm hip, his feet almost dangling.

He shot—he didn't have a choice, didn't have a chance in hell. He just gave it up and creamed his jeans like a virgin at a peep show.

"Oh fuck, darlin'. I can smell you." Galen hauled his ass over to their lounge chair, sat down, and pulled him down to straddle Galen's long thighs before going to work on Shane's other arm. From the top down.

"Galen. Fuck. Your mouth...." His head tossed, the fucking world spinning.

"Mmm. You wanna fuck my mouth later, I'll let you.

Right now I want...." Those lips moved down his arm, leaving stinging kisses. God.

"Anything." His fingers wrapped around the edge of the lounge chair, heart pounding like a jackhammer on a sidewalk.

"Good." That satisfied growl worked all the way down to his toes, all shivery. He had no idea the outside of his forearm was so sensitive, but the little hairs stood up as Galen bit him hard.

"Oh. Oh Christ." His eyes rolled back in his head like dice, tongue caught between his teeth.

"No. Not Christ." Chuckling, Galen moved back up, pulling his arm out, bubbling up almost to his underarm to leave a lurid mark there too.

He rolled his eyes. Asshole. And he fell for it every time and.... Oh.

God, yeah.

Good.

Galen eased him down on the lounge, flat on his back with his legs still draped over Galen's thighs. Then Galen bent, spreading his legs back as that mouth found his wrist, teeth scraping.

The chair creaked and his fingers curled, his cock filling again. Hell, maybe it hadn't ever gone down.

"Mmm. Let's get these open, huh?" His button and zipper gave way under Galen's hands, his wet cock pushing out as Galen touched him, thumb pressing his slit. "Oh yeah, darlin'. Pretty."

"Yours. You make me fucking crazy." He grinned through his moan, trying to focus on those fine fucking eyes.

"Mine," Galen agreed, pulling his hand down and putting it around his own cock, then bending to bite the top of that arm, making his hand squeeze. Damn, that was a hell of a sensation.

"Yes. Don't stop?" He was going to fix that fucking roof all the damned time.

"Not gonna." No, Galen wasn't stopping, was moving his hand on his cock with every fucking slip and slide of that mouth. He was gonna be sore as hell, with all those bruises.

"You're not. What about. I. Uh." Damn, he was befuddled.

"Not what, Shane?" A soft chuckle drifted over the spot on his elbow that throbbed, made his clenched fingers twitch.

"Huh?" Oh, man. That was. Uh-huh.

"Nothin'." Licking, Galen moved over to the other arm again, hand closing over his to make him stroke, make him pull. God, the man made him crazy, he truly did. Galen started pushing up against his ass too, pulling him up and over a little more so Galen's cock could poke his ass through their jeans.

He stopped even trying to think, just followed Galen's touch, let the heat inside him ratchet higher and higher.

"God, Shane. Want you. You just... fuck." Okay, good, Len wasn't thinking either. That made him feel better. They rocked together, their hands moving on him, his ass moving on Galen, that mouth sending him flying higher and higher.

"Yours. Yours...." He jerked as he shot again, heat flushing through him in a wave.

Galen growled low, the sound almost a cry, and jerked under him, hips rocking. Shane could smell him too. Hot and male, pure Len.

"Uhn...." He nuzzled in, rubbing his lips against Galen's jaw. "Like the beard."

"Yeah? I got lazy." Galen laughed, kissing him hard. "I like you in my old shirt. Whatever possessed you to pull the sleeves off, I approve."

Well, no wonder. It was Len's shirt. He'd thought it was a bit big around the chest.

"One was ripped." He thought. Maybe it hadn't been. He didn't remember. "I'll wear it again."

"You will. Soon." Galen chuckled. "We need to bathe. Or maybe soak. Or even hose off."

"Uh-huh." Soaking sounded good.

"Come on, darlin'." They were all pretzeled, but Galen unbent them, got them up and moving.

"You get your business done?" Man, his legs were like Jell-O.

"Uh-huh. Done for at least a day. Wanna play with you instead. I like that part of being done with work." Galen supported his weight, sorta dragging him in.

He grinned down at his arms. Man, he looked like a leper. Toothy bastard. Hot, toothy bastard.

"Looks good, darlin', you wearing my marks. Never thought about how pretty your arms were from all that bartending before." One hand slid up his arm, fingers pressing marks.

"Hey, eighty hours a week lifting bottles." He flexed, part to show off and part because of how it felt.

"Mmm-hmm. You're a stud." Bathroom, bathtub, water. Good stuff.

"Yeah, yeah. Not only that? I'm damned handy." He winked over, both of them chuckling.

"As long as it's the roof and not the bathroom sink, right?" Galen rubbed his ass, almost companionably.

"Don't make me beat you, Len." He turned his face up for a kiss. That bad smell was a long, long time ago.

Len gave him his kiss and then some, just pushing into his mouth with that hot tongue, fucking his lips. Damn. He never got tired of that, ever.

He cupped Galen's jaw, arms stinging wherever the little marks were.

"Mmm. Oh, darlin'. What you do to me." Yeah. Galen did it for him too. It worked well.

Sorta like it was supposed to be.

Chapter Twenty-Four

S HANE WAS bebopping around, humming, flitting from thing to thing. He'd fed Goober enough bacon to give the poor little guy the stinkiest farts known to man. He'd started working on an alligator pool to save his own inflatable one, just in case Victor came back. He'd even cleaned the tub, ass swinging as he scrubbed.

Galen figured Shane needed something to focus on. So he got up, all casual like, and started herding.

Shane was in the kitchen. Galen wandered out and got between him and the sink, which was about to get a dose of scrubbing bubbles.

"Hey, darlin'."

He got a grin, Shane bouncing on his toes. "Hey. How's it hanging?"

"It's kinda starting to stand up." Galen grinned, groped Shane's crotch. "You need to catch up."

Shane went up on his tiptoes a second, wiggling some. "Mmm. What's got you all riled up?"

"You. You've been giving attention everywhere but here, darlin'. Time for me to take a little of that giving." He grinned, waiting for that look. That one, with the heavy eyes and pink cheeks.

Oh, there it was. That flush crawled right up Shane's abs, hitting those cheeks as Shane's teeth sank into that bottom lip. "I wouldn't want you feeling neglected, Len...."

"No." Circling, he started backing Shane out of the kitchen and down the hall.

Shane went, eyes on his, cock starting to fill, hips swaying a bit. "I've been getting shit done."

"I know, but it's time for intermission, darlin'. Something fun. You know what they say about all work and no play...." He stripped his shirt up over his head and tossed it into the guest bedroom as he went by.

"Uh-huh. Something about dull boys, I think." Shane reached for him, fingers brushing his belly, following the line of dark hair down to his waistband.

"Exactly." He grinned, flexing his muscles, really putting on a show. "And we wouldn't want that. You deserve a reward, Shane."

"Yeah?" Oh, Shane was caught, licking his lips, little rings shifting as those pretty nipples went tight.

"Mmm-hmm." Ah, the bedroom. Galen sauntered to the bed, unbuckling his belt, unzipping his jeans. He turned, showing off his ass as he bent to push them off.

Those hands landed on his ass, squeezing and rubbing. "Pretty, pretty." Shane's kiss brushed his shoulder, teeth teasing his skin, making him jump a little.

God, that man made him insane. Galen straightened, kicking out of his jeans, then grabbed Shane and tossed him up on the bed to start stripping off Shane's tight cutoffs. "Got plans for you, darlin'."

"Mmm.... What plans?" Shane arched up, tight denim rolling right off that tight little ass.

Once they were both naked, he got the little box he needed

out of the nightstand and crawled up on top of Shane, holding him down with his weight. "Gonna tie you up. Love you all afternoon."

"Oh."

Oh fuck, yes. He loved the way Shane rippled, rubbing up against him. Loved the way those eyes rolled. Loved how he turned Shane on. "You think so, huh?"

"I do." He got the box open, rubbing his cock against Shane's, his eyes trying to roll right back. The cuffs felt warm and soft. "Remember these?"

"Vaguely. Think I saw them once or twice." He snorted. Once or twice. Right. Once in the front room, bent over the sofa, while Galen worked that sweet ass with a dildo. A half dozen times on the front porch.

In the bathroom. In the kitchen.

Once in the Jeep.

Mmm. That time had been out by the ocean, a storm blowing in. They'd cut it close.

Galen gathered up Shane's hands, secured one, then the other to the bedposts. Then he dug out the cock ring, along with the little chain that connected it to the little decoration between Shane's nipple rings.

Oh, somebody remembered that too. That strong little body went tight, thighs hard as rocks beneath him.

He stroked Shane's chest with his free hand, tugging the nipple chain. "Yeah. Yeah, you like that, huh, darlin'?"

That little groan was enough to make a dead man hard, the way those nipples went dark even better. "You know I do. Like how it makes you look at me."

"And I like how it makes you look." He sat back, straddling Shane's thighs so he could snap the cock ring into place, then traced the chain up to clip it where it belonged. "Oh fuck, Shane."

Shane took a deep breath, stopped when that pulled, tugged that chain, those nipples stretching. "Len...."

"So fucking fine, Shane. So damned mine." Galen bent, carefully not brushing the chain, and kissed Shane hard.

Shane opened right up, tongue pushing and sliding against his, not backing down even a bit.

Galen kissed him, loved on him, tasted him. Yeah, that got Shane to focus, got him pulling at the cuffs, got that hot body writhing under him.

One of those legs caught him, wrapped around his hip and held him close, giving Shane something to rub against. Oh no. It wasn't gonna be over like that.

Grinning, Galen moved away, prying Shane's leg off him so he could move aside and kneel next to Shane's hip. "Naughty, darlin'. I told you I have plans."

He got a little pout, Shane twisting toward him, then stopping short as the long chain tugged again.

"Uh-huh. I can see you, darlin'. I can see every little movement of your muscles." And of that sweet cock too, as it quivered. Galen touched the tip of it with one finger, listening to Shane's breath.

Hot, wet—his fingers slipped over the slit, pressing in. Shane's thighs parted, hips rolling right up toward the touch.

The way Shane responded to him always awed him. Galen chuckled, bent to touch his tongue to one of Shane's nipples before blowing air across it, watching for a reaction.

Oh, pretty. The skin wrinkled up, sliding against the ring as it went hard. The skin goose pimpled up, Shane shivering for him.

He grinned, rubbing his stubbly chin against it. "I do love that, Shane. I surely do. You have the prettiest shivers."

"Galen." The chains rattled, Shane trying to reach for him. "Fuck."

"Wait, darlin'. Have a little patience." He growled,

rewarded Shane with a kiss, fingers rising to tug the chain between cock and nipples.

Shane dug his heels into the mattress, arched up into him, just like that.

Galen used his free hand on Shane's hip to hold him down, mixing it up with leaning to bite the flesh on the inside of Shane's arm, lightly, but enough to leave a tiny mark.

"Oh. Shit. Galen. Again." Shane bucked against his hand, starting to rock, hips wanting to roll.

"No. Not gonna do the same thing twice." He was going to keep Shane guessing. He moved back, licking across Shane's belly, chin pressing the little trail of hair down to Shane's cock.

Fuck, but Shane smelled good. All hot and male with a hint of soap. Musky. "Driving me crazy, Len."

"Am I? You were driving me nuts, Shane. All that wiggling and dancing and scrubbing and all...." He moaned, skipped down to Shane's thighs, nuzzled the tender skin on the insides. Those thighs spread so pretty, giving it up for him. Shit. Cock high and hard, balls drawn up between, Shane was like a feast. Galen tugged that little chain again, watching Shane's cock bob with the pressure.

Soft babble started, Shane promising the goddamn world to him. The man meant it too. Oh, hell, yes. That deserved something, like maybe the flat of his tongue lifting Shane's balls, tasting the salt-musky flavor of his very own lover. Addictive.

The tiny soft hairs tickled his tongue, the skin wrinkling up, shifting on his tongue as Shane moaned. Galen hummed, nudging the sacs back and forth, hands stroking Shane's thighs, the backs of those cute-as-fuck knees.

Every so often he'd hit a ticklish spot or a hot spot and he'd get a jerk, a twist. Then the sudden stop would come, Shane moaning as the chains pulled. So good.

Finally Galen spread Shane's legs as wide as they would go,

straining those fine muscles, and moved up to kneel between, his cock against Shane's balls as he pulled that chain sharply. "Wanna fuck you, darlin'."

Shane nodded, lips parted, eyes wide as all get-out. "Yeah. In me. Deep. Now."

He nodded, reached for the little tube of lube they kept in their box of tricks, and got his fingers good and wet. Then he slipped two into Shane's body, pushing nice and deep. Shane rolled, riding his fingers immediately and furiously, so there, so into him it damn near ached. Galen moaned, growled, his cock twitching and throbbing so he hurried, moving his fingers in and out, stroking lube over his own cock with his other hand. Damned near yanking it. *Come on, come on.*

"Fuck. Fuck, you're hot. Want you, Len. Please. Come *on*."

Shane's body told the same story, and Galen pulled his fingers free, putting his cock where they'd been, holding it steady so he could slide right in. Soon he was seated deep, hips against Shane's ass and thighs, his fingers reaching, twisting Shane's nipples.

"Shit. Len. I." Shane was fucking vibrating, tugging at the cuffs, ass squeezing him.

"Yes, you do. Goddamn, Shane. You fucking kill me. Love you." He did. With every damned bit of him. Galen started moving, finding a rhythm, watching every move make Shane shake and groan.

"Love. Galen." Shane stretched, managed to get a kiss, tongue sliding right into his lips, fucking them in time with his thrusts.

The kiss got hard, desperate, their lips bruising right up. Galen thrust harder, faster, knowing Shane's cock had to be aching, knowing he was driving Shane nuts.

Shane jerked his head back, keening. "Len. Len. For you. Please. Please!"

"Uh-huh." Rearing up, he snapped the cock ring open, letting Shane go, letting him feel every little thing as Galen thrust and stroked in time, loving on him. Needing Shane to come for him now.

Spunk sprayed over Shane's pretty belly, Shane going tight enough around him to ache.

Hollering, Galen shot hard into Shane's body, pulling that little chain one last time, getting one last contraction of Shane's muscles for his trouble. Fuck, yes, his Shane could focus when he needed to.

The sweet as fuck little moans got slower and softer, Shane lax and sated beneath him. Oh, hell, yes. That was pretty.

He let Shane's arms loose, knowing they'd be sore if he didn't, wanting to feel them around him. "You make sure you put me on your to-do list from now on, darlin'."

"Mmm-hmm. The top of it." Shane wrapped all around him, nuzzling right in like a sleepy pup, making him grin.

"Love." He squeezed, tossing things back in their box of toys and putting it aside before curling in tight and covering them with the sheet. "Always."

He got a nod, a sweet little sigh, and then Shane was gone, sound asleep and holding on tight.

Galen smiled up at the ceiling. He figured they were getting better at this talking-shit-out thing. Or at least poking each other when the need was up.

That was good enough for him.

Next time he'd have to do Shane over the kitchen table.

Chapter Twenty-Five

S OMETIMES ALL a man needed was a beer, a nice warm
day, a half-naked lover, and a phone that had gone into
the lagoon. *Sploosh*.

In fact, Galen couldn't remember seeing Shane so het up
since, well, since events that were best left unremembered. It
had been fucking cute. Shane had taken that phone, stuffed it
right up that thawed chicken's butt, and tossed it, hollering for
old Vic at the top of his lungs.

Once Shane had settled, well, things had gotten a lot
calmer, and now they were both out on the deck, the sun
baking them, the heat almost too much to move in. Almost.
Galen flicked some cold drops of condensation at Shane.

Shane stretched; the water and the sweat on that flat belly
rolled right on down. "Mmm... hey, Len."

"Hey, darlin'. This was a good idea." Even if Shane had
gone to... extremes.

"I have tons of 'em. Good ideas." Shane grinned, the look
smug as all get-out. Little shit.

"Uh-huh." The way the sweat outlined Shane's muscles,

made his skin shimmer, Galen wasn't gonna be in any mood to bitch.

Shane slid his hand down, unsnapped the button on those cutoffs, and eased the zipper right on down. Oh. Hello.

His eyes widened, and Galen licked his lips. "Shane, darlin'? You forget I'm here?"

He was there. He could help.

"Not even a bit. I was sorta hoping you were paying attention...." That pretty cock pushed free, heavy and hard, skin shining in the sun.

"Umm-hmm. I am paying attention, darlin'. I promise."

Smooth, tanned skin. Sweet cock. Musky male scent. Hoo yeah.

"Yeah?" Shane spread a little wider, thighs falling off either side of the deck chair, hand starting to move, teasing him.

"Uh-huh. I...." His mouth went dry, and Galen sipped his beer. "You look good, Shane. Real good. Edible."

"Mmm. Edible. I like that." One hand moved to those little gold rings, twisted and tugged, showing off for him.

"Hot. God, darlin'." Galen's cock pushed against the zipper of his cutoffs, putting the pressure on, really letting him know it was there.

"It is." Those eyes met his dead-on, hotter than the hinges of hell. "And all yours."

"Uh-huh." Before he even thought about it, Galen was out of his chair and on his knees next to Shane, rubbing his cock through his shorts. And bending to suck on Shane's.

"Yes." The word was bitten out, Shane's feet planting on the deck as the man arched, hips thrusting up toward him.

"Mmm-hmm." Galen opened his mouth and pulled Shane in, his head sliding down, lips sealing tight around Shane's prick. God, yeah. His.

There was nothing like watching those muscles ripple,

seeing the sweat turn that skin shiny, and hearing the deep, rough cries that tore out of Shane's throat.

That and the taste, the feel of Shane's skin. Oral? Him? Galen chuckled, his free hand coming up to yank at Shane's shorts, searching for Shane's balls, needing the different texture. Shane spread even farther, balls just as soft as anything against his fingers. That delicate skin wrinkled right up, moving and tightening as he touched.

So responsive to him. Shane awed him, he really did. Galen sucked harder, closing his eyes and really pulling, cupping the warm balls, cradling them.

"Been needing you. So bad." The words were whispers, low enough he could ignore them as Shane's fingers slid through his hair. The motions of those lean hips got rough, random, graceless as Shane got close. Tuning out everything but the taste, the feel, the movement of Shane's body, Galen moved, up and down, pulling Shane in and out.

He could feel it, feel the heat and the tension filling Shane, feel the snap of Shane's hips the second before bitter-salt flooded his mouth.

Galen sucked it all down, running his tongue along the underside of Shane's prick, massaging those sweet sacs. God, he loved this.

The chair creaked as Shane relaxed down into it, going all melty and boneless.

Shane's cock finally slid out of his mouth, Galen taking one last taste of the slit at the tip. He leaned his head on Shane's hip.

"See? Told you I was paying attention."

"Mmm-hmm. Amazing what you see when you're not on the phone."

He nipped one hipbone. "Yeah, yeah. The phone is in the chicken." That sounded so ridiculous that he snorted.

"The chicken is in the gator." Shane hooted, eyes just dancing.

"And the gator isn't gonna give it back." Putting his faith in the strength of that stupid lounge chair, Galen crawled up with Shane, rubbing a little.

"No fucking way. And I ain't giving you back yet either." Shane's hands landed on his ass with a smack, pulling him down harder.

His skin jumped, his eyes going wide again. Damn. That stung. Galen grinned, kissing Shane hard, the angle awkward as hell but working for him anyway.

Shane kissed him back, just as hard, stealing his breath clean away as those hands squeezed his ass tight enough to bruise.

Someone was hungry. Someone was worrying. Galen cupped Shane's head, leaning into the kiss, saying all sorts of shit with his mouth. *I need you too, darlin'*, he thought. *So bad.*

The sweetest fucking moan pushed into his lips, Shane giving it up for him, letting him hear. Then those hands on his ass started moving him, rubbing him against all that hot, smooth skin.

Galen struggled some with his shorts, not wanting to let go of Shane but needing to let his cock rub too, wanting the fabric gone.

Shane didn't help; those hands were fastened on his ass, squeezing good and tight.

"Darlin', I have to. Oh, there." He heaved a sigh of relief as the cutoffs slipped down and he could get full-on friction going. God, yeah.

"Yeah." Shane nodded, arching right up into him, giving him those muscles, that skin to push against.

"Oh." Galen moaned and went for it, the chair creaking

under them as he thrust and thrust. His head was gonna explode. It really was.

Shane's teeth slid on his jaw, and then he heard the whispered, "Mine," before Shane's mouth fastened on him, the suction starting up.

Crying out, Galen humped Shane's belly, his cock jerking as he shot, coming hard enough to kinda hurt. Oh, so good.

"Yeah. Yeah, just like that." Shane was purring, holding on tight.

"Yours, darlin'." He needed to remember that sometimes. Maybe every time he got too wrapped up, Shane would call his old cell phone and Victor would ring somewhere and it would remind him.

Shane nodded, cheek sliding against his. "Yeah. And everybody best start remembering it, before I get grumpy. Cell phones are probably gonna give Vic the trots."

"Yeah. But he likes the chicken." Personally, Galen figured Vic could consume an entire electronics store and not get the shits.

"I don't think he even tastes it." Shane leaned up, kissed him, nice and slow.

"Mmm." That kiss settled him. Made him hum. He stroked Shane's back, feeling the silkiness of sweat under his fingers.

"You want to go run a bath, get all cooled off and soapy?"

"Uh-huh. Sounds great, darlin'." That meant moving, but hey. He could do that. Eventually.

Shane nodded again, settling with a happy little hum.

They'd nap. Bathe. Eat something not chicken. And then they'd go to bed, and Galen would spend the night making up to Shane for a touch of neglect.

It was the least he could do before he had to go buy another phone.

Want More?

Interested in learning more about BA's cowboys? Want free fiction and news? Join my newsletter or follow me on Ream!

About BA

Western to the bone and an unrepentant Daddy's Girl, BA Tortuga spends her days with her hounds and her beloved wife, having mother-daughter dates, and eating Mexican food. When she's not doing that, she's writing. She spends her days off watching rodeo, knitting, and surfing Pinterest in the name of research. Following their own personal joys, BA and Julia heard the call of the high desert and they now live in the New Mexico mountains. BA's personal saviors include her wife, her best friends, and coffee. Lots of coffee. Really good coffee.

Having written everything from fist-fighting cowboys to rural single dads to werewolves, BA does her damnedest to tell the stories of her heart, which is committed to giving everyone their happily ever after. With books ranging from heart-warming stories of found families, to rodeo cowboys that are fighting to make a mark, to fiery passionate love affairs, BA refuses to be pigeon-holed by anyone but the voices in her head.

Bombs and Guacamole

Ammo and Enchiladas

The Cereus Series

Cereus: Building

Cereus: Opening

Cereus: Training

Cereus: Rescue

The Cowboy Wanted Series

Cowboy Healing

Second Chance Cowboy

The Foster Ranch Series

The Cowboy Contract

The Cowboy Guardian

Leanin' N Ranch Series

Commitment Ranch

Finding Mr. Wright

Whiskey to Wine

Come Back Around

This Old Wind

Perfectly Seasoned

Love is Blind Series

Ever the Same

Real World

Midnight Rodeo Series

Welcome to the Pack

Tails and Whiskers

Above the Fold

Brownie's Sway

Thack's Angel

Here, Kitty Kitty

The Recovery Series

Refired

Slip

The Release Series

The Terms of Release

The Articles of Release

Catch and Release

The Road Trip Series

Racing the Moon • Steam and Sunshine

Under Pressure • Walking on the Sun

Roughstock Series

Blind Ride

And a Smile

File Gumbo

Back to Back

Pulled from All Sides

Coke's Clown

Leading the Blind

Mud, Movies, Bullets, and Bulls

Needing To

Old Town New

Rainbow Rodeo

Rough in Wranglers

Say Something

Seashores of Old Mexico

Soft Place to Fall

Stetsons and Stakeouts

Truth or Consequences

Wicked in Wranglers

Historical Standalones

Cabin Fever

Hammer and Tongs

Oranges and Peppermints

Paranormal Standalones

Baker's Dozen

Calling His Bluff

Forged in Magic

Long Black Cadillac

Luck of the Draw

Redemption's Ride

Roman and Cage

Setting His Sights

Things that Go Bump in the Night

Unearthed

Wolf Run

Lesbian Romance

Summit Springs Series

Christmas Bizarre w/ Jodi Payne

Honeymoon in the Cards w/ Jodi Payne

Tipping the Barrel

Contemporary Standalones

Bright Lights and Boobjobs

Games Girls Play

Historical Standalones

Bustles and Doeskins

With Jodi Payne

The Collaborations Series

Refraction

Syncopation

The Cowboy and the Dom Series

First Rodeo

Razor's Edge

No Ghosts

The Soldier and the Angel

The East Meets Westerns Universe

Temptation Ranch

Les's Bar Series

Just Dex

Hide Bound

Wholly Trinity

Lone Star Series

Tending Tyler

Roped In

Merry Everything Series

Window Dressing

Cowboy Protection

Cowboy and Cupcakes

Wrecked Series

Wrecked

Flying Blind

Special Delivery

Seeds and Sunshine

Pick Up Man

The Higher Elevation Series

Land of Enchantment

Keeping Promises

Bigger than Us

Heart of a Cowboy

Home Free

The Sin Deep Series

Sin Deep

The Trouble with Cowboys

The Triskelion Series

Breaking the Rules

Making a Mark

Making the Rules

Hey, y'all!

Thank you for giving Tropical Depression a try. I hope you enjoyed the story, and will consider leaving a review at the eBook retailer website where you made your purchase.

Don't forget to "like" my BA Tortuga page on Facebook to keep up with new releases, author news, special discount codes and sale announcements. And if you're interested in sneak peeks, rodeo pictures, and general fun, please come see the BA's Cowboys on Facebook. We'd love to have all y'all!

Yeehaw!

BA